FLY ME TO THE MORGUE

The Rat Pack Mysteries from Robert J Randisi

EVERYBODY KILLS SOMEBODY SOMETIME
LUCK BE A LADY, DON'T DIE
HEY THERE – YOU WITH THE GUN IN YOUR HAND
YOU'RE NOBODY 'TIL SOMEBODY KILLS YOU
I'M A FOOL TO KILL YOU *
FLY ME TO THE MORGUE *

*   *available from Severn House*

FLY ME TO THE MORGUE

A 'Rat Pack' Mystery

Robert J. Randisi

Tacoma Public Library
TACOMA, WA 98402-2098

Severn House

This first world edition published 2011
in Great Britain and the USA by
SEVERN HOUSE PUBLISHERS LTD of
9–15 High Street, Sutton, Surrey, England, SM1 1DF.
Trade paperback edition first published
in Great Britain and the USA 2011 by
SEVERN HOUSE PUBLISHERS LTD.

British Library Cataloguing in Publication Data

Randisi, Robert J.
   Fly me to the morgue.
   1. Rat Pack (Entertainers) – Fiction. 2. Gianelli, Eddie
   (Fictitious character) – Fiction. 3. Horse owners – Crimes
   against – Fiction. 4. Las Vegas (Nev.) – Fiction.
   5. Detective and mystery stories.
   I. Title
   813.5'4-dc22

ISBN-13: 978-0-7278-8015-4 (cased)
ISBN-13: 978-1-84751-341-0 (trade paper)

All Severn House titles are printed on acid-free paper.

Severn House Publishers support The Forest Stewardship Council [FSC],
the leading international forest certification organisation. All our titles that
are printed on Greenpeace-approved FSC-certified paper carry the FSC logo.

MIX
Paper from
responsible sources
FSC
www.fsc.org   FSC® C018575

Typeset by Palimpsest Book Production Ltd.,
Falkirk, Stirlingshire, Scotland.
Printed and bound in Great Britain by the
MPG Books Group, Bodmin, Cornwall

To Marthayn, who
Flies Me To The Moon
every day

PROLOGUE

Las Vegas, December 2004

My long-time buddy, Danny Bardini, had shown up at my door with the DVD in his hot little hand.

'Merry Christmas,' he said.

'Christmas is next week.'

'I know, but Penny has us committed to some family gathering, so this was my only chance to give this to you and have a Christmas drink with my old pal.'

'Old' being the operative word. We were both in our early eighties at this point in our lives. Danny hadn't handled a case in ten years; not since his wife Penny – for many years his secretary – had forced him into retirement.

I popped the cork on some champagne and he regaled me with the problems he had being married to a younger woman. After all, Penny was only sixty-eight.

'I swear, Eddie,' he said, 'she wants it twice a month. I tell ya, she's tryin' to kill me.' He put his feet up on my coffee table. 'Put the DVD in.'

'What? Open my Christmas present now?'

'What part of I'm not gonna be here for Christmas did you miss?'

'OK,' I said. 'Early Christmas present for me.' I tore it open, and found myself holding a DVD of *The Frank Sinatra Show*. 'Hey, all right. The perfect gift.'

'That's what I thought.'

I went to my fifty-inch flatscreen and went down to one knee to access the DVD underneath. Both had been gifts from Vegas high rollers.

'How do you do that?' Danny asked.

'What?'

'Go down on one knee like that. Can you get up again?'

With the disc in the machine I stood up easily.

'Show off,' he said. 'My knees are killing me.'

'I walk,' I said, 'a lot.'

'I walk,' he insisted.

I sat next to him and said, 'I mean further than from the sofa to the refrigerator and back again. Oh wait, you don't do that, either. Penny gets your beer for you.'

'Hey,' he said, 'I earned that kind of service with a lot of years of hard work and devotion.'

'What did Penny ever see in you?' I asked.

'I was Mike Hammer, and she was Velda,' he said. 'Who else would she go for? You?'

'Not me. She was too young for me.'

'You're only two years younger than me.'

'Yeah, I know.'

Danny was my older brother's best friend when we were kids in Brooklyn. When my brother died he kind of took me under his wing. He moved to Vegas after I did, telling me I was his only friend. I was never sure, but I found out over the years he was right. He didn't trust people easily, and when you can't trust, you can't befriend.

'Hey, turn this thing on,' he said. 'Mitzi Gaynor's on the show with them.'

'Ah, Mitzi . . .' I said.

'You knew her?'

'No.'

'But she played Vegas a lot.'

'What can I tell you? You can't meet them all.'

'But you met these guys,' he said, gesturing at the TV.

Frank, Dino and Bing were sitting on something that looked like a jungle gym for adults, singing together. It was *The Frank Sinatra Show*, circa 1958, and they were performing *Together*.

At one point Bing referred to them as 'three vagrant minstrels'. He also referred to Frank as 'Bones'.

'Sure, but that was easy. They were all part of the Rat Pack.'

'Bing Crosby?'

'Well, sort of,' I said. 'He did do *Robin and The Seven Hoods* with them. And before that he and Frank did *High Society*. And this' – my turn to gesture – 'came in between those two things. *High Society* was fifty-six, this was fifty-eight and Robin was . . . sixty-four.'

'Jesus, even your memory is better than mine,' he complained.

'Yeah, but you still got your looks.' And most of his hair, I noticed.

'Yeah, I do, don't I?' He raised his chin. 'But what about the whole JFK thing?'

'I've always wondered about that, too,' I said. 'Frank never got mad at Bing when JFK stayed at his house, instead. Never even got mad at Kennedy. He took it all out on Peter.'

'Sounds kinda unfair.'

'Maybe . . .'

'You want help turnin' the DVD player on, old timer?' he asked.

'I've got it,' I said, pointing the remote.

When the screen came to life so did my friends . . .

ONE

August 4, 1962, Del Mar Race Track, Del Mar, California

My invitation to Del Mar Race Track for the Bing Crosby Handicap came from Dean Martin. Del Mar was founded by Bing Crosby himself in 1937, and every summer the elite showed up there for thoroughbred horse racing by the sea.

Singers like Dino, Frank Sinatra, Perry Como and Tony Bennett had for years talked about the debt they all owed to Bing Crosby. In fact, in 1950 Dean even recorded a song called 'If I Could Sing Like Bing.'

In point of fact Dino was the one who was most like Bing. Not only could he sing, but he also shared Bing's flair for comedy. Frank could be funny in the movies and on stage, but it didn't come naturally to him like it did for Bing and Dino.

Dean had played Vegas in September of '62 and wasn't scheduled to come back to the Sands until '64. But he called me in July of '63 and asked me if I wanted to go to the track . . .

'Gonna be quite a bash,' he told me on the phone. 'Bing will be there for the race, and he's invited Jack Benny and Bob Hope.'

'He won't mind if I just show up?'

'Hey, pally,' he said, 'Der Bingle invited me and I invited you. And bring somebody if you want. The more the merrier. It's supposed to be a party.'

Dean even offered to send me a plane ticket but I told him I preferred to drive.

'I'd like to bring Jerry Epstein, if that's all right?'

'The leg breaker?' Dino laughed. 'I thought you'd bring a broad with you.'

'Jerry's a big horse player,' I said. 'This'd be right up his alley.'
'Then bring 'im,' Dean said. 'Sure, why not? It'll be great. And pack for a couple of days. I'll get you rooms in the Hotel Del Mar. That's where a lot of us will be staying instead of driving home.'

When I hung up with Dean that day I called Jerry and he got excited. The chance to go to Del Mar to watch and bet on the Bing Crosby Handicap *with* Bing Crosby? The big guy loved it.

So at the end of July, Jerry came to Vegas, we did the town for a couple of days, and then headed for Del Mar in my Caddy. Naturally, he drove.

'A month ago I never expected to be spending the first weekend in August in Del Mar,' Jerry said, during the ride.

'It's a big deal, huh?'

'You kiddin'?' he asked. 'The two places I'd most wanna be in the summer are either Del Mar or Saratoga. I can't thank ya enough, Mr G.'

We drove to the Hotel Del Mar, checked into our rooms and had dinner, then Jerry said he had to go to his room to handicap.

'I don't wanna embarrass myself tomorrow,' he said. 'I gotta pick some winners.'

'I hope so,' I told him. 'I'm gonna be betting your horses.'

When we got to the track the next day, we were immediately shown to the Clubhouse, where Dino welcomed us and made the introductions.

First he introduced us to our host, Bing Crosby, who had his wife of six years, Kathryn Grant, on his arm. It caused a stir in Hollywood when they married, as she had been twenty-three at the time and he fifty-four. But they looked like a happy couple that was very much in love.

'Thanks for coming,' Bing said, shaking hands with both of us.

'It's a real pleasure, Mr Crosby,' I said.

'Bing,' he said, 'just call me Bing.'

'Mr Crosby,' Jerry said, sounding nervous.

'You, too, son,' Bing said. 'Call me Bing.'

'Oh, I couldn't do that,' Jerry said.

'Sure you can—'

'No, he really can't,' I said. 'He still calls me Mr G., and we've known each other for years.'

'Are you two an act?' Bing asked, laughing. 'Should Hope and I be worried?'

'I don't think you and Mr Hope should worry about anybody,'

Jerry said. 'You guys are funnier than Abbott and Costello, and they're my favorite.'

'High praise, indeed,' Bing said, his arm around his beautiful wife's waist. 'I've gotta check a few things, so you boys just mingle, huh?'

'Thanks, Bing.'

He walked off, looking more like he was dressed for golf than the track, but that was probably just his style. His wife, like many of the women around us, was decked out in an expensive sundress, others in halter-tops, all there to enjoy the sun as well as the horses. Some of them passed close enough for us to smell the ocean on them, indicating they had come to the track right from the beach.

Jack Benny was next, with his wife Mary; then we met Bing's partner in Del Mar, Pat O'Brien. There were others, friends of Bing's and O'Brien's, not Hollywood types, all of whom were very nice and very rich.

A spread had been laid out for the guests, which I nibbled at but Jerry made full use of. I stood off to one side with a Bloody Mary in my hand and watched him pile a plate high with cold cuts, potato salad and several other types of salad.

'He really appreciates a smorgasbord, doesn't he?' Dean asked.

'He has a big appetite, all right.'

'You got any horses picked out for today?'

'Jerry's my guy for that,' I said. 'He's a good handicapper.'

'Is that so?' Dean asked. 'How good?'

'Real good.'

'I usually rely on Bing for my tips.'

'Jerry doesn't give out tips,' I said. 'He just picks winners.'

'I might give him a try.'

'Well, he did a lot of his handicapping last night, but as he explained to me on the way here, that's only half the job. When he's actually at the track he watches the horses in the paddock.'

'Sounds like a lot of work,' Dino said.

'Why do you think I'm counting on him to do it?' I asked. 'Where's Frank, by the way?'

'Bing invited him, but he's got other obligations.'

'It's not because of the, uh, JFK thing, is it?'

'What? Hell, no. Frank doesn't hold Bing responsible for that.'

'Or Jack Kennedy, I notice,' I said. 'Just Peter.'

'Peter, and the rest of the Kennedy family, especially Joe. No, Bing means too much to Frank for him to get mad at. You don't know what a thrill it was for Frank to work with Bing in *High Society*. In fact, he's asked Bing to take the part that Peter was

going to play in our new film, *Robin and The Seven Hoods*. He
wishes he could have come, but he couldn't. Same for Sam and
Joey. Other plans. So, lunch?'

'It's too early.'

'It's almost noon. Almost first post.'

'I know, but working and living where I do I sometimes eat at
odd hours.'

'Well,' Dean said, 'Bing usually leaves this spread out all day.'

'Good to know.'

'If Jerry leaves any of it for us.'

TWO

B y the fifth race Jerry had picked three winners, and cashed a
place bet. So had I, and Dean had followed. Bing, on the other
hand, was oh-for-four, but not ready to toss in the towel yet.

'You kiddin'?' he said, when Dean suggested he followed Jerry's
picks for the rest of the day. 'I'm just gettin' warmed up. And I
have the winner in the big race.'

'Are you sure?' Dean asked.

'Positive,' Bing said. 'I got the word from the trainer.'

He walked off to make his bet on the fifth race.

'He's stubborn,' Kathryn said, with a wry smile, 'but I know
when I'm licked. Jerry, who do you like in this race?'

Jerry gave her his pick and she went off to play it, as did Dean.
Jerry had already bet, for both of us.

'Who do we like in the big race?' I asked him.

'Crazy Kid.'

'What?'

'The horse's name is Crazy Kid, trained by John G. Canty for
Vista Hermosa Stable.'

'You know all of that?' I asked.

'You gotta have as much information as you can to make your
pick,' Jerry said. 'This ain't casino gamblin', ya know.'

'Oh? And what's wrong with casino gambling?'

'Most of it is luck,' he said. 'This is skill.'

'You've played poker and blackjack, and you can still say that?'

'You still gotta have the cards.'

'Well, here you've got to have the horse.'

'And the jock, and the trainer, and the track condition—'

'OK, OK,' I said. 'I give. Crazy Kid it is.'

'I gotta get somethin' ta eat,' Jerry said, and headed for the spread. Actually, I was finally hungry, so I followed him.

We were standing off to one side with plates when Pat O'Brien came walking over. Had anybody in Hollywood played more priests in the movies than Pat O'Brien?

As he approached I could see how much thicker and greyer he'd gotten with age. I was used to seeing him on the screen, and hadn't seen him like this. But after all, he *was* sixty-four. He reminded me of George Raft, who'd had a similar career.

From 1930 through 1952 I don't think there was a year that Pat O'Brien wasn't in a movie. Lately, he'd been plying his trade on TV in things like *Playhouse 90*, *Studio 57*, and his own show for one season, *Harrigan and Son*.

He looked around, like he was worried someone would see us.

'Hey, big fella,' he said, 'I hear you been pickin' winners today.'

'I've had a few.'

'So, whataya like in this race?'

Jerry told him.

'That horse is ten-to-one,' O'Brien said.

'He's due,' Jerry said. 'He's droppin' in class just enough to put him over.'

'You got a tip?'

'I don't believe in tips, sir,' Jerry said.

'OK, son,' the actor said. 'Thanks.' He started away, then stopped and turned back. 'No reason Bing has to hear about this conversation, hey?'

'You got it, Mr O'Brien,' I said.

As he walked away I said to Jerry, 'I hope that horse wins.'

'He will,' Jerry said, around a mouthful of macaroni salad.

And he did.

Bing Crosby looked around as the horses crossed the finish line, wondering why everybody was so happy. Then he got it, and took the news with good grace and humor.

'You're all a bunch of traitors,' he said, laughing.

When he saw the look on Kathryn's beautiful face he said, 'You, too?'

She shrugged and he laughed again.

*   *   *

Jerry cooled off, though, missed two races in a row before the feature. I went to the paddock with him to look at Crazy Kid.

'He looks good,' Jerry said. 'Should run in better than one-oh-nine.'

'If you say so,' I said.

'Look at his legs.'

'I'm better with showgirls' legs.'

'Well, this horse may not be able to kick like a showgirl, but he can run.'

'Then we better go and bet.'

'You think Mr Crosby will be mad when my horse wins and his doesn't?' he asked as we walked to a betting window.

'No,' I said, 'I think he'll congratulate you.'

'Why won't he play my horse?'

'I guess some men just like to pick their own,' I said. 'After all, he founded this track, even owns some horses of his own. He probably considers himself an expert.'

'Then he should be better at pickin' winners,' Jerry said.

'Yeah, I suppose he should,' I said, 'but how about we don't tell him that, hmmm?'

Jerry shrugged and said, 'OK by me.'

We placed our bets and made our way to Bing's box so we could watch the race with the others.

'There you are, big fella,' Bing said. 'I thought you were gonna miss the race.'

'No, sir,' Jerry said. 'Not a chance.'

Everyone had their tickets in their hands. All but Bing had bet on Crazy Kid, the horse Jerry had picked.

'This horse's first race was a twenty-seven hundred dollar claiming race,' Bing reasoned. 'There's no way he's come this far.'

But Jerry remained silent and stuck to his guns. So did the rest of us.

It was post time.

And they were off . . .

'I can't believe it!' Bing Crosby said.

It was hours later. The spread in the clubhouse had been changed from cold cuts to hot food. Jerry had a plate stacked sky high and was looking very uncomfortable as he was also the center of atten-tion. He had not only given out the winner of the Bing Crosby Handicap but the last race as well. The people surrounding him were now the Faithful. Dean was standing off to one side with an amused grin on his face.

'A track record,' Bing said to me. 'One-oh-seven and three. I can't believe it.'

'Jerry told me in the paddock the horse looked like he'd run a sub one-oh-nine.'

'Where did you find this guy?' he asked.

I shrugged and said, 'Brooklyn,' and went to rescue Jerry.

THREE

Las Vegas, April 1963

Bob Hope teed off and we all applauded as the ball sailed straight and true down the fairway.

I was playing at the Desert Inn Golf Course as part of a foursome that included myself, Hope, Dean Martin and Bing Crosby. Dean had taken me out on the golf course several months before. I had played occasionally, but now I was hooked. I tried to get out two or three times a week, and I prided myself that my game was improving. Dean said I had a natural talent for it. Still, when he invited me to play with Benny and Bing I hesitated . . .

'Come on, pally,' he said. 'It's just a friendly game.'

'Friendly?' I asked. 'I heard you guys play for high stakes.'

'Well,' Dino said, 'that depends on what you consider high stakes. I tell you what I'll do. I'll cover you.'

'Dean—'

'We'll play teams,' he said. 'You and me against Bob and Bing. Whataya say?'

I said yes, of course . . . but I told him we might be on the Road to Losing. Which I thought was a pretty good joke.

'Don't quit your day job, Eddie,' he said.

When it was my turn to tee off I held my breath, let it out slow, did what Dean had taught me to do, and shanked it.

'He's got the shanks,' Bob Hope punned in that deadpan way he had.

A 'shank' is the worse shot in golf. You hit the ball with the heel of the club rather than the face, and it goes off to the right.

'The kid's just nervous,' Bing said.

'Golf is a hard game to figure,' Hope said. 'One day you will go out and slice it and shank it, hit into all the traps and miss every green. The next day you go out and, for no reason at all, you really stink.'

As we got into our golf cart Dino put his arm around me and said, 'Don't worry about it, kid. We got 'em right where we want 'em.'

I did better the rest of the way. At least, I never shanked another one. I hit a couple of sand traps, but so did the others. It goes without saying there was a lot of joking and laughter, and even some advice, good and bad.

By the time we got to the eighteenth hole we were only two shots back.

'We can do this, Eddie,' Dean said to me, as we got out of our cart. 'You're putting OK, but you've got to concentrate on your tee shot and your drives.'

'OK,' I said . . .

I think one of the problems was I was meeting Bob Hope for the first time. I'd known Dean for a few years by then, and had spent a whole day with Bing the year before at Del Mar. When I got to the golf course Bing greeted me like an old friend, and then introduced me to Hope.

Hope had played Vegas, and had even attended some of the shows the guys performed at the Sands, but somehow I had missed meeting him.

On this day I was not only meeting him, but on the golf course, where he might have spent even more time than he did on stage.

When we shook hands he said, 'You didn't bring any ringers with you, did you, kid?'

I figured he was referring to me bringing Jerry to Del Mar the year before, where he had showed Bing up by picking a lot of winners.

'No ringer, Mr Hope,' I said. 'Just me, and I only started playing golf a few months ago.'

'Is he puttin' me on?' Hope asked Dean, still shaking my hand.

'No, he's a beginner, but a talented one,' Dean testified.

'Well,' Hope said, releasing my hand, 'maybe we should discuss increasing the stakes.'

'Let's talk about that, Bob,' Dean said, putting his arm around Hope's shoulders and walking away with him.

'Higher stakes?' I said to Bing.

'Don't worry, Eddie. Dino won't hold it against you if you cost him a bundle.'

I wondered if Bing Crosby had somehow orchestrated this little match to get back at me for bringing Jerry to Del Mar?

He smiled at me, though, in that Father O'Malley way he had, like in *The Bells of Saint Mary*.

By the time we got to the eighteenth hole, Hope had me calling him Bob, but he was also keeping up a running string of one-liners that had to do with my skill as a golfer.

'He's just tryin' to get under your skin,' Dean told me, at one point.

'He's succeeding,' I said.

So at eighteen I was nervous. The hole was a par five. Dean said, 'If you can do it in four, I might be able to get there in three. We could force a one hole sudden death play-off.'

'Really?' I asked. 'It wouldn't just end in a tie?'

'No,' Dean said, 'somebody's got to win, Eddie.'

'I thought this was for fun, and some small stakes.'

'Well,' he said, squirming, 'the stakes have gotten a little bigger.'

They had been making some side bets along the way, which I hadn't taken part in because I was so new at golf. But my score probably would have the biggest impact on the final score.

'No pressure, Eddie,' he said, 'but I really would like to beat these two.'

I looked over at Hope and Crosby, who were laughing, totally relaxed.

'Yeah,' I said, 'yeah, so would I.'

'Let's do it, then.'

FOUR

Hope and Crosby continued their jibes as I approached the tee, but, to give them credit, they kept quiet each time I addressed the ball, and the final hole was no different.

I'd had a couple of decent drives, mostly mediocre, but I hadn't shanked a ball since the first hole. Now I took my turn, stared down at the ball, concentrated, and swung.

I had heard golfer before talk about 'kissing' a ball. Hitting it so well that it felt like a kiss. I'd never known what they were talking about until that moment.

I kissed it.

I heard Dean let out a breath. I looked over at Hope and Crosby and they were just staring, watching the ball soar, arc, and land.

Bing looked at me and said, 'Nice drive, kid.'

Hope just shook his head.

We walked back to the golf cart with Dean's arm across my shoulder.

'That drive should knock one stroke off,' he said. 'You can get it on the green now, and then it's just a good putt. We have a shot at this, pally.'

As we got in the cart I felt bad. What if I disappointed Dino?

I made it to the green in two. Best hole of the day for me already.

Dino made it in two, also.

So did Bing.

Hope shanked it.

But with Hope, everything was an excuse for a good joke.

'I get upset over a bad shot just like anyone else,' he said. 'But it's silly to let the game get to you. When I miss a shot I just think what a beautiful day it is. And what pure fresh air I'm breathing. Then I take a deep breath. I have to do that. That's what gives me the strength to break the club.'

We all laughed, but I knew he was seething inside.

Once on the green I putted last. Bing missed a ten footer by inches, then bumped it in. Dino sank one from about fifteen. Hope got himself on the green and left an eight footer.

We had made up one stroke with Bing's missed putt, and another because it took Hope four to make the green. We were tied.

I had to sink an eighteen footer for a birdie. Hope had to sink his for par, and a tie, forcing a play-off.

'Go ahead,' Hope said to me. 'Shoot it.'

'Age before beauty,' I said.

He had to smile at that.

'You fit right in, don't you?'

He lined up his putt, stood over the ball. I saw him bite his lip just before he swung. The ball went straight and true, right for the cup . . . and stopped just on the lip.

He walked up to it and dropped it in. No joke. Then he walked away. A golfer would rather miss by a mile than have the ball hang.

If I made my putt, Dean and I would win. If I missed, we'd have a play-off, which I didn't want. I wanted to end it now. I was afraid I'd choke in a play-off.

The three of them stood off to the side, watching. I looked over at them. Three showbiz legends. Suddenly, I felt that if I missed I'd be disappointing all of them.

I lined up the putt, addressed the ball, held my breath . . . and swung.

I had watched Dean's fifteen footer. It had curved slightly, and I adjusted for that.

The ball went right into the cup.

Dean and Bing came over and slapped me on the back, congratulating me. Bob Hope walked over and shook my hand.

'Clubhouse,' Dean said. 'Drinks, on Hope and Crosby.'

'Were those the stakes?' I asked.

Dean patted my cheek and said, 'You kill me, kid.'

Back at the clubhouse we lined up at the bar for drinks. Mack Grey was there, too. Dean's majordomo had been waiting there for his master, his friend.

'You should've seen it, Mack,' Dean said. 'What a shot on the eighteenth. The kid's a natural.'

Mack looked at me and said, 'Golf bores me.'

'Me, too . . . or, at least, it used to.'

Hope and Crosby had to leave and Dean walked them to the exit. They both came over, shook hands with me and Bing said, 'Great seein' you again, Eddie.'

'You, too, Bing.'

'I'll get you next time, kid,' Hope said with that crooked grin of his.

They left and I looked at Mack.

'I won,' I said, proudly.

He slapped me on the back hard enough to dislodge some fillings and said, 'Don't get overconfident, Eddie. They made you a thirty handicap.'

'Thirty?'

Mack grinned.

'They gave you a thirty shot head start, and you won by a single stroke.'

FIVE

I had become the 'go to guy' for Frank, Dean and Sammy when they had a problem they needed handled discreetly. It was my own fault, really. Jack Entratter, my boss, had put me in that position a couple of times and I had come through. At the same time I liked to think I had formed a friendship with those guys, specifically Dino and Frank. Of course, I was never friends with each of them the way they were friends with each other, but when they were in town – together or separately – they usually invited me to dinner.

This time, however, Dean calling and inviting me to play golf was a surprise. More of a surprise to find that the invitation included Bob Hope and Bing Crosby.

Something was up.

When I got word in the afternoon that Entratter wanted to see me in his office I figured this was it.

'Go right in,' his girl said to me as I entered. For some reason I didn't rate the usual look of disdain I got from her.

'Jack,' I said, as I entered.

Jack and I had always had a cordial boss/employee relationship, during which I had never referred to him as anything but 'Mr Entratter.' But ever since I had become 'that guy' for him – the one who kept his 'friends' safe – I had become much more comfortable calling him 'Jack'. Sometimes.

'Siddown, Eddie,' he said. 'I heard you played golf with Dino, Bob Hope and Bing Crosby.'

'That's right,' I said, taking a seat. 'Dean invited me.'

'You didn't beat them too bad, did you?'

'One stroke.'

'Yeah,' he said, 'I heard they gave you a thirty handicap and you beat 'em by one.' He shook his head. 'You almost blew a thirty shot head start?'

'Hey,' I said, 'I just started playin' a few months ago. I think I did pretty good.'

He started laughing.

'What's so funny?'

'I'm sorry,' he said, 'I can just see you struttin' around the course like you accomplished somethin'.'

'Did you bring me up here just to laugh at me?'

'Pretty much. Want a drink?'

'I've got to get back to my pit—'

'Bourbon?' he asked, getting up.

'Sure.'

He poured two bourbons, added ice and handed me one.

'Dean's in town and he's not playin' anywhere,' I said. 'What's that about?'

'Frank Junior,' he said, sitting back down.

'What?'

'Frank Junior is opening next door,' Entratter said, 'at the Flamingo.'

'Why is he opening there and not here?' I asked.

'Frank didn't want any favors for the kid,' he said. 'He made Frankie get his own deal.'

'And he got it next door? Kid's got balls. Is that why Hope and Crosby are in town?'

'That's about the only thing that would bring Crosby here,' Entratter said. 'He doesn't play Vegas. Doesn't want to play gaming establishments. But he's stayin' with us. So is Hope.'

'So if Dean, Bing and Hope are here for the kid's opening,' I said. 'Where's Frank?'

'Frank's playin' a gig in Atlantic City for Skinny D'Amato. He's comin' to Vegas in a few days to play two nights here, and see the kid's last performance.'

'I didn't know he was comin' here.'

'It wasn't planned,' Entratter said. 'We're movin' Vic Damone back two nights to make it work.'

'Vic doesn't mind?'

'Not when I told him it was Frank.'

I sipped my drink. So I was wrong about something being up. Dean wasn't here to ask for my help. He was just here to support Frankie.

'Wait a minute,' I said. 'How old is the kid?'

'Nineteen.'

'Isn't he a little young?'

'Wayne Newton was younger when he started,' Jack said. 'And the first time Frank Junior came here he was ten. He grew up in this business.'

'You goin'?'

'Openin' night,' he said.

'When is that?'

'Tomorrow.'

'Maybe I'll go.'

'If I'm not mistaken,' he said, 'you're workin'.'

I stared at him.

'Nah, I'm kiddin',' he said. 'You can go. Now get back to work.'

'Yeah,' I said, 'right.'

I left the office, wondering why I was so uncomfortable with the fact that Jack Entratter had suddenly developed a sense of humor.

SIX

D ean was in Vegas without his wife, Jeannie, but both Hope and Crosby had brought their wives along. The four of them went out to dinner together, leaving Dean alone so he came down to the casino floor to find me.

'Wanna get somethin' to eat?' he asked.

'Didn't they invite you to the Road to Dinner?' I asked.

'You gotta stop that,' Dean said.

'Yeah, OK. Sure, I can go. What do you have in mind?'

'I like the food in the Garden Room.'

'Garden Room it is. Gimme ten.'

'I'll go and get a table.'

As he headed for the Garden Room I went to get myself a replacement in the pit for a couple of hours. There was still a chance something was on Dean's mind, and maybe he was going to bring it up over dinner.

Dean was working on a cup of coffee when I got there.

'I was thinkin' about the prime rib special,' he said as I sat down.

'Always good,' I said. I waved a waitress over and ordered two prime rib dinners.

'Right away, Mr Martin,' she said, even though I was the one who spoke.

'Sitting with you always makes me feel so important,' I said to him.

'Sorry, pally,' he said, looking down at his resplendent self. 'It's the suit.'

'I'm wearing a suit,' I pointed out.

'It's the *expensive* suit,' he said, with a grin.

'OK, you got me there,' I said, pouring myself a cup of coffee from the pot on the table. 'I heard about Frank Junior opening next door.'

'Yeah, I'm gonna catch the kid's act tomorrow night,' Dean said.

'You gonna go?'

'I think so.'

'He sounds a lot like Frank.'

'That's not necessarily good, is it?' I asked. 'I mean, there's already a Frank.'

He winced and commented, 'That's what some people are sayin', but they should give the kid a break.'

Our prime ribs came and Dean asked for an iced tea to wash it down. I went the same way.

We caught up because we hadn't really seen each other since earlier in the year. He told me he and Frank were making another film together, a western called *Four For Texas*.

'Four?' I asked.

'Yeah, the other two are Ursula Andress and Anita Ekberg.'

'Wow,' I said.

'Joey'll have a part in it, too. It'll be fun. I've decided I'm only gonna make movies that are fun from now on.'

'But why? Your dramatic films have been great. You get good reviews.'

'Mostly,' he said, 'but I don't have anything to prove to anybody, anymore. Actors like Brando and Monty Cliff give me respect. That's all I need. I'm just gonna make fun movies and not worry about critics. Westerns. I'm gonna make a lot of westerns. Oh, and those spy movies I told you about.'

'You gonna do those like James Bond?'

He laughed.

'Naw, I'm gonna be the anti-Bond,' he said.

He went on to talk about his daughter, Claudia. She wanted to be an actress, and Frank had been kind enough to give her a part in a film he was producing for his daughter, Nancy, through his film company. It was called *For Those Who Think Young*.

'It's a beach movie with James Darren.'

'Bikinis and sand, huh?'

'You said it.'

I remembered meeting Nancy the year before. She was a good-looking young woman, and would probably do justice to a bikini. I didn't know about Dean's daughter, Claudia. I suddenly felt bad that I considered us to be friends, and I had never seen his daughter. Young Dino, yeah, he had come to Vegas a time or two, but Claudia . . .

'How old is Claudia?' I asked.

'Nineteen,' he said. 'Old enough to be running around on screen in a bikini; or so I've been tellin' her mother. She's not so sure about it.'

I told Dean I'd make sure to see the film when it came out.

'That's OK,' he said. 'I'd just as soon you didn't see Claudia running around in a bikini.'

Seemed to me Dino wasn't so sure about this movie, either.

We had coffee and pie for dessert and we started to talk about Bing. I don't recall who brought him up. Maybe I did after mentioning being at Del Mar the year before.

'It killed Bing to have to give up Del Mar,' Dean said, 'but he had to cover the inheritance tax on Dixie Lee's estate when she died. He still owns some horses, though. Supposed to be lookin' at one while he's in Vegas.'

'Where?'

Dean shrugged.

'Red Rock Canyon, I think he said. He's supposed to be meetin' his trainer here.'

'When?'

'I'm not sure,' he said. 'Probably after Frankie's opening night.'

'How long are you stayin' in town?' I asked.

'I'll probably leave after a couple of Frank Junior's shows,' he said, thoughtfully. 'I'm just supposed to give him enough morale to last until Frank gets here himself.'

'And when is that?'

'A few days,' Dino said. 'Closing night.'

'I'm sure it'll give the kid a thrill to have his father in the audience.'

'I told Frank I could stay that long. So I'll be around.' He finished his coffee, pushed away his empty pie plate. 'He also wanted me to ask you if you'd look out for Frank Junior while he's here.'

If that was what Dean had been leading up to, it wasn't much to ask.

'Sure,' I said. 'No problem.'

'Good. I told Frank I didn't want you to think I only came to town to ask for favors.'

'I think we're past that, Dean,' I said. 'We've had enough dinners together over the past few years that were just friendly dinners.'

'Yeah, you're right,' he said.

Teaching me golf and inviting me to Del Mar, those were also acts of friendship. He hadn't asked me for anything either time.

Looking out for Frank Junior might not be as much fun as squiring Nancy around town might have been, but it wasn't a big deal.

SEVEN

F rank Junior put on a hell of a show the next night. And he did it without singing more than two or three of his father's songs. He wanted to stand on his own two feet; I gave him credit for that.

After the show I was granted backstage access and found myself awash in celebrities. Not only Hope, Crosby and Dino, but Jack Benny, George Burns, Keely Smith and Louis Prima, Alan King.

'Hey, Eddie, how ya doin'?' Somebody grabbed my arm. There was no mistaking that voice. I turned and looked into the cock-eyed face of Buddy Hackett, who was grinning at me.

'Hey, Buddy!' He shook my hand enthusiastically. 'Boy, Frank pulled out all the stops tonight, huh? Got all his friends to show up here.'

'Most of 'em,' Buddy said. 'The ones that aren't workin' somewhere themselves tonight. Like Sammy.'

'What about Joey?'

'He's in this mess, somewhere,' Buddy said. 'You meet the kid yet?'

'No,' I said, 'and Frank asked me to look after him while he's in town.'

'Well, if anybody can do that, it's you,' Buddy said. 'Come on, let's find 'im.'

Buddy forged into the crowd, which parted for him, and I followed. With an unerring sense of direction he made his way right to Frank Junior, who looked for all the world like a young Frank Sinatra. Same shock of hair, same thin frame, same big smile. Not identical, but you could sure see the resemblance.

I met the young man quickly, but he was in demand, so we agreed to meet the next day and see what kind of trouble I could get him into.

He was carried away into the crowd and when I turned I was face-to-face with Joey Bishop.

'Hey, Joe!'

'Eddie!'

We shook hands, slapped each other's backs.

'Been a while,' I said.

'I'm still busy with my show,' he said, 'but I couldn't miss this. I wouldn't want Frank putting a hit out on me.'

Only Joey Bishop could get away with making a remark like that.

'I gotta find Buddy,' he said.

'He's in here someplace,' I told him. 'He just introduced me to Junior.'

'He's a good kid. You gonna keep an eye on 'im?'

'Best I can,' I said. 'I'll show him Vegas.'

'Frank'll appreciate it,' Joey said. 'And he'll be here in a few days. Closing night, as a matter of fact.'

'Yeah, I heard that from Dino,' I said. 'That'll be a big night for Frank Junior.'

'Maybe bigger than tonight,' Joey said.

I slapped Joey on the shoulder and sent him into the crowd to find Buddy.

'Eddie!'

I turned to see who was calling me this time. It was Bing Crosby, with Kathryn alongside. She was stunning in a low-cut gown, showing smooth, pale cleavage, making Bing the envy of the room.

'I've been wanting to talk to you, Eddie,' Bing said, 'but it's too noisy here. Can we get together later? At the Sands?'

'Sure, Bing,' I said. 'How about the Silver Queen lounge?'

'Great? In an hour?'

'In an hour you'll be in bed, darling,' Kathryn told him.

'Don't ever marry a younger woman, Eddie,' Bing told me. 'She's always tryin' to get you to go to bed early. Even in Vegas!'

She slid her hand through his arm and he put his hand over hers.

'Can we make it half an hour, Eddie?' he asked.

'Sure, Bing,' I said. 'I'm headin' back to the Sands now.'

'Just let me take this lovely lady to our suite and I'll join you at the bar, post-haste.'

'See you there.'

Bing and Kathryn melted into the crowd and I headed for the exit, wondering what was on Bing Crosby's mind.

I thought Dean might be able to fill me in, but I wasn't able to get close to him backstage at the Flamingo. So I went directly to the Silver Queen Lounge when I got to the Sands.

The bartenders in the lounge came and went like they were in a revolving door. This one's name was Ted. The same went for the waitresses, but I happened to know the one working the floor. She was a nifty little redhead named Didi, and she waved when she saw me and came trotting over. She had a taut little body, but trotting still made her breasts do interesting things.

'Hi, Eddie.'

'Hello, Didi. How're you doin'?'

'I'm fine. What brings you in?'

'I need a beer. Tryin' to get the new guy's attention.'

'I'll get it for you,' she said, then lowered her voice. 'He's a little slow.'

She went down the bar, spoke to the bartender, who drew a beer and set it on her tray. Then she carried it back to me.

'I clued him in who you are,' she said. 'He'll take better care of you, now.'

'Maybe he'll take good care of me when my friend gets here,' I said.

'Who's your friend?'

'Bing Crosby.'

'Really?' she asked. 'You know Bing Crosby?'

'I do.'

'And he's comin' here tonight?'

'In about ten minutes.'

'Wow.'

'Do you want to meet him?'

'I wanna see him,' she said, 'but I'd be too nervous to meet him.'

'Come on, Didi,' I said, 'everybody likes to meet stars. And stars like to meet pretty girls.'

'Well, maybe,' she said.

'You better make up your mind,' I said, 'because he just walked in.'

EIGHT

Didi turned and caught her breath as Bing approached us. 'Hey, Eddie,' he said, putting his hand out long before he got to me. 'Thanks so much for meetin' me.'

'Sure thing, Bing,' I said. 'Oh, this is Didi. She's a big fan of yours.'

'Didi,' Bing said. He took her hand and held it gently. 'I'm always happy to meet a fan, especially one so pretty.'

'Oh my God!' Didi said.

'Didi,' I said, 'say hello to Bing.'

He still held her right hand so she put her left hand over her mouth and said, 'Oh my God!'

Bing threw me an amused look and released Didi's hand.

'OK, Didi,' I said, 'you've got some customers lookin' for you.'

Didi looked at me, then at Bing and said, 'Oh my God.'

I grabbed her tray from the bar, handed it to her, then turned her around and patted her on the butt.

Bing got up on a stool and looked toward the bartender.

'Drink?' I asked.

'A cup of coffee, I think.' He took out his pipe and gestured to me. 'Do you mind?'

'No, go ahead.'

He got the pipe going and the bartender brought him a cup of coffee and served him as if he was Joe Blow from Kokomo on vacation in Sin City.

'Frank Junior had a good show,' I said, as an icebreaker. Bing seemed to have settled into puffing on his pipe and gone away to a place all by himself.

'Hmm? Oh, yeah,' Bing said. 'He's got to develop, but he's got some talent. He has a lot to live up to, though, with Frank as a father. It's not easy, you know, being a famous father and trying to raise sons.'

He had sons of his own, but I didn't know anything about Bing Crosby as a father. Not then.

'Well, maybe I should get to the point,' he said, finally. 'My wife is waiting for me upstairs.'

'OK.'

'Aside from singing and my wife,' he said, 'I have two loves. Golf and horses. You've seen me around both.'

I nodded.

'One of the reasons I came to see Frankie's show was because I was also coming out here to look at a horse. I may not own Del Mar anymore, but I still like to own thoroughbreds.'

'Dino mentioned something about Red Rock Canyon,' I offered, to help him along.

'Yes, I'm supposed to go out to where this fella has a ranch.'

'Is there a problem gettin' out there?' I asked. 'Transportation? The Sands can provide . . . or I can drive you . . .'

'I appreciate the offer, Eddie, but my problem is this: my trainer hasn't shown up. He was supposed to meet me here today. Then we were supposed to go out and look at the horse tomorrow.'

'I see.' I didn't see, but I didn't know what else to say. 'You want me to check around, see what I can find out?'

'Actually, that wasn't what I was gonna ask, but maybe that would be a good idea. What I wanted to ask you was about your friend.'

'My friend?'

'The big fella who was with you at Del Mar last year.'

'Jerry?'

He pointed with his pipe and said, 'That's him.'

'What about him?'

'He seemed to know a lot about horses.'

'I suppose.'

'I mean, he picked winners, but he also went to the paddock to look them over. Seemed to me he knew what he was doin'.'

'He did.'

'Do you think he'd go with me to Red Rock to look at this horse? I always like to have a second opinion – a professional opinion.'

'Jerry's not a professional, but I suppose he has a certain amount of expertise . . .'

'Would you ask him for me?'

'Well, sure, but he lives in New York, Bing.'

'I'll fly him out,' Bing said. 'That's no problem. If he says yes I can have a plane bring him here tomorrow. I'll cover all his expenses, too.'

I nodded and said, 'I'll call him in the mornin'.'

'Great! I appreciate it. And if you could find out something about my trainer . . . he was supposed to fly in this morning. I called him at home and there was no answer. Nobody at his barn seems to know where he is.'

I pulled a notepad from my pocket and asked, 'What's his name?'

'Fred Stanley. Also goes by the name of 'Red'. Don't know why. There's nothin' red about him.'

He gave me his address in San Diego, phone number, and the same information for his barn.

He got down off his stool then and said, 'Goodnight, Eddie. I appreciate your help with this.'

'That's OK, Bing. That's what I'm here for. The Sands does its best for its guests.'

'No,' Bing said, gripping my arm and shaking my hand, 'I'm gonna consider this a personal favor from a friend, if you don't mind.'

'I don't mind at all, Bing.'

He nodded, turned and left, being nice enough to throw a wave at Didi on his way out.

I stuck the notepad back into my jacket pocket and looked up at Didi, who came over to me, shaking her pretty head.

'Oh my God!' she said.

I looked at my watch. It wasn't late, but I didn't really feel like driving home.

'Didi,' I asked, 'what time do you get off?'

NINE

I stayed in a room at the Sands that night, after grabbing a change of clothes I kept in a locker. When I woke up there was a firm rump pressed into my crotch, which was not an objectionable way to start the day.

When Didi turned into me I got a glimpse of her pubic hair, as fiery red as the hair on her head. She also had the green eyes and pale, freckled skin of a real redhead.

'Good-mornin',' she said.

''Mornin'.'

'You workin' today?' she asked.

'Bright and early,' I said. 'I've got to shower and change, then go home before I come back and start. Also got some phone calls to make. So . . .' I slapped her on her bare ass.

'You tellin' me to get up and out?' she asked.

I rubbed her butt where I'd smacked it, then ran a finger up and down the crease between her cheeks.

'Nope,' I said, 'not just yet.'

Eventually we both got up and out. She also had to go home, shower and change, run some errands and then come back for a shift. I told her I'd see her later in the lounge.

Before she left she put her hand against my chest and said, 'Don't worry, Eddie. This doesn't mean we're goin' steady, or anythin'.'

I kissed her on the tip of her nose and said, 'I'll try to console myself.'

I put on chinos and a t-shirt, tossed my suit into the back seat of my car, then drove toward my little house. I stopped first to get some take-out breakfast from a diner down the street – bacon and egg on a bagel, and coffee.

I hung the suit up in the closet, figuring I'd get it cleaned before I wore it again. After that I ate my breakfast, took a shower and dressed, again. This time trousers and a polo shirt. I'd be changing still again before I went to work later.

I called my buddy, Ted Silver, at McCarran Airport and gave him Fred Stanley's name. He said he'd check flights for me.

Next, I called Jerry.

'Hey Mr G.,' he said. 'You caught me havin' a second cup of coffee. What's up?'

'How'd you like an all expense paid trip to Vegas, Jerry?' I asked.

'What's the beef?' he asked. 'You got trouble?'

'Not me,' I said. 'Somebody else asked for you.'

'Who?'

'Bing Crosby.'

'You shittin' me?'

'I shit you not.'

'What's he want with me?'

'He was impressed with the way you handled yourself last year at Del Mar. He wants you to go with him and help him buy a horse.'

'Ain't he got trainers for that?'

'His trainer didn't show up. He doesn't want the trip to go to waste. Says he can fly you here today and cover all your expenses.'

'Jeez . . .'

'You got somethin' else to do?' I asked.

'Nothin' important,' he said. 'Hell, Bing Crosby, huh?'

'Yup.'

'Whataya think, Mr G.?'

'Hell, come on out, man,' I said. 'Help the guy buy a horse and then we'll do the town.'

'You got it, Mr G.,' he said.

'I'll get Bing to make the arrangements, then call you and let you know where to go.'

'I'll be here. See you soon, Mr G.'

*   *   *

I hung up and called Bing right away. He said he'd arrange for a plane to pick Jerry up at Idlewild Airport, which had actually been changed to New York International Airport, Anderson Field in 1948, but most people in New York still called it Idlewild.

I called Jerry back with the info and he had just enough time to get out of his place. Apparently, Bing had assumed he'd say yes, and the plane was standing by.

I hung up, all the plans made. Now all I had to do was wait for Jerry to arrive, then let him accompany Bing to Red Rock Canyon.

I was about to leave my house to run some normal errands – laundry and groceries – when the phone rang.

'Hello?'

'Eddie, Ted Silver.'

'Ted, so quick?'

'Your man was booked on an early flight yesterday from San Diego.'

'And?'

'According to my info he used the ticket.'

'Well then,' I said, 'he disappeared somewhere between the airport and the Sands.'

'Looks like. You gonna call the cops?'

'Not yet,' I said. 'I've got somebody better. Thanks, Ted.'

I immediately dialed a number and waited two rings.

'Bardini Investigations.'

'Hey, Penny, it's Eddie. Is he in?'

'Well, hello to you, too. And yes, he is.'

'Sorry, honey,' I said. 'I'm just in kind of a hurry.'

'Trouble?'

'Maybe.'

'I'll put him on.'

She did, and we arranged to meet near his office, in the coffee shop in Binion's Horseshoe. I'd learned from Jerry that there was always room for another breakfast.

TEN

Danny was waiting for me when I got to the Horseshoe Coffee Shop.

'How come,' he asked, when I sat opposite him, 'you never invite me to meet you up in the steak house?'

'Next time,' I promised. 'I guess I probably owe you that after all this time.'

'Jesus,' he said, 'I was just kiddin'. You don't owe me a thing, Eddie. We're friends. We do things for each other. Sometimes, you even pay me.'

'Well, maybe this will be one of those times.'

'Not with your money, though,' Danny said. 'Bing Crosby's dime, right?'

'We'll see,' I said.

A waitress came over and I ordered bacon and eggs. Danny wanted pancakes.

I took out my notebook and passed it over.

'That's his name, and his addresses. Home and barn.'

'Fred 'Red' Stanley,' he read. 'What's red about him?'

'Nothin', according to Bing. It's just a nickname.'

'Well, maybe when I find him I'll ask him,' he said. He tore the page out of my book and put it in his pocket. 'What else is goin' on?'

'Well, Bing is flyin' Jerry in to help him buy a horse.'

'I know the big guy plays the horses, but what's he know about buyin' them?'

'I don't know,' I said, 'but he impressed Bing last year at Del Mar.'

'When I find the trainer I may be puttin' Jerry out of a job.'

'He's gettin' an all expenses paid trip out of it,' I said. 'He won't mind.'

'That is, if I find Red alive.'

'Now what made you go and say that?'

'Maybe it's our track record,' Danny said. 'It seems when you and me and Jerry get involved, there's a body close behind.'

'I guess I can't argue with you there.'

The waitress came with our plates, set them down, filled our coffee cups and hip bumped Danny when she turned to leave.

'Thanks, Lacy,' he said. He looked at me. 'Guess I better eat my fill here before Jerry gets here and cleans out the kitchen.'

Over breakfast I told Danny about playing golf with Dino, Hope and Crosby.

'What's Hope like?' he asked.

'Same as he is on the TV and in the movies,' I said. 'Got a joke for every occasion.'

'And Crosby?'

'He's funny,' I said, 'but it doesn't come as easily to him. I get the feeling he's got things going on in his private life that the public doesn't know about.'

'What's so bad?' Danny asked. 'He's married to a gorgeous woman thirty years younger than him.'

'Well, twenty-four or five, but I get what you mean,' I said.

'What is she like up close?' he asked. 'Have you met her?'

'She takes your breath away, Danny,' I said. 'Beautiful skin, and her eyes.'

'Better than bein' close to Ava Gardner?'

I grinned.

'Nothin's better than that.'

I had spent some time the year before with Ava Gardner, and still didn't have my breath back from that.

'Come on, tell me the truth,' Danny said. 'You slept with her, didn't you?'

I didn't answer. He'd been asking me that for months, but that was my business, and Ava's.

'How's Penny?'

'Still buggin' me to make her a detective.'

'When are you gonna give in?'

'I don't know,' he said, 'but I'll probably have to at some point.'

'And what about . . .'

'What?'

'. . . marryin' the girl.'

'Are you nuts?' he asked. 'Whatever made you ask that?'

'She's in love with you.'

'You're crazy.'

'If you don't know that, my friend,' I said, 'then you're stupid.'

He paused a moment, then said, 'Besides, she's too young for me.'

'Whatever you say,' I replied.

'Finish your breakfast,' he said. 'I've got work to do.'

ELEVEN

After breakfast I drove to the Sands and put in a few hours in my pit before heading to the airport to pick up Jerry. But before I left, Jack Entratter came down to the floor to see me.

'Had a talk with Bing Crosby this mornin',' he said. 'Seems he wants to use you for a few days.'

'Use me?'

'You know what I mean.'

'I'm supposed to be showing Frank Junior a good time.'

'You can do both,' Jack said, 'but only if I give you time out of the pit.'

'And will you?'

'Whatayou think?' Jack asked. 'I gotta keep both Frank and Bing happy.'

'Dino's gonna be in town a couple of more days, too,' I said.

'Look, you do what you gotta do,' Jack said. 'And do me another favor.'

'What's that?'

'You pick your replacement in the pit,' he said. 'You know the talent down here better than I do.'

'Am I gettin' a promotion to management?' I asked.

'Yeah, right,' Jack said, and walked away.

'I'll take that as a no,' I called out to his retreating back.

Due to the time difference, Jerry left New York late in the morning and arrived in Vegas early afternoon. He came into the terminal with a big smile on his face, dropped his carry-on and lifted me in a big bear hug.

'Great to see you, Mr G.,' he said. 'Ya didn't have to come and get me.'

'Door to door service, Jerry,' I said, picking up his bag.

'With the Caddy?'

'What else?' I asked.

When we got to the car I tossed him the keys, dropped his bag into the back seat, and got into the passenger's seat. He slid behind the wheel, took a deep breath and let it out slowly.

'I love this car,' he said, caressing the steering wheel.

When we first met I'd had a '52 Caddy that he loved. After that one got blown up I got the '53, which he also loved. I always got a kick out of letting him drive.

He started the engine, admired the purr for a few moments, then put the car in drive and pulled away from the curb.

'Where to?' he asked.

'The Sands. Might as well meet Bing Crosby first thing.'

'Am I stayin' at your place?'

'Since Bing's footin' the bill I got you a suite at the Sands.'

'A suite? You mean, like Dino gets?'

'Yup.'

'Jeez,' he said.

We drove in silence for a while and then Jerry said, 'So whataya think about the Mets gettin' The Duke?'

'What?'

'Duke Snider,' he said. 'The Mets bought his contract from the Dodgers.'

The Mets had broken the record for losses in their very first season. They were about to start their second.

'It's about time Snider went back to New York,' I said. 'I mean, after LA stole the whole team from Brooklyn. The Mets are gonna need more than him to help them.'

'I guess so,' he said, glumly. 'So when does Mr Crosby wanna go see this horse?'

'I don't know,' I said. 'We'll have to ask him.'

'What about his trainer?'

'Looks like he made the flight,' I said, 'he just didn't make it to the hotel.'

'You lookin' for him?'

'I got Danny on it.'

'The Vegas Dick,' Jerry said. 'How's he doin'?'

'Good,' I said, 'he's doin' good.'

'He make that little gal who works for him a dick yet?'

'Not yet.'

'Marry her?'

'Nope.' Even Jerry could see how Penny felt about Danny.

We drove for a while, Jerry enjoying the feel of the power under his foot.

'Will you be comin' with us?' he asked. 'To look at the horse, I mean?'

'I don't know,' I said. 'I guess that'll be up to Bing. I'm not the one who impressed him by pickin' so many winners.'

'Yeah, that was a good day,' he said. 'I ain't had a day at the track like that in a while.'

'In a slump?'

He shrugged.

'Gets like that sometimes.'

'Well, do me a favor,' I said. 'Don't tell that to Bing.'

TWELVE

When we got to the Sands we parked and I walked Jerry to his suite. It was identical to the ones Dino always stayed in.

'Wow,' he said.

'This is how the other half lives. Why don't you put your stuff in the bedroom and I'll call Bing.'

'Sure thing, Mr G.'

I picked up the phone and dialed Bing's room. Kathryn answered.

'Oh, hello, Eddie,' she purred. 'Bing is over at the Flamingo. He's helping Frank Junior with some arrangements.'

'The kid must be thrilled.'

'That kid's father is Frank Sinatra,' she said, laughing.

'Kathryn,' I said, 'Frank himself would be thrilled to have Bing's help.'

'That's a very nice thing for you to say, Eddie,' she answered.

'Listen, I was, uh, doin' somethin' for Bing—'

'I know about Bing and Red Rock Canyon, Eddie, and what he asked you to do.'

'Well, Jerry's here, in the hotel,' I said. 'He's ready to see Bing whenever he's ready.'

'Bing should be back within the hour. Why don't you and Jerry just come up in an hour?'

'Both of us?'

'Well, of course. We'll have drinks.'

'OK.'

'Make it an hour and a half, Eddie,' she said. 'I look forward to seeing you both.'

'Thank you, Kathryn.'

As she hung up, Jerry came walking back into the room.

'We're gonna go to Bing's room in an hour and a half,' I said. 'I just spoke to Kathryn.'

'His wife?'

'Yeah.'

'She's gonna be there?'

'Yes,' I said. 'She said we'll have drinks.'

'Drinks?' he asked. 'With Bing Crosby and his wife?'

'That's right.'

'Mr G.,' he said, anxiously, 'I don't got nothin' to wear.'

'That's OK,' I said. 'Let's go downstairs and do some shopping.'

An hour and forty minutes later we were at the door of Bing Crosby's suite. Jerry was wearing a sports jacket and pants we bought at a big and tall store. He had combed his hair a couple of times, and was feeling nervous.

In fact he said, 'I ain't been this nervous since I met Miss Ava last year.'

'You didn't seem nervous then.'

'I was shakin' inside.'

'Well, then, just keep it inside this time, too.'

I knocked and the door was opened by Kathryn Crosby. She was wearing a peach-colored silk blouse, white hip-hugging pants and open-toed sandals with just enough heel.

'Eddie,' she said. 'And Jerry. So nice to see you again.'

'Yes, Ma'am,' Jerry said, ducking his head.

'Well come in, both of you,' she said. 'I'll make the drinks. Bing will be out in a minute.'

She walked to the bar and situated herself behind it. We entered and closed the door behind us.

'What can I get you?' she asked.

'Uh, bourbon,' I said.

'Do you have beer?' Jerry asked.

'Yes, we do.' She held up a shaker. 'But I made martinis.'

'I'll have one, then,' I said.

'Uh, just beer for me, if that's all right,' Jerry said.

'It's fine, Jerry,' she said, with a smile.

Kathryn Crosby was not yet thirty, and had possibly the most beautiful skin I'd ever seen, pale and smooth. She almost glowed.

'Well, there are my boys,' Bing said, entering the room. He wore grey trousers and an open-necked polo short. He came right up to us with his hand out, shook with both of us.

'It's nice to see you again, Jerry.'

'Yes, sir, same here.'

'Oh, don't start callin' me sir,' Bing said. 'We're gonna be workin' together. Just call me Bing.'

'Um—'

'Oh that's right, I forgot,' he said. 'OK, then Mr C. it is, right?'

'Yes si—yes, Mr C.'

'As long as Como doesn't show up we won't get confused,' he said.

He walked to the bar and kissed his wife on the cheek. She handed him a martini, then held one out to me. She put a can of Piels on the bar for Jerry. Then picked up her martini and sipped it.

'You gentlemen have business,' she said. 'I'm going to sit on the sofa and keep quiet.'

This time she kissed Bing on the cheek, and went to the sofa.

'Jerry, my man,' Bing said. 'You know horses, don't you?'

'Yes, si—yeah, I do.'

'And I mean, you don't only know how to play them, but you know the animals.'

'Yes.'

'How?' Bing asked.

'Huh?'

'Why do you know about horses?'

'Because I bet money on them,' Jerry said. 'I don't bet my money unless I know what I'm doin'. So when I decided I liked betting the horses, but I liked winnin' better, I got to know horses.'

'Humor me,' Bing said, 'but I'd still like to know how?'

'I went to work for a trainer,' Jerry said.

'As what?'

'I did a little bit of everything,' Jerry said. 'I mucked stalls, I was a hotwalker . . . I did everything but be a jockey.'

Kathryn laughed at that.

'So you know horseflesh.'

'I do.'

Bing looked at me.

'Have you been able to find out anything about Stanley?'

'He did fly into Vegas. He just never made it from the airport to here. I've got a friend of mine checkin' it out.'

'OK,' Bing said. He looked back at Jerry. 'There's a guy out in Red Rock Canyon who's got a horse to sell. I wanna go out and take a look at it. My trainer was supposed to tell me whether or not the horse would be a good buy. Do you think you could do that for me?'

'Well,' Jerry said, 'I ain't a trainer, but I can give ya my opinion.'

'And I would value that opinion,' Bing said, 'because I've seen what you can do at the track.' He turned to Kathryn. 'Remember how this man picked so many winners.'

'I sure do,' she said. 'Maybe he can come to the track with us another time.'

Bing looked at Jerry.

'Whataya say? Would you like to do that again?'

'Del Mar?' Jerry asked.

'Del Mar, Santa Anita, Hollywood Park, wherever you wanna go.'

'That sounds great,' Jerry said.

'OK,' Bing said. 'So we'll drive out to Red Rock Canyon tomorrow mornin', huh? I've got the address.'

'Whatever you say.'

'Let's meet in the lobby,' Bing said. Then he looked at me. 'Eddie?'

'You want me to come, too?'

'Why not?' Bing asked. 'You interested?'

'Sure I'm interested.'

'Should I rent a car?' Bing asked. 'Get a limo?'

'Mr G.'s got a sweet Caddy,' Jerry said. 'I can drive it.'

'A Caddy, huh?' Bing asked.

'Fifty-three,' Jerry said.

'OK,' Bing said. 'The Caddy it is. Let's meet in the lobby at eight a.m.'

'Bing, make it nine,' Kathryn said. 'You need more sleep than that.'

Bing gestured toward his wife and said, 'I usually listen to my wife, guys. So how about nine?'

'Nine's good,' Jerry said.

'Nine it is,' I said.

We drank up, and then left Bing and Kathryn to their day.

Bing walked us to the door and said, 'We're gonna go and have a look at Lake Mead.'

'Enjoy it,' I said.

Out in the hall Jerry said to me, 'Lake Mead? That a new casino?'

I laughed, because after all this time, I knew Jerry wasn't as dumb as he made out. But he was funny.

THIRTEEN

I left Jerry at the Sands. He had the rest of the afternoon to do whatever he wanted. I figured he'd be in the Book, playing the horses.

I wanted to drive home, make some calls, and change my clothes, so I told him I'd come back and we'd go out to dinner.

When I got home I called Danny's office.

'He's out, Eddie,' Penny said. 'Says he's working on your case.'

'OK, sweetie,' I said. 'Just tell him I called. He can reach me at the Sands, leave a message there if I'm out.'

'OK, doll.'

I blew her a kiss and hung up.

I got back to the Sands; Jerry was in his suite, watching TV when I called up there.

'What are you doin'?' I asked as I walked in. 'I thought you'd be playin' horses.'

'I tol' ya,' Jerry said. 'I'm in a slump.'

'So you've been watchn' TV?'

'Westerns,' he said, nodding. 'Jimmy Stewart. You know him?'

'Never met him.'

'I thought you knew everybody?'

'Everybody who comes to Vegas to gamble.'

Jerry stood up. Turned off the TV and asked, 'Where we goin' to eat?'

'Italian?'

'Sounds good to me.'

'Then let's go.'

Since I knew where we were going I got to drive my own car. I took Jerry to an Italian place off the strip that Frank Sinatra really liked. He ordered a huge plate of spaghetti and meatballs to go with a plate of chicken parmagiana. I went for some veal picata. We split a bottle of red wine, but also had some beer.

Jerry told me some of what he'd been doing the past few months since we'd seen each other. Most of it he edited for content, and some of it he didn't tell me at all. He was, after all, a legbreaker for the mob.

'What about your personal life?' I asked.

'What personal life?'

'You know what I mean. Women.'

'Mr G., come on. You know me and women don't mix, unless they're strippers or whores.'

'Jerry,' I said, 'I don't see why you can't find a nice girl—'

'Nice?'

'OK,' I said, 'a girl, period. One who's not a whore or a stripper. Look, I've seen you interact with women—'

'You seen me stumble over my tongue with Miss M. and Miss Ava,' he said, referring to Marilyn Monroe and Ava Gardner. 'And now with Mr C.'s wife.'

'OK,' I said, 'but those are famous women. What about Penny? You got along with her when you met?'

'She don't count, Mr G.,' he said. 'She's the Vegas Gumshoe's girl.'

Jerry's nicknames for Danny were piling up. That's how I knew he liked him.

The waiter came with another basket of Italian bread and Jerry asked for a small bowl of meat sauce. When it came he soaked his bread in it and chewed thoughtfully. He was thinking about what to have for dessert.

After dinner I let Jerry drive back, and he tried to tit me for my tat.

'What about you, Mr G?'

'What about me?'

'Any women?'

'Nobody steady.'

'Waitresses, showgirls?' he asked. 'You're not so different from me, you know, Mr G. You spend your time with women you meet on the job, like I do.'

Unfortunately, he was right.

'Anybody lately?' he asked.

'Well, there's this little readhead in the lounge, but we've only been together once.'

'Good for you, Mr G.'

When we pulled up in the Sands' parking lot I asked, 'Wanna hit some casinos?'

'When I was watchin' TV this afternoon I saw a commercial for the movie tonight. I think I wanna watch it.'

'What is it?'

'Jimmy Cagney.' He held up two sausage-like fingers. 'Two of 'em.'

'Can't compete with that.'

'I'm gonna get some popcorn,' he said. 'You wanna watch?'

'No thanks,' I said. 'I still need to talk to Danny, and then I think I'll check in with my pit.'

'You can't stay off the floor, can you, Mr G?' he asked. 'Even when you're supposed to be off.'

'What can I tell you?' I said. 'It's home away from home.'

He looked at me across the car and said, 'I wish I had one of those. I just got home, and work.'

'Hey,' I said, 'you can have Vegas as your home away from home. It's my gift to you.'

He looked genuinely touched by what I meant to be a flip remark.

'Gee, thanks, Mr G.'

'Come on,' I said. 'I know a place you can get some popcorn, even though it's late.'

'Regular and caramel?' he asked.

I grinned and said, 'You got it, big boy.'

FOURTEEN

The lack of an office never kept me from getting or making phone calls in the Sands. Sometimes I used some of the office phones on the second floor. Other times – like now – I just checked with the front desk to see if I had any messages.

'Yes, sir,' the young man on the desk said. 'Right here.' He passed me two message slips.

'You're new, right?' I asked him.

'Yes, sir. My name's Chris.'

'OK, thanks, Chris.'

'Yessir.'

Both slips were from Danny. I went to the front desk to use a phone and dialed his apartment.

'Hey, Danny,' I said, when he answered. 'You alone?'

'Unfortunately. I'm gettin' ready to watch some Cagney movies on TV.'

'You and Jerry both,' I said.

'Thanks,' he said, 'now I'm really depressed.'

'What'd you find out for me?'

'Your trainer got off a plane here yesterday, but he never got into a cab.'

'And he never got to the hotel,' I said. 'Then what happened to him?'

'I asked around,' he said. 'You know, porters, valets, drivers. If your guy was a redhead like his name implies it might've helped. You got a description of him?'

'No,' I said, 'I don't. Sorry. I should've asked Bing.'

'Well, do it tomorrow, will you?' he said. 'Then I can circulate it and see what I can come up with.'

I had the feeling somebody was speaking behind him.

'What was that?'

'Nothin'.'

'You sure you're alone?'

'Why would I lie to you?'

'You might lie to me,' I said, 'if Penny was there with you.'

'It's the TV, butthead,' he said. 'It's a beer commercial.'

'Yeah, OK,' I said. 'I'll talk to you tomorrow after I get that description from Bing. I'm meetin' him and Jerry in the lobby at nine.'

'Where you off to?'

'Red Rock Valley to look at a horse.'

'Well, OK, but call me before you leave so I can get started. Hey, here's Cagney.'

'Yeah, you and Penny enjoy the movie.'

'What are you—'

I hung up with a smile on my face.

I checked in at my pit to see how my hand-picked replacement was doing. His name was Vince Elliott and he'd been a dealer at the Sands for several years. There were others who had been there longer, but Vince had shown signs right from the beginning of being smart and capable. This would be a good test for him.

'Hey, Eddie,' Vince said, as I approached, 'come to check on me?'

He was a tall, fit man in his thirties. Jack Entratter might say he was too young, but I was willing to give him a chance. After all, Entratter had given me one.

'I just had some spare time,' I said. 'Thought I'd walk the floor before headin' home.'

'Well, things are goin' OK,' he said.

'How are the dealers takin' it?'

'I think some of them think they should've gotten the nod over me,' he said, 'but for the most part everybody's cooperatin'.'

'That's good,' I said. 'That's what comes from havin' professionals work for you.'

At the Sands we tried to weed out the troublemakers and malcontents. The last dealer who had been found to be cheating had paid a heavy price at the hands of Entratter and his security boys. He had let me watch, since I was the one who had spotted the cheat. They didn't kill the guy. They left him alive to spread the word about what happened to cheaters at the Sands. Especially those who tried to cheat from the inside. Jack Entratter took that very personally.

'Hey, Eddie,' one of the dealers called out. 'We got one of your regulars here, looking to increase the limit.'

'Talk to Elliott,' I called back. I looked at Vince. 'Your call, brother.'

'Thanks, Eddie,' he said, and walked over to the table to make the decision.

I decided to head for the parking lot, point the Caddy home, and maybe catch a Cagney movie.

FIFTEEN

I called Jerry the next morning and arranged to meet him for breakfast in the Garden Room. He was already there, working on a pot of coffee when I arrived.

'You order?' I asked.

'No,' he said. 'I waited for you.'

I waved over a waitress and we ordered. I ordered bacon and eggs, Jerry surprised me and ordered a Spanish omelet with a side of bacon, and potatoes.

'No pancakes?'

'Maybe after,' he said. 'I'm tryin' to mix it up. I had one of these last week in Brooklyn, and it was really good.'

He asked me what I ended up doing last night and I told him I went home and caught one-and-a-half Cagney movies. Half of *White Heat* and all of *Blood On The Sun*.

'*White Heat* was great,' Jerry said. 'I made it, Ma. Top of the World.' Hey, has Mr C. ever been in a movie with Cagney?'

'I don't know,' I said. 'I guess we can ask him later. I also have to ask him to describe this guy Fred Stanley. Danny needs it to pass around. I should've asked him earlier.'

'Don't worry, Mr G.,' Jerry said, as the waitress came with our orders. 'We'll just get it after breakfast.'

He picked up his fork and dug in.

'Fred?' Bing Crosby said, in the lobby. 'Well, sure, he's kind of . . . how do I put this.' He waved a hand in front of his face. 'He's not tall, kind of . . . short-legged, ya know? Thick in the body. Big ears.'

'That should do it,' I said. 'Just wait here while I give Danny a call and tell him.'

I left Jerry and Bing in the center of the lobby and called. Danny was in his office, even before Penny arrived.

'How was that movie last night?' I asked him.

'It was good.'

'You watched the Cagneys?'

'Sure.'

'Which ones?'

'You know . . . two of the famous ones.'

If he had been with Penny – or someone else – doing something other than watching TV he wouldn't be able to tell me the names of the movies.

'Um, yeah, *White Heat* and . . . the one about the Japanese.'

Good guess?

I gave him Stanley's description and he promised to get in touch as soon as he knew something.

'Say hi to Penny.'

'Enjoy your horse hunting.'

I hung up and walked over to Jerry and Bing, who were sharing a laugh.

'What'd I miss?' I asked.

'We can't tell you,' Jerry said.

'Why not?'

'Because we were talking about you,' Bing said. 'Come on, boys. Let's go look at a horse.'

Jerry drove and we followed some directions Bing had gotten from the owner. Red Rock Canyon was to the West of Las Vegas. Eventually we were on highway 159 out in the middle of nowhere.

'Is this right?' Jerry asked, looking around warily. 'Looks to me like we're in the middle of the desert.'

'We are,' I said.

'Mr G., I hope you been takin' good care of this engine,' Jerry said. 'I don't wanna get stuck in the desert.'

'Come on, you big cry baby,' I said. 'You've been spendin' too much time in Brooklyn and Manhattan. You need some wide open spaces.'

'I'm happy with the wide open spaces I can see from my hotel window.'

'Relax, Jerry,' Bing said. 'This ain't so different from Palm Springs.'

'Beggin' your pardon, Mr C.,' Jerry said, 'I been to Palm Springs to Mr S.'s house, and it's a lot different. At least there's buildings there.'

'Have you bought any horses from this guy before, Bing?' I asked.

'I never heard of him until last week.'

'What's his name?'

'Chris Arnold.'

'He called you out of the blue?'

'He called my trainer, Red Stanley,' Bing said. 'Said he had a horse he thought we'd like to look at.'

'And is anybody else gonna be lookin' at it?' I asked.

'I don't know that,' Bing said.

'I mean, if the horse is for sale there's got to be other buyers, no?' I asked.

'You'd think so,' Bing said, 'but like I said, all I know is I've got an appointment to look at the horse today. I don't know if anyone else will be there.'

'What's that up ahead?' Jerry asked.

Bing and I both looked. Coming at us seemed to be a dust cloud. As it got closer, we saw there was a vehicle in the center of it. It was moving fast, kicking up a lot more dust than we were.

'This guy's a nut,' Bing said. 'He's comin' right at us.'

'Who thought we'd hit traffic out in the middle of nowhere?' I asked.

'If he wants ta play chicken he came to the right guy,' Jerry said, gripping the wheel.

'Not with my car, Jerry.'

'Aw, Mr G. . . .' he whined.

'Give him some room.'

'Spoilsport.'

As the car came closer Jerry slowed, moved over and reluctantly stopped. When the car went by us it must have been doing seventy. It pelted us with sand and rocks, which meant I was going to have to have my interior cleaned. We covered our heads and faces, but our clothes still got covered with sand. Bing was wearing his ever-present hat, so he didn't have to worry about sand in his hair like Jerry and I did.

'Anybody see the driver?' I asked.

'No,' Jerry said. 'I thought I saw something . . . but no . . .'

'Too busy covering up,' Bing said.

'He's gotta be goin' to Las Vegas,' I said. 'I'd like to find him again, if only to give him my cleaning bill.'

'I'd like to clean his clock,' Jerry said.

'Let's mush on, boys,' Bing said. 'We've still got a horse to see.'

Jerry put the car in drive and we started off again.

SIXTEEN

Before long we spotted some low, flat buildings in the distance. As we got closer it became clear there was a house and a barn.

'Finally,' Jerry said. 'Civilization.'

'Hey, we did this in Reno one time, remember? Had to ride out to the middle of nowhere?' I said.

'Yeah,' Jerry said, 'and it didn't end well, did it?'

'Don't be such a cynic.'

We drove beneath a sign that said 'Red Rock Farm'. It was like no farm I'd ever seen, and I said so.

'Lots of thoroughbred outfits use the word farm,' Bing said. 'Doesn't mean the same thing. This is more of a ranch than anything else.'

Jerry drove up to the front of the house and stopped. Next to the barn was a corral with three horses in it. I wondered if one of them was the one Bing had come to look at. I hoped not. Who'd leave a valuable – or potentially valuable – thoroughbred in a corral with other horses?

'OK,' I said, as we got out, 'so where's your guy?'

Bing checked his watch.

'We're on time,' he said. 'He should be around here, somewhere.'

'Should we look around?' Jerry asked. 'Or wait?'

'Let's knock on the door, for starters,' I suggested.

We mounted the front steps and Jerry knocked a little heavier than I would have. Not that he could help it.

'Try again,' Bing said.

Jerry did. No answer.

'Try the doorknob,' I said.

'That's not a good idea, Mr G.'

'Why not?' Bing asked.

'Because if it's unlocked, we'll go in,' Jerry said. 'That ain't legal.'

Bing looked at me.

'Jerry's had a run in or two with the law in the past.'

'Well, I haven't,' Bing said. He reached for the knob and turned it. 'Huh, it's unlocked. Whataya think about that?'

'We should keep knockin',' Jerry said. 'Or check the barn.'

'Jerry, you check the barn,' I suggested. 'I'll go into the house with Bing.'

'Suits me,' Jerry said.

He went down the stairs and walked toward the barn. I pushed the door open and Bing and I stepped inside.

It was a ranch-style house, all on one level, pretty big by my standards, but not by Bing Crosby standards.

'Jerry's been in trouble with the law?' Bing asked.

'Let's say he's had . . . experience with them,' I said.

'That how you met him?'

'How do you mean?'

He looked at me thoughtfully, then said, 'Never mind.' He raised his chin and called out, 'Hello? Chris?'

We stood there a moment and got nothing.

'Maybe he's in the shower?' I suggested. 'Or out back, barbecuing something.'

'Damn it,' Bing said. 'We drove all the way out here and the guy isn't even around.'

'Well, let's look around.'

'I see a kitchen,' Bing said, pointing.

'I'll look for a bedroom.'

We split up. I walked through the dining room and found the bedroom. The bed was unmade. I went into the master bath and found wet towels. He'd been around earlier in the day.

I went back to the front door, found Bing standing there.

'Dishes in the sink,' he said.

'How many?'

'Just breakfast for one,' he said. 'A small plate, one cup.'

'I got an unmade bed and wet towels. He was here. So where is he?'

'In the barn.'

We turned and looked at Jerry, who had slipped in through the open door. I knew something was up because he had his .45 in his hand.

'What?' I asked.

'He's in the barn.'

'What the hell is he doin'?' Bing asked. 'Why didn't he hear us yelling for him.'

'Because,' Jerry said, 'he's dead.'

SEVENTEEN

J erry led us over to the barn. But first I blocked Bing's view and said to Jerry, 'Stow the piece, will ya?'

'Sorry, Mr G.' He put it away.

'Where'd you find him?' Bing asked, as we walked.

'I had to poke around a bit, but I found him in one of the stalls. They covered him with hay, but they didn't do a good job.'

'They wanted him to be found?' I asked.

'Maybe.'

We entered. There was a horse standing in a stall, staring balefully at us. No other horses were around. This one was bigger than the ones in the corral.

'That it?' I asked. 'The horse?'

'I don't know,' Bing said, looking unnerved. 'Could be.'

'Where is he, Jerry?'

'Over here.'

We started over and then I stopped.

'How bad?'

'Bad.'

'Why don't you stay here, Bing?' I said.

'What, you think I'm squeamish?' he asked, already looking a little green around the gills.

'Why take a chance?' I asked.

'Good point. I'll go and look at that horse.'

'Good idea.'

I followed Jerry to another, empty stall.

Empty except for a battered, bloody man.

'Do we know that's him?' I asked.

'No.'

'You go through his pockets?'

'No, Mr G. I found him and went to tell you. Ya want me to?'

'Why not?' I said. 'Let's see if it's him before we call the cops.'

'We gotta call the cops?'

I turned and looked at Bing, who was bent over, checking the horse's legs.

'Let's talk about that later, too.'

Jerry bent over the body. The man was lying face down in the hay. Jerry went into his jeans, came out with a wallet.

'License, and credit cards in the name Christopher Arnold,' he said.

'Put it back.'

He did and stood up.

'What's it look like, Jerry?'

'Like somebody went at him with something,' he said. 'A two-by-four, a baseball bat, a tire iron . . .'

'Hey guys?' Bing called. We both looked over at him. 'What's going on?'

'It's him,' I said. 'Chris Arnold. Somebody beat him to death.'

'Jesus.'

We backed away from the stall and joined Bing.

'Wow,' Jerry said. 'That looks like a thoroughbred. Good formation, looks about three. You want to buy a three year old, Mr C?'

'I'd buy a horse who looked like he could win, no matter what age,' he said.

'This one would never get you to the triple crown.'

'Why not?' I asked.

'Because they're over for this year. And next year this horse will be four.'

'That doesn't matter,' Bing said. 'In fact, none of this really matters if that's Chris Arnold. What do we do now?'

'We have two options,' I said.

'What are they?'

'We can get in the car and get out of here, or we call the cops.'

'What do you suggest?' Bing asked.

'We get outta here,' Jerry said.

'We should call the cops,' I said.

'Mr G.,' Jerry said. 'The car.'

'What about it? The tracks would be kinda hard to wipe out.'

'No, not your car,' he said. 'The other car. The one that passed us.'

'Ohhh, yeah.'

'You mean, they saw us?' Bing asked.

'Well, they probably saw us the way we saw them,' I said. 'But I think what Jerry means is, somebody in that car could've been the killer.'

'Oh.'

'Bing, this is gonna be your call,' I said. 'There's bound to be publicity.'

'But if we leave, there might be somebody who knows that we were supposed to meet today.'

I shrugged.

'We can say you couldn't make it. You called to reschedule, and nobody answered.'

'But they'd still want to question me, right?' He looked at Jerry. 'Right?'

'Mr C., if he's got your name in an appointment book or some-thin', yeah, they'll still wanna talk to ya.'

'And I'd have to lie – I mean, if I didn't want them to know I was here.'

'Well, yeah,' Jerry said.

Bing rubbed his chin and said, 'I don't know how good I'd be at that.'

'Ain't you ever lied before?' Jerry asked.

'Yeah, but not to the police. And you don't want to be here for the cops, right, Jerry?'

'I'd rather not, Mr C.'

'We could just leave this poor joker here to be found by someone else,' I said.

'Have you boys done this sort of thing before?' Bing asked. 'I mean, with some of the stuff you've done for Dino and Frank?'

Jerry and I exchanged a glance. I knew he was wondering, like I was, how much Bing knew, and who had told him.

'Let's just say we did whatever was necessary,' I said.

'OK,' Bing said, 'I shouldn't've asked. Forget it. Let's just decide what we're going to do in this instance.'

If it had been just Jerry and me there would have been no problem. We'd walked away from dead bodies before. But with Bing Crosby involved, we had to do the right thing. Keep everything on the up-and-up.

'Bing,' I said, 'the fact is we haven't done anything wrong here.'

'That's true.'

'They'll talk to you, they'll question me and Jerry a little more because we've been through this before. But you, they'll probably just let you go back to the hotel.'

'Well, I don't want you boys to get into trouble.'

'Don't worry, Mr C.,' Jerry said. 'We can handle the cops.'

'Well, then . . . where should we do this from? Drive back to civilization? I mean, this being the scene of the crime and all.'

'I think we can risk calling the police from the house,' I said. 'Jerry, maybe you should wait here and . . . watch the body.'

'Wouldn't want him to get up and walk away,' Jerry said. 'Would we?'

EIGHTEEN

Bing and I walked to the house and called the police. It took a while but eventually some deputies arrived, and then they called for two detectives from the Sheriff's Department. Thankfully, we weren't in the city limits, so Jerry and I wouldn't be seeing any familiar faces. It would take the detectives some time before they found out our history.

As it was they seemed impressed by Bing Crosby, and treated him and – by extension – us with respect.

'So, Mr Crosby,' Detective Harry Lewis said, 'you didn't have a definite time for your appointment with Mr Arnold?'

'We just said it would be this morning,' Bing said.

He gave us all a look.

'And none of you saw the driver of the car that sideswiped you?'

'It didn't exactly sideswipe us,' I said, 'but no, there was too much dust and dirt bein' kicked around.'

'That's right,' Bing said.

Jerry just nodded.

'You don't say much, do you, Mr Epstein?' Detective Lewis said.

'I guess not.'

Lewis' partner, a man named Perry, came out of the barn and walked over to us.

'The M.E. says he was bludgeoned to death,' he said. 'Also said the killer would have been covered with the victim's blood.'

Pointedly, the two detectives looked the three of us over.

'Clean as a whistle,' Bing said.

'Yes, it would seem,' Lewis said. He was the older of the two men – forties as opposed to thirties – and also seemed to be the man in charge.

'Well, we can reach all three of you at the Sands Hotel in Vegas?'

'That's right,' Bing said.

'Did any of you touch the body?' Detective Perry asked.

'I looked at his wallet,' Jerry admitted.

'Why?'

'We wanted to be sure who he was,' Bing said. 'I asked Jerry to look.'

Bing effectively took the pressure right off Jerry with that admission.

'Not exactly what you're supposed to do when faced with a body, Mr Crosby,' Lewis said. 'We prefer witnesses don't touch the victim.'

'Well,' Bing said, 'we didn't really witness anything, did we?'

'It's . . . just a word we use,' Lewis said. 'You found the body, and saw the car hurrying away.'

'I see,' Bing said.

'And the house?' Perry asked.

'What about it?' Bing asked.

'Did anyone go in?'

'Well, yeah,' Bing said. 'Eddie and I went in to look for Mr Arnold. Jerry went to look in the barn.'

'Touch anything in the house?' Lewis asked.

'Just the front doorknob,' I said.

Lewis made a note.

'We'll be bringing the body out in a few minutes,' Perry said. 'If you don't want to see it, you're free to go.'

'You won't be leaving Vegas anytime soon, will you, Mr Crosby?'

'We should be here a couple of more days,' Bing said. 'If there's family around I might still want to buy the horse.'

'I see,' Lewis said.

'Is that a little cold-blooded?' Bing asked.

'Not at all, sir,' Lewis said. 'After all, you didn't know the man . . . did you?'

'Never met.'

'All right, then,' Lewis said. 'The three of you can leave. We'll need to take formal statements from you at some point.'

'We'll be available.'

We started for the car and then Lewis called, 'Mr Crosby?'

'Yes?' We all turned.

'You said you never met the deceased.'

'That's right.'

'What about your trainer, Mr . . . Stanley?' he asked, referring to his notebook. 'Had he ever met him?'

'They spoke on the phone,' Bing said, 'but they never met.'

'Would I be able to question Mr Stanley about it?' Lewis asked.

'That might be a problem,' Bing said.

'Why's that?'

'We don't know where he is,' Bing said. 'He was supposed to meet me at the Sands, but he never showed up. We're pretty worried.'

'I see. Have you made a report to the Vegas police?' Lewis asked.

'No,' Bing said, 'we thought he might show up today. Still might, I guess.'

'All right,' Lewis said. 'We'll be in touch.'

We got in the car with Jerry behind the wheel. And drove away.

We rode a while in silence and then I said, 'Thanks, Bing, for taking the lead.'

'I noticed how they reacted to me,' he said. 'Respectful. Thought I might as well trade on that.'

'Once they get back to their offices and check on us, they'll come around a little less respectfully,' I said.

'Well, if they do, let me know if I can help.'

'When they're less respectful,' I said, 'it'll probably be best if you're not around.'

'I wonder,' Bing said, 'if Red Stanley showed up, yet?'

NINETEEN

When we got back to the Sands Bing went straight up to his suite. It had seemed like a long day already, but it was only early evening. There was plenty of day left, by Vegas standards.

'We gotta get your car cleaned,' Jerry said, in the lobby.

'We can do that later,' I said. 'I want to check and see if Danny called.'

'I'll go to my suite, then,' Jerry said. 'I need a shower.'

'OK,' I said. 'I'll call you later.'

'OK, Mr G.'

'Jerry.'

'Yeah?'

'I'll have one of the valets get the car washed,' I promised. 'It'll be clean next time we use it.'

He grinned and said, 'OK.'

I went to the front desk and found a message there from Danny. I went to a phone and called his office. Penny answered.

'He's been waiting for your call, Eddie,' she said. 'I'll put you through.'

'Eddie?'

'What's up, Danny?'

'How was your meetin' with the horse guy?'

'Not good,' I said. 'When we got there he was dead.'

'What? Tell me.'

I explained, told him we called the cops after a lot of procrastination, and then relayed to him our conversation with them.

'They let you go?' he said, when I was done.

'Yeah, they don't know our history, yet,' I said. 'And they were pretty respectful to Bing.'

'This isn't good, Eddie.'

'Don't I know it.'

'Well, you don't know the half of it.'

'Whataya mean?'

'I found your trainer, Red Stanley.'

'Where?'

'In a hotel room.'

'What the hell—'

'He's dead, Eddie,' Danny said. 'He's dead, too.'

Danny came to the Sands so we could talk face-to-face. We decided on drinks in the lounge.

We sat at the bar and each had a beer.

'Did you call the cops?' I asked.

'Oh, yeah,' he said. 'I've got a license to protect.'

'OK,' I said, 'tell it to me from the beginning . . .'

Danny started at the airport.

He found what flight Red Stanley came in on, what gate the passengers would have disembarked through, then talked to ticket agents, flight attendants, baggage handlers, security people, other than Ted Silver. Outside he talked to cab drivers, and one of them said he saw a man who matched Stanley's description.

'He came out the front, carrying his suitcase,' the driver said. His name was Frankie. 'I was next in line, but instead of coming to my cab he got into another car.'

'He got in on his own?'

'No,' the driver said. 'Another man came up alongside him, they talked for a minute, and then the sedan pulled up. And they both got in.'

'Did you see a gun?'

'A what?'

'Could the other man have had a gun?'

The driver thought then said, 'I suppose he could have. Yeah, out of sight, like. Maybe jammed into the guy's side? Was it a kidnapping?' he asked. 'Did I see a kidnapping?'

'Maybe,' Danny said. 'Did you see which way the sedan went?'

'It just pulled away from the curb and kept going.'

'Toward town?'

'That's what it looked like.'

Danny handed the man a fiver and said, 'Thanks. Could you pass the word to other drivers? Maybe somebody saw the sedan arrive at its destination, saw the two men get out? Funny lookin' little guy with big ears? Fiver in it for them, too.'

'I'll pass the word,' the driver said. 'You ain't a cop, are ya? You're private.'

'That's right.'

'I'll pass the word.'

'If I get somethin' today, there'll be a ten in it for them and for you.'

'Right, boss.'

Danny gave the cab driver his number, then drove to his office to tell Penny not to leave.

'We've got cab drivers all over the city lookin' for this guy,' he told her. 'If he went to a hotel – willingly or unwillingly – we'll find out.'

'You think he was taken?'

'Yeah,' he said. 'The Sands didn't send a car for him. And he's a stranger in town. The only reason he wouldn't take a cab is if he couldn't.'

'What if he's a regular at one of the other casinos and they sent a car for him? Do you know for certain he's a stranger to Vegas?'

Danny stared at Penny and said, 'Shut up.'

She laughed.

'You didn't think of that?'

'I thought of it,' he said. 'If he gets dropped at another casino some cab driver there will see him.'

'So what are you going to do in the meantime?' she asked.

'Paperwork,' he said. 'I want lunch at my desk.'

'The usual?'

'Yes.'

TWENTY

Danny was at his desk eating his usual lunch – a burger platter from the Horseshoe Coffee Shop – when the phone rang.

'This Danny Bardini?' a voice asked.

'That's right.' Stupid question, he thought. Penny would have already told the caller that this was the office of Bardini Investigations.

'Yeah, this is Frankie? The cab driver you talked to at the airport, this morning?'

'Yeah, Frankie, whataya got?'

'One of my drivers saw your guy.'

'Where?'

'Ten for me and ten for him, right?'

'Right.'

'If this is the right guy, could you make it twenty?' the driver asked.

'For you or for him?'

'Well, me.'

'Let's see if it pans out.'

'OK. My guy saw him gettin' out of a dark sedan in front of the Hotel Raleigh. You know where that is?'

'I do,' Danny said. It was a rundown hotel in a seedy part of town. This didn't bode well.

'I'll get back to you, Frankie.'

'Twenty would be a big help,' Frankie said.

Danny hung up.

When he passed through the outer office Penny said, 'Are you going down there?'

'Yes,' he said, on the way to the door.

'Alone?'

'Yes.'

'Without backup?'

He stopped, turned and looked at her. 'You want me to give you a forty-five and let you come with me?'

'Would you?' she asked, excited.

'No,' he said. 'Stay by the phone.'

* * *

When Danny got to the Hotel Raleigh it was even worse than he remembered. There was a homeless guy out front, a drunk sleeping on the steps. There were two more guys sleeping in the lobby, and one of them was the desk clerk.

'Hey!'

The guy's head jerked up off the desk.

'Welcome to the Hotel Raleigh,' he mumbled. 'Can I get you a room?'

'Jesus, no,' Danny said. 'I'm lookin' for a man who was brought here by a dark sedan. Short, thick, big ears—'

'No, man—'

'Don't interrupt me!' Danny snapped. 'We can do this the easy way or the hard way. The easy way you make five bucks. The hard way costs you more than five bucks' worth of dental work.'

'Take it easy, man,' the young clerk said, leaning back.

'Which way you wanna go?'

The clerk reached behind him, taking a key off the wall.

'Upstairs, room five, man.'

Danny took the key, then pointed his finger at the clerk.

'You call ahead and I'll come down and provide that dental work. Get me?'

'I gotcha, man.'

'Go back to sleep,' Danny told him. 'It's safer.'

He went up the stairs and down the hall to room five. He listened at the door, heard nothing. He knocked. Still nothing. Then he used the key and opened the door . . .

'. . . and there he was, lyin' on the bed,' Danny said. 'The sheets were a bloody mess.'

'Shot? Stabbed?'

Danny shook his head and said, 'Beaten.'

'Damn.'

'Why?'

'Arnold was beaten, too.'

'You're thinkin' the same person killed them both?' he asked.

'We don't know who was killed first, right?' I asked. 'We don't even know if Arnold was killed yesterday or today. So we don't know if one person could've done it.'

'I can get the autopsy results from the coroner here in Vegas,' Danny said. 'The county might be a little harder.'

'How did it go with the police?'

'Two detectives from Homicide responded.'

'Hargrove?'

'Not this time.'

'Well, that's good,' I said. 'We won't have to deal with his . . .'

'Prejudices?'

'Yeah, I guess that's the word.'

'What's gonna happen when the Sheriff's detectives look up your history? And Jerry's?'

'They'll probably want to talk to us both again,' I said. 'We'll deal with that when the time comes. Right now, we need to figure out what's goin' on.'

'Why?'

'What do you mean?'

'Why do we need to figure it out?' Danny asked. 'Let the county dicks work on the Arnold murder and the city dicks work on Stanley's murder. Why do we have to be involved, at all?'

I opened my mouth to answer then realized he was right. Did we really have to get involved, at all?

'I better talk to Bing,' I said. 'He'll want to know about Stanley's death.'

'Can I come?'

'Sure, why not?' I said. 'After all, you found him. But I better call and ask.'

I asked the bartender for a phone and called Bing's room. We talked for a few seconds.

'Well?' Danny asked.

'He said to come right up,' I said, getting off my stool. 'Both of us.'

TWENTY-ONE

When we knocked on the door Bing answered.

'Come on in, boys,' he said, backing away. 'Katy's out getting her hair done.'

'Have you told her—' I started to ask.

'Not yet,' he said. 'I thought I'd . . . wait. For what, I don't know. A better time?'

'What'd you tell her about the horse?'

'That I was thinking about it.'

'Bing, this is Danny Bardini, the private detective I told you about.'

They shook hands.

'Did you find Red Stanley?' Bing asked him.

'I did, Mr Crosby,' Danny said. 'He's dead.'

Bing looked shocked, then said, 'Damn. You fellas want a drink? I'm gonna have one.'

'Sure,' Danny said.

'Bourbon,' I said.

'All around,' Bing said, and poured out three bourbons.

We sat at the bar, with him behind it.

'So what do we do now?' he asked.

'We were just talkin' about that downstairs in the bar,' I said.

'What did you come up with?' Bing asked.

'Well, the police in both jurisdictions are workin' on the murders,' Danny said. 'Do we need to do anything?'

Bing looked at me and I shrugged.

'The cops are still gonna come lookin' for us, aren't they?' Bing asked. 'To question us some more?'

'Yes,' I said, 'but they'll have to make the connection between Arnold and Stanley.'

'I'm the connection,' Bing reminded us. 'The detectives from this morning already know about Red Stanley.'

'He's right,' I said to Danny. 'He had to tell them why he was there.'

'Then unless Mr Crosby—'

'Just Bing, Danny.'

Danny smiled at Bing and said, 'If Bing doesn't tell them that Red Stanley is dead, they're gonna wanna know why.'

'Then I better call them,' Bing said. 'That one detective, Lewis, gave me his number.'

'OK,' I said. 'Call him. Tell him you just found out that your trainer is dead.'

'They'll wanna know how he found out,' Danny said.

'He can tell them you told him,' I said.

'Then do we tell them that you hired me on Bing's behalf to look for him? Or should we just say that Bing hired me and keep you and Jerry out of it?'

The three of us were staring at each other, trying to figure out the best course of action, when the phone rang.

'Hello?' Bing said. 'Oh, really? Well, yes, I suppose you'd better. Thank you.' He hung up.

'What?' I asked.

'I think the question just got answered for us,' he said. 'That was the front desk. They said the police are here to talk to me. They asked if they should let them come up.'

'And you said yes,' Danny said.

Bing nodded.

'OK,' I said, 'look, none of us has done anything wrong. Why should we be worried about talking to the police?'

'What about Jerry?' Danny asked.

'Jerry doesn't have to be here,' I said. 'He had nothing to do with Red Stanley. All he did was ride out to that ranch with Bing to look at a horse.'

'Right,' Bing said.

'So there aren't even any questions we have to avoid,' Danny said.

'Is this an unusual situation for you two boys to be in?' Bing asked.

'Actually,' I said, 'it is.'

TWENTY-TWO

'm not a hood, or a member of the Mafia; although Detective Hargrove of the Las Vegas Police would probably argue against it. Still, I have, on occasion, had to lie to the police.

In Danny's job he has to lie to the cops, a lot.

On this day, neither one of us had to lie.

So yeah, it was kind of unusual when Bing let the detectives in that we were able to relax and tell the truth.

They introduced themselves as Detectives Freeman and Moore.

'Mr Crosby, we're here about a man named Fred Stanley. I believe you know him as Red?'

'Yes,' Bing said. 'And I also know that he's dead.'

'Yes,' Freeman said. He looked at Danny. 'I assumed that when I saw Mr Bardini here.'

Freeman had a Marine crew cut, and the bearing of a military man. He was respectful enough to all of us that I thought he had probably been an officer.

Moore was silent, but I got a feeling of impatience from him. Like he didn't want to be as polite as his partner when he saw Danny there.

'And who are you?' Freeman asked me.

'My name's Eddie Gianelli,' I said. 'I'm a pit boss in the casino.'

'And you're here because . . . ?'

'He's a friend of mine,' Bing said. 'He was helping me try to find my trainer by introducing me to Mr Bardini. Also, he drove me out to meet with the man my trainer and I were supposed to see about buying a horse.'

'A horse?' Moore asked.

'A race horse,' Bing said.

'Let me see if I understand this,' Freeman said. 'You called Mr Gianelli when your trainer didn't show up.' He looked at me. 'You, then, called Mr Bardini and put him together with Mr Crosby.' He looked at Bing. 'You, then, hired Mr Bardini to try to find out what happened to your trainer, Mr Stanley.'

That wasn't exactly the right progression, but Bing said, 'That's right.'

'It didn't occur to you to call the police?'

Bing spread his hands. 'For all I knew Fred Stanley decided not to make the trip. When I couldn't get him on the phone, I asked Danny to find him for me. If he hadn't found him, then I would have called the police.'

'So you found him in that hotel, dead,' Moore said to Danny.

'And called the police right away.'

'How did you find him?' Moore asked.

'Legwork.'

'That's it?'

'Good detective work,' Danny said. 'Contacts.'

'Mr Gianelli,' Freeman said, 'we don't need to talk to you, so you can leave. And Mr Bardini, we've already talked with you, so there's no need for you to stay. We just need to interview Mr Crosby.'

'I'd like them to stay,' Bing said.

Freeman looked at Bing curiously.

'And why is that?'

'Well . . . something happened when Eddie and I drove out to Red Rock Canyon.'

'Red Rock,' Moore said. 'That's where the guy with the race horse was?'

'Yes.'

'And you went without your trainer?'

'I did.'

'But with this guy,' Moore said, indicating me. His lack of respect was starting to show. Maybe he was getting frustrated. He was about to become even more frustrated.

'So why is that important?' Moore asked.

Bing looked at me.

'Because, detective,' I said, 'when we got to the place, we found the horse owner, Chris Arnold, dead.'

'Dead?' Freeman asked. 'How?'

'He had been beaten to death.'

Both detectives turned to face me.

'Did you call the police?'

'Of course we did,' I said. 'Two Sheriff's detectives responded.'

'You have their names?'

'I do,' Bing said. 'I wrote them down.'

He took a slip of paper from his pocket, walked up to Freeman and handed it to him.

'I don't know these guys,' Freeman said, 'but we'll get in touch.'

'But we do know you, Gianelli,' Moore said.

'Well, I don't know you guys.'

'We know a friend of yours,' Moore said. 'Detective Hargrove?'

'Hargrove's no friend of mine.'

'We heard,' Moore said. 'So you just happened to find a dead body, huh?'

'Hey, hey, what's this about?' Bing asked. 'The only reason Eddie was even out there was as a favor to me. So why's he being badgered?'

'You don't know who you're dealin' with, Mr Crosby,' Freeman said. 'Gianelli's got a history here in Vegas with the police, and it's not a good one.'

'I don't care about that,' Crosby said. 'Eddie's a friend of mine, has been for some time. I certainly do know who I'm dealing with. And I think any further dealings I have with you guys will be through my lawyer.'

'That's the way you wanna play it?' Moore asked Bing.

'Easy, Ray,' Freeman said to his partner. 'If Mr Crosby wants us to talk to his lawyer, that's his privilege.'

'I'll have him get in touch with you, Detective Freeman,' Bing said. 'Today.'

'That'll be fine, sir,' Freeman said. 'Let's go, Ray.'

They headed for the door, but before he could leave, Moore decided to get in my face. He got almost nose to nose with me.

'This ain't over for you, boyo.'

'Boyo?' I repeated. 'That's the best you got?'

'Why you—'

'We're leavin' Ray,' Freeman said, grabbing his partner's arm, 'now!'

As they headed for the door Bing's wife, Katy, decided to use her key to enter. She stopped short as the two men almost bowled her over.

'Oh, excuse us, Ma'am,' Freeman said. 'We're so sorry.'

'Sorry, Ma'am,' Moore said.

Kathryn Crosby's beauty drained the two men of all their animosity.

'That's quite all right,' she said to them. 'Good day.'

'Good day, Ma'am,' Freeman said, closing the door behind them.

Kathryn, holding several shopping bags, looked at the three of us and said, 'Would anybody like to tell me who the men were who almost trampled me?'

'Katy, this gent is Danny Bardini, a friend of Eddie's.'

'The detective who's looking for Red Stanley?' she asked.

'That's right, honey. Why don't you take your bags into the bedroom,' Bing suggested. 'I'll be right in to explain everything to you.'

'Did you find him?' she asked Danny.

'Ma'am—' Danny said, somewhat tongue-tied.

'Katy?' Bing said. 'Honestly, I'll explain everything. Just let me finish with Eddie and Danny.'

TWENTY-THREE

'They never asked about Jerry,' Bing said, when Kathryn had gone into the bedroom.

'So you didn't have to lie,' Danny said.

'But once they talk to the Sheriff's detectives,' I said, 'they'll know about Jerry. And when they talk to Hargrove, they'll come lookin' for him.'

'I can fly him back to New York,' Bing offered.

'Probably not a good idea,' Danny said. 'They'd make him come back, even if they had to call the NYPD to do it.'

'And Jerry probably wouldn't go back,' I said to Bing.

'Why not?'

'It's not his style,' I said. 'He'd feel like he was runnin' out on both of us.'

'So what do we do?' Bing asked.

'We wait and see what happens,' I said. 'Meanwhile, you better stick to your guns and have your lawyer contact all the detectives involved.'

'I'll call him as soon as you gents leave,' Bing said, 'and I finish explaining everything to Katy. I don't know if you fellas noticed, but she ain't happy.'

'We'll leave you to it, then,' Danny said. He shook hands with Bing.

'Thanks for everything, Danny,' Bing said. 'You'll send me the bill, huh?'

'Not a chance,' Danny said. 'This one's on Eddie. He owes me.'

'Well, if you're ever in Palm Springs give me a call. We'll have you out to the house.'

'I'll take you up on that,' Danny said. 'You comin'?' he asked me.

'In a minute.'

'I'm headin' back to the office. See you later.'

I nodded, and he left.

'This is a mess,' Bing said.

'It'll take some cleanin' up, that's for sure,' I said.

'Can you stay with it?' Bing asked. 'I mean, the cops'll be back.'

'You'll have your lawyer.'

'I want you, Eddie.'

'You'll have to clear it with Jack, Bing.'

'Jack won't be a problem,' he assured me.

'As long as you're in Vegas, Bing, you can count on me.'

'Good man!' He grabbed my hand and pumped it warmly. 'Why don't you plan on having dinner with me and Katy tonight.'

'Oh,' I said, 'will that go over OK with her?'

'Sure, sure,' Bing said. 'She likes you. And bring Jerry. She's real interested in him.'

'Well, OK,' I said. 'We can do that.'

'I'll have a car pick us up in the front of the hotel,' he said. 'Eight o'clock OK?'

That was two hours away. 'I'll check with the big guy, but it should be fine.'

'This may sound cold,' he said, 'but I'm still interested in that horse. I came all this way to see her.'

'I suppose Chris Arnold might have a wife, or family,' I said. 'You want me to check?'

'No,' Bing said, 'that might bring you into contact with the cops. I'll have my lawyer check on it.'

'OK,' I said. 'We'll meet you in the lobby.'

'I'll pick the place, OK?'

'You're the host.'

He walked me to the door and we shook hands again.

'Sorry to get you mixed up in all this, Eddie.'

'That's OK, Bing. Listen, I'll check in with Jack so he knows what to expect.'

'OK.'

I grabbed the elevator and took it to the second floor to Jack's office. His girl's desk was unoccupied, so I knocked on his open door.

He looked up from his desk, waved and said, 'Eddie, come on in.'

I walked to his desk and sat down across from him.

'What's goin' on?' he asked. 'Or am I gonna regret askin' that question.'

'Um, yeah,' I said, 'you pretty much are, Jack.'

'Two dead bodies?' he repeated after I'd finished my story.

'I'm afraid so.'

'You bring Jerry in from Brooklyn and find two dead bodies?'

'First of all, Jerry's got nothin' to do with either one,' I said. 'Me and Bing were with him when we found Chris Arnold. And Danny found Fred Stanley for Bing.'

'Yeah, yeah,' he said, waving his hands, 'forget I said that. It just seems when you and him get together—'

'That's the way the cops are thinkin', Jack,' I said. 'I don't need for you to be thinkin' the same way.'

'OK, I said forget it!' he snapped. 'Look, I'm sorry. Where's Jerry?'

'Bing got him a suite.'

'Great,' Entratter said. 'Glad to hear he's comfortable.'

'Jack—'

'OK, OK,' Jack said. 'So, the Vegas cops don't know about Jerry yet.'

'Right.'

'And when they find out, they'll come callin'.'

'Right again.'

'Is he heeled?'

'He is.'

'Well, tell him for Chrissake to leave the piece in his room somewhere.'

'I'll tell him.'

'And you know Hargrove is gonna be all over you.'

'It's not his case.'

'That don't matter,' Jack said. 'If he sees a chance to come down on you and Jerry, he'll take it.'

'Bing's gettin' his lawyer involved.'

'I'll call our lawyers, too,' Jack said. 'Keep them on call.'

'Probably smart.'

'Just try to keep your ass and Jerry's ass clean on this.'

'So far we haven't done anything we could be faulted for, Jack,' I said. 'All we did was ride out there with Bing.'

'Is he stayin' in town?'

'The cops want him to stay,' I said, 'plus he's still interested in that horse.'

'Is there family he can deal with?'

'He doesn't know,' I said, 'but he's gonna have his lawyer find out.'

'Well, I guess you won't be goin' back to your pit any time soon,' he said. 'How's your replacement doin'?'

'He's doin' great.'

'You better hope he don't do that great.'

'Why?' I asked. 'You'll promote me?'

'Yeah, right,' he said. 'Look, clear this up as soon as you can.'

'Clear what up?' I asked. 'The cops are investigating both murders. I'm just gonna try to stay out of the way.'

'Funny,' he said, 'tell me another one.'

I started for the door.

'Oh, by the way.'

'Yeah?'

'Aren't you supposed to be showing Frank Junior a good time?'

'Oh, crap,' I said. 'I forgot. Hey, you think he'd like to have dinner with Bing Crosby?'

'When are you going?'

'About an hour.'

Jack shook his head.

'He'll be on stage. Give him a call and arrange to meet him after.'

'I'll do that.'

TWENTY-FOUR

I found Jerry in his suite, watching TV. He was sitting on the big, overstuffed sofa. I had the feeling he was really comfortable in his suite. Going back to his little apartment in Brooklyn might not be so easy.

On the bar was a demolished tray of food, so he'd availed himself of room service.

'Just a snack,' he said, when he saw me looking. 'Don't mean I don't want dinner.'

'That's what I came to see you about,' I said. 'Bing wants us to have dinner with him and Kathryn.'

He sat up straight.

'You and me?'

'That's right.'

'Jeez, Mr G., I don't know. Mr C.'s wife is a real lady.'

'So? You managed to choke down your food last year with Ava Gardner.'

He smiled.

'Miss Ava ain't no lady. She's a broad, if you know what I mean.'

'I know.'

'When's dinner?'

'About an hour.'

He leaped off the sofa.

'I gotta take a shower and get dressed.'

'Yeah,' I realized, 'so do I. I'll stop by here and pick you up in about fifty minutes.'

'OK, Mr G.'

'Oh, and Jerry?'

'Yeah.'

'Leave the rod home.'

'I'll feel naked.'

'Do it, anyway.'

'OK,' he said, glumly.

I went to the room I was using at the Sands and took a quick shower. I'd already grabbed a suit out of my locker first. Checking myself out I had to admit, I was cooking.

Before I left I called the Flamingo and got Frank Junior's room. I asked him if he wanted to meet me in the lounge at the Sands after his show. He told me he already had a date, but if he could make it he'd meet me there. I hung up, thinking that Junior was apparently seeing to his own good time.

I knocked on Jerry's door and he answered, looking very proud of himself. He was wearing a suit, his hair was slicked down, and I smelled cologne.

I stared.

'What?'

'Nothin',' I said. 'I'm just . . . not used to seeing you so . . .' I waved my hands, words failing me.

'I look OK?' he asked, worried.

'You look great, Jerry.'

I frisked him.

'I left the gun in the room, Mr G.,' he said.

'Hidden?'

'Naturally. I always figure some cop is gonna toss my room, even if it's just for the practice.'

I frowned. He may have been right. Once Hargrove heard from Freeman – or the Sheriff's detectives – that Jerry was in town, that wasn't something I'd put past him.

'We better go,' he said, looking at his watch.

I was wearing a sports jacket and no tie. Jerry made me feel underdressed as we walked to the elevator.

We got to the lobby before Bing and Kathryn, which suited us. We didn't want to make them wait for us.

Bing was wearing a jacket and tie, a fedora and his ever-present pipe. Kathryn wore a dress that showed bare shoulders and great legs, and looked stunning.

'Jerry,' Bing said. 'I didn't recognize you. You look . . .'

'He looks very handsome,' Kathryn said. 'Hello, Jerry, good to see you again. How about you call me Katy?'

Jerry was speechless. Kathryn had extended her hand so he took it and shook it delicately.

'Ma'am,' he finally managed.

'Shall we go?' Katy further flustered Jerry by sliding her arm into his and having him walk her to the car.

'If she gets him to call her Katy it'll be a miracle,' I said.

'She's pretty good at miracles,' Bing said.

*   *   *

We went to the Sahara to eat in the Congo Room. Sheckey Green was playing and he introduced Bing from the stage, then came by to say hello.

This was Katy's first trip to Vegas, so Bing wanted to show her the town. We began with the Congo Room, then started to hop from casino lounge to casino lounge. Finally she claimed she was tired, but I figured she wanted to get Bing back to the hotel fairly early.

We drove back to the Sands in the limo. As we got out Katy said, 'Oh, I've lost an earring.'

Bing turned but Katy waved him off and said, 'Eddie can help me find it, Sweetie. Go on inside.'

I knew this was a ruse, because I noticed both her earrings were right where they belonged, on her ears. She wanted to talk.

'Eddie,' she said, putting her hand on my arm, 'Bing told me about the . . . the dead men. I'm worried about him being involved in this.'

'He hasn't done anything, Katy,' I said. 'It'll probably make the papers, and the wire services, but all he did was drive out to meet a guy who turned out to be dead.'

'I know, but you also know how Hollywood can blow things out of proportion.'

'What do you want me to do?'

'I've heard Frank and Dean talk about you,' she said. 'They trust you. Can I trust you?'

'Of course.'

'Can you just . . . watch out for him?' she asked. 'Without telling him that I asked you to?'

She still had her hand on my arm, so I put my hand over hers and said, 'Don't worry, Katy. Everything will be OK.'

'Thank you, Eddie,' she said, squeezing my arm. 'Thank you very much.'

TWENTY-FIVE

When we went inside, Bing Crosby asked, 'Did you find it?' She touched her ear and said, 'Yes, it was in the seat. Eddie found it. Thank you, Eddie.' She leaned over and kissed my cheek.

They said goodnight to us and went up to their suite, arm-in-arm.

'They make a nice couple, even though he's a lot older.'

'Yeah, they do,' I said. 'Let's get a drink in the lounge.'

'OK, Mr G.'

On the way Jerry took off his tie, tucked it into his pocket and undid the top button of his shirt. When we got to the lounge Jack Jones was singing 'Lollipops and Roses,' his hit from the year before. When he saw me, he waved, never missing a beat. I waved back, then stopped to look the place over. In a corner booth sat Frank Junior with a young lady.

'There's Frank Junior,' Jerry said.

'I see him.'

'Who's that he's with?'

'I'm not sure,' I said, 'but it looks like . . . Joey Heatherton.'

'Are either one of them twenty yet?'

'Probably not. Come on, let's just sit at the bar.'

We went to the bar, got the bartender's attention and ordered two beers. Didi came over to say hello, and I introduced her to Jerry. Jack Jones did a few more songs, then came over to say hello, also.

Finally, just before Jack did another set, Frank Junior came over and introduced us to Joey Heatherton, who was a kittenish blonde with more sex appeal than one girl should have.

Frank agreed to have lunch with me the next day, and then he and Joey left.

Jerry finished his second beer and said, 'I'm gonna go to my suite, Mr G.'

'Already?'

'Who knows when I'll ever have a suite again,' he said. 'I'm kinda enjoyin' it.'

'Jerry,' I promised, 'I'll get you a suite from now on whenever you come to town.'

'Nah,' he said. 'This time is good enough. Makes it special, Especially knowin' that Mr C. is payin' for it.'

'OK,' I said. 'Wanna meet for breakfast in the coffee shop?'

'Sure,' he said. 'Eight?'

'That's good. We can talk about what we're gonna do when the cops start comin' after us.'

'Mr G.,' he said, putting his massive paw on my arm, 'this time we didn't do nothin'.'

'You know it,' I said, 'and I know it . . .'

TWENTY-SIX

Rather than stay overnight in the hotel I decided to drive home and sleep in my own bed, even though I'd arranged to meet Jerry early for breakfast. It would only be about an hour's drive from my house in the morning.

Because there had been more than one occasion over the past few years when I found some strangers in my house, I used my key and entered very carefully. I felt silly, though, and quickly switched on a light. What reason would anyone have to lie in wait for me in my own house? We'd said it more than once, Danny, Jerry and I, that we hadn't done anything this time. We were actually in the clear, hadn't shot at anybody, hadn't killed anybody.

I shucked my clothes, hung up what had to be hung up and tossed the rest into the hamper and noticed that it was laundry time. Maybe Frank Junior would like to accompany me to the laundry when I dropped my clothes off the next day.

Yeah, that'd be the day.

I decided not to worry about anything until morning and went to bed.

I woke at six, wondering whatever possessed me to agree to meet Jerry for breakfast at eight.

I showered and brushed my teeth, put on jeans, a polo shirt with a collar, and sneakers. Real casual. Then I put all my laundry into a bag and carried it out to the car. On the way to the Sands I dropped it at a Chinese laundry.

I found Jerry in the Garden Room, working on a pot of coffee and waiting for me, like the morning before. Only this time we didn't have to drive to the desert. He was wearing a sports jacket and pants. I hoped the jacket wasn't to hide his gun.

''Mornin', Mr G.,' Jerry said.

'Jerry,' I said, sliding in the booth across from him. 'Pancakes today?'

'You know it, Mr G.'

'I think I'll join you.'

When the waitress came over I told her two orders of pancakes for Jerry, and one for me.

'Comin' up, Eddie.'

I watched her as she walked away, but couldn't remember her name.

'They all know you, Mr G.'

'Yeah, Jerry,' I said. 'I guess they think they do.'

'What are we gonna do today?' Jerry asked.

'I'm not sure,' I said. 'I guess we should talk to Bing. His lawyer is supposed to find out if there's any family for him to buy that horse from.'

'He still wants to buy the horse?'

'Is it worth buying?'

'I don't know, Mr G.,' he said. 'I never did get a real good look at it.'

'So if Bing is still interested, he'll want you to check it out.'

'Hey, as long as he's payin' the freight, I'm willin' to stay.'

'Jerry, we're gonna have to deal with the cops, pretty soon,' I said. 'Maybe even our old buddy Hargrove.'

'Hey, I figured that, Mr G., when I found the dead guy. I even thought about coverin' him and leavin' him there.'

'Without telling me?'

'Well, it was a just a thought. What's the dick doin' today?'

'Nothin', as far as I know,' I said. 'There's nothin' *for* him to do.'

'He could solve the murder.'

'Not while the cops are workin' on it,' I said. 'He's got a license to consider. Besides, nobody's payin' him to solve it.'

'What about Mr C?'

'I think he's happy to let the police work on it,' I said. 'He knew the man as a trainer, but I don't think they were friends.'

The waitress came with the pancakes, set them on the table in front of us, provided syrup and a fresh pot of coffee.

'Anything else, Eddie?'

'No, thanks a lot.'

She left and we dug in. We were only halfway done when a man I wasn't looking forward to seeing, walked in the door.

'Jerry.'

'Yeah, Mr G?'

'You don't have your gun on you, do you?'

'No, Mr G. It's still hidden in my suite.'

'That's good.'

'Why?'

'Remember we were talkin' about Hargrove before?'

'Yeah.'

'Well, speak of the devil and up he pops.'

'Damn,' Jerry said, 'is he gonna ruin my breakfast?'

Hargrove spotted us and came walking over.

'I think he's gonna give it the old college try.'

TWENTY-SEVEN

Hargrove stopped at our booth, another man behind him. He was younger, looked uncomfortable in his suit, like he hadn't been out of uniform for very long.

'Eddie,' he said. 'Looks like your Gunsel is in for another visit.'

'You're gettin' older, Hargrove,' I said. 'Or are your partners gettin' younger?'

'Probably a little bit of both,' he said. 'You mind if I sit down?'

'Sure, why not?' I asked. 'Have a cup of coffee. Want me to slide over?'

'No.' He grabbed a chair from another table. 'This is good.'

His partner just sat at a chair at the table behind us. He knew his place, already.

'Keep eatin', fellas,' Hargrove said. 'I don't want to ruin your breakfast.'

'Thanks.'

'Where's your other buddy? Bardini?'

'He doesn't check in with me every day.'

'No, huh? Off on a case maybe? Already?'

I shrugged.

'I talked to a colleague of mine yesterday,' Hargrove said. 'Freeman. Know him?'

'I know Freeman.'

'Seems you and the Gunsel, here, got yourselves involved in another murder.'

'We're not involved,' I said.

'Your buddy Bardini is.'

'He just found the body, that's all,' I said. 'He was lookin' for a missin' person, and he found him dead.'

'He was workin' for you, though.'

'Not me,' I said. 'Bing Crosby.'

'Yeah,' Hargrove said, 'another one of your Hollywood bigwig buddies. But in the end he was working for you.'

I looked at him.

'It's not gonna do me any good to keep sayin' no, right?'

'Right.'

'So what do you want, Hargrove?' I asked. 'This isn't your case.'

'I'm helping my friend Freeman,' he said, 'since I know some of the principals involved.'

'That's us, right?' Jerry asked.

'Smart boy.'

There was an empty cup on the table. Hargrove poured himself a cup of coffee.

'Heard you fellas found a body out in Red Rock Canyon, too,' he said.

'Now I know that's not your case,' I said. 'Still helpin' some friends?'

'Naw, I don't know those Sheriff's men,' Hargrove said, sipping his coffee. 'I just find it interesting how you guys always stumble across bodies when you're together.'

'Not always,' I said.

'Enough.'

I ate the last of my pancakes, pushed the plate away.

'What's this about, Hargrove?' I asked.

'I'm just curious, Eddie,' he said. 'I was going to ask you the same question.'

'All I know is what I told the Sheriff's boys, and what I told your boys. Bing Crosby needed some help, we tried to give it to him.'

'Then why the Gunsel?' Hargrove asked.

I saw a muscle jump in Jerry's jaw, but he covered it with a mouthful of pancakes.

'Actually, Bing met Jerry at Del Mar last year and was impressed with his knowledge of horses. When his trainer didn't show up he asked me if Jerry would take a look at the horse for him. Jerry agreed, and Bing flew him out.'

'He's coverin' my expenses,' Jerry said. Then he did something I'd never seen him do before. He smiled at Detective Hargrove. 'He put me in a suite.'

'Nice,' Hargrove said. 'A free flight, free suite, and free pancakes, huh?'

'You got it,' Jerry said.

'Pretty good deal,' Hargrove said, then looked at me and asked, 'but are we sure Crosby didn't bring Jerry in to off the horse owner?'

'Oh yeah,' I said, 'Bing made an appointment to meet the guy. Then we showed up and clubbed him to death before they could make a deal for the horse. And then we called the cops. Tell me something, Detective? What does Bing Crosby gain from that?'

'Gee, I don't know, Eddie,' Hargrove said, 'but maybe I'll poke around and see what I can find out.' He put his cup down. 'Thanks for the coffee. I'll be seeing both of you guys . . . soon.'

'Hargrove,' I said, before he could leave, 'I really like this new quiet, understated technique of yours. Maybe your new partner is rubbing off on you.'

Hargrove just smiled, tossed us a salute and then led his partner out of the coffee shop.

'What the hell . . .' I said.

'I don't like that,' Jerry said. 'He was way too calm. Usually he's yellin' at us.'

'I know,' I said. 'Something's up. We better talk to Bing.'

'After breakfast?' Jerry asked hopefully, looking at the rest of his pancakes.

'Of course, after breakfast,' I said.

TWENTY-EIGHT

I asked the waitress – whose name, I finally remembered, was Jeannie – to bring a phone to the table. When she did I called Bing. When he answered I told him we'd had a visit from the police, and they had something up their sleeve.

'Why would they have it in for me?' he asked. 'I hardly ever come to Vegas.'

'Well, you had the misfortune of gettin' mixed up with Jerry and me,' I said. 'We would have warned you, but we had no idea that your wanting to look at a horse would lead to two dead bodies.'

'No, that's not your fault.'

'Maybe not, but it's us that Hargrove has it in for,' I said. 'That's got to spill over on to you, and that's what I'm apologizing for.'

'OK, look,' Bing said, 'I had my lawyer make some calls. He found out there's a family and they're still willing to sell that horse.'

'Don't tell me you want to go back out to Red Rock Canyon,' I said.

'That's the only way for me to see the horse,' Bing said. 'If I don't at least take a good look at the animal, my trip here is wasted. I mean, as much as I like Frank, and want to support Frankie, I came here to try and buy a horse. Is Jerry still willing to do it?'

I looked at Jerry, who had been listening to my end of the conversation while working on some bacon and toast he'd ordered after he finished with his pancakes. He simply nodded.

'Jerry's willing.'

'What about you, Eddie?'

'I'm with you, Bing.'

'OK,' he said. 'I made an appointment – I mean, an actual appointment – to meet with Chris Arnold's sister, Adrienne, at noon today. We got time to make that, right?'

'Just about,' I said.

'OK, then I'll meet you guys in the lobby in ten minutes. After we see the horse I'll buy lunch someplace expensive. How's that?'

'Jerry's always up for lunch.'

'Great. While we're driving out there I'll tell you what else my lawyer said.'

'OK,' I said. 'See you in ten.'

'Ten?' Jerry asked as I hung up.

'Finish your bacon,' I said. 'I want to make a quick call to Danny.'

I dialed and got Penny.

'It shocked me,' she said, 'but yeah, he's here this early. Hold on.'

'What's up, Bud?' he asked, coming on the line.

I told him about our visit from Hargrove, and warned that he should be on the lookout.

'He's got something up his sleeve,' I said. 'He was way too calm, which makes me think he's confident. Which makes me real uncomfortable.'

'Can I point out that this time we're actually in the clear?' Danny said. 'What could he possibly be confident about?'

'I don't know,' I said, 'but a smug Hargrove is not a pretty sight, so be careful.'

'I will. What're you guys up to?'

'Going back to Red Rock Canyon to see a horse,' I told him, knowing what he would say.

'Again? You're a glutton for punishment.'

'Hey, it's Bing's call.'

'Well, look out for falling bodies,' Danny said. 'Call me if you need me.'

'Hopefully, we won't,' I said.

TWENTY-NINE

'My lawyer said the family owns the horse,' Bing said, 'but that some of them are not in agreement about selling it.'

'Wouldn't be the first time family killed family,' Jerry said, 'over a lot less than a horse. What's the askin' price, Mr C?'

'Two hundred thousand.'

'Wow,' I said. 'This must be some nag.'

'You remember that horse who won at Del Mar last year when we were there?'

I didn't, but Jerry said, 'Crazy Kid.'

'Right. This one is supposed to be a half brother to that one.'

'Makes him worth the money,' Jerry said, 'if he's sound.'

'Sound?'

'If he ain't a cripple,' Jerry said.

'I getcha,' I said.

'Hopefully, we'll get a better look at him today,' Bing said.

When we reached the point in the road where we had encountered the other car we all had our eyes peeled, but we were alone out there. Nobody spoke, but I sensed two sighs of relief to go along with my own.

We reached the ranch at eleven fifty-five, five minutes early for our noon appointment. As we drove up to the house I saw a woman waiting for us with her arms crossed. She was wearing pants and what looked like riding boots, and had a very nice shape on her, from a distance with long, red hair that hung past her shoulders, pulled back into a ponytail. As we got closer, she only got better. The pants and boots really showed off what appeared to be showgirl quality legs.

As Jerry stopped the car she dropped her arms and walked towards us. She was wearing a man's shirt tucked into her jeans, which pulled the material taut over full breasts.

'Mr Crosby,' she said, as we got out of the car. 'I'm Adrienne Arnold.'

They shook hands and Bing said, 'Miss Arnold, I'm so sorry about what happened to your brother.'

'Thank you,' she said. 'I appreciate that you found him and called the police.'

I thought this woman had a lot of sand to be meeting us here the day after her brother had been bludgeoned to death on the grounds.

'This is my trainer, Jerry Epstein,' Bing lied, 'and Eddie Gianelli, who works at the Sands Hotel, where I'm staying.'

Jerry nodded, didn't blink once when Bing called him his 'trainer'.

'Miss Arnold,' I said, 'my condolences.'

Up close we saw how beautiful she was. She had big brown eyes and a gorgeous wide mouth. A prominent nose did nothing to ruin the effect and, in fact, gave her a very strong profile. I hadn't seen enough of the dead man's face to see if there was a strong resemblance.

'Shall we go and look at the horse?' she asked.

'Of course,' Bing said.

She and Bing walked ahead of us, and I noticed Jerry was watching her denim-encased butt as closely as I was. She was statuesque, the boots making her almost six feet tall.

As we got to the barn I couldn't help looking over at the stall where Jerry had found her brother. She seemed to have no trouble at all ignoring it, though, and walked right to the horse.

'Why don't we take him out to the corral so you can get a good look?' she asked. 'I moved the other horses out of there.'

'Good idea,' Bing said.

'Do you think your man could do that for me?' she asked. 'It was always my brother who handled the horses.'

'Jerry?' Bing said, looking at the big guy.

'No problem, Mr C.,' Jerry said.

I stood back. I knew nothing about horses. Didn't know how to ride them, judge them or – as was obvious at Del Mar the year before – how to bet them.

Jerry actually put a halter on the horse before leading him out of the stall, through the bar and out the back into the corral. I saw Adrienne Arnold watching him closely, and decided she knew more about horses than she was letting on. She wanted to see how much Jerry knew.

Bing walked out with Jerry.

'Why don't we go out the front, Mr Gianelli,' she said. 'We'd only be in the way inside the corral.'

'Suits me,' I said, following her out.

'What's your job at the Sands, if I may ask?'

'I'm a pit boss.'

'That's an important position in a casino, isn't it?' she asked.

'I like to think so. Do you gamble?'

'Only on horses,' she said.

'Well, if you played blackjack and wanted to increase the stakes at your table, that would have to be OKed by me.'

'I see,' she said. 'That puts a lot of money in your hands, doesn't it?'

'Usually, yes.'

'You must be very trustworthy.'

'And loyal,' I said. 'I'm a regular boy scout.'

'Oh,' she said, 'somehow I doubt that, Eddie.'

THIRTY

We watched from outside the corral as Jerry and Bing checked the horse's legs, and looked in his mouth. She explained to me that you could tell a lot about a horse by looking at its teeth.

I had noticed last year at Del Mar that Jerry referred to the horses as 'he' and 'her,' while most of the other folks around us called them 'it.' Adrienne Arnold was one of the 'it' people.

But I had a hard time listening to her talk about horses. I found myself zoning out and just staring at her profile when she wasn't looking at me. Except once when she caught me and gave me a long look back. I managed not to turn away, which I think won me some points.

'Oh, no,' she said, looking past me at one point.

I turned and saw a man stalking towards us, obviously angry. He was dressed similarly to Adrienne, was also very tall, but was very thick through the middle. Nevertheless, I assumed this was another family member.

'Problem?' I asked.

'My brother,' she said. 'He's not in favor of this sale.'

'He does look mad,' I said, and as he got closer I added, 'and big.'

'Yes,' she said, 'he uses his size to intimidate people. Did it to Chris and me as kids, and he's still trying.'

'Get away from that horse!' he shouted, attracting Bing and Jerry's attention.

When he reached us I saw that he was at least six-three, in his forties, which put him at least ten years older than his sister. He was barrel-chested, with arms that strained at his long-sleeved shirt, and legs like tree trunks. His eyes were narrowed in anger, his mouth twisted, but he shared the prominent nose with his sister, which made it pretty obvious that they were related.

Bing looked to Adrienne Arnold for guidance.

'Keep examining the horse, Mr Crosby,' she said. 'I'll handle my brother.'

By the time the man reached us his face was crimson with fury, and his big hands were closed into fists.

'Philip,' Adrienne said, 'don't make a scene.'

'I'll make a scene if I want to, Adrienne,' he snapped. 'Who are these people?'

'They're here to look at the horse,' she said. 'In case you don't recognize the man in the corral, that's Bing Crosby.'

'Crosby!' he said. 'Are these the men who found Chris yesterday.'

'That's right.'

'Well, you sure didn't waste any time gettin' them back here, did you?' he demanded.

'This is what Chris wanted, Philip.'

'What he wanted? What do you know about what he wanted? This is what you want, and you bullied him into selling.'

'I'm not the bully in this family, Philip.'

'You can't let that go, can you, Adrienne?' he asked. 'We were kids—'

'You've hardly grown up, Philip. You still think your size gives you the advantage.'

'I'll show you an advantage,' he said, coming at her, fists raised, looking as if he was going to hit her.

I stepped into his path to stop him, said, 'Hey—' but that was as far as I got before he brushed me aside with a swipe of one arm.

As I hit the ground I thought for sure he was going to strike his sister but, out of nowhere – I never saw him move – Jerry was there. He grabbed Philip Arnold's raised arm by the wrist and the two big men's eyes locked.

Arnold was muscle-bound, but Jerry was slightly bigger, and rawboned. He didn't work on his strength in a gym, it came to him naturally. He was big and strong by the grace of God, not Charles Atlas.

If possible, Philip Arnold's face got even redder as he strained to pull his arm free of Jerry's grip. Finally, Jerry released his hold with his right hand, but stiff-armed the man with his left, driving him back. Arnold's arms windmilled as he tried to stay on his feet, but in the end he ended up sitting on his ass in the dirt, staring up at Jerry.

'Looks like you've finally met your match, Philip,' Adrienne said, with great satisfaction.

Arnold switched his hate-filled glance to his sister. I got back to my feet and went to stand alongside Jerry. Bing was still in the corral, holding the horse's reins, patting his neck to keep him calm.

'Take it easy, man,' Jerry said. 'Don't raise your hands to the lady.'

We all waited to see what Philip Arnold's reaction was going to be.

THIRTY-ONE

P hilip Arnold slowly got to his feet, but I was watching him closely, as was Jerry. If he charged, Jerry would be ready, but instead he stood there, brushing the dirt off his butt, seeming to gain control of himself.

'This ain't over,' he said, maybe to all of us, but definitely to his sister. He pointed a thick finger at her. 'My lawyer says you can't make this sale without my signature.'

'Then you better have your lawyer talk to my lawyer, Philip,' Adrienne said. 'I think you'll find I can.'

'You can bring in all the bully boys you want,' he said, 'it ain't gonna make a difference.'

'You can't stand that you're not the biggest, strongest man in the room, can you?' she asked, mocking him.

'We'll see who the bully boy is, Adrienne,' Philip said. Unconsciously he was rubbing the wrist that Jerry had grabbed. 'We'll see.'

He turned and stalked away.

Adrienne looked at Jerry and said, 'Thank you. I've never seen anyone overpower my brother like that before.' Then she looked at me. 'And thank you for stepping between us.'

'Didn't do much good,' I said. 'He swatted me aside like a fly.'

'It doesn't matter,' she said. 'He might have hit me if you hadn't given Jerry time to step between us.'

She turned and looked at Bing in the corral.

'Shall we go inside and talk. I have lemonade, or something stronger.'

'Lemonade sounds good,' Jerry said.

'Come on, Jerry,' Bing said. 'Let's walk this big boy back into the barn.'

'Right, Mr C.'

I saw how Jerry had been able to get to us so quickly when he vaulted back over the fence to grab the reins from Bing.

'Just come up to the house when you've secured the horse,' Adrienne called out to them. To me she said, 'Shall we walk inside?'

'Sure.'

As we walked back she asked, 'My brother didn't hurt you, did he?'

'Only my pride,' I said. 'I've never really thought of myself as a little guy.'

When she looked at me our eyes were about even, but I consoled myself with the fact that she was wearing cowboy boots.

'Do you have any more relatives we have to worry about?' I asked.

'Actually, I have quite a large family,' she said, 'but Philip is the only one to worry about. I have a younger brother and sister, but they're not the least bit interested in horses.'

'Is your sister anything like you?' I asked.

'How do you mean?'

'I mean beautiful.'

'Oh.' She surprised me with a slight blush. I had thought she was being playful, but apparently she actually didn't know what I'd meant.

'Well, she's younger than I am and, yes, quite pretty,' she said. 'But she's not here today.'

We reached the house and entered through the unlocked front door. I hadn't heard a vehicle leave, and half expected to find big Philip somewhere inside, but it seemed empty.

'Lemonade?' she asked.

'Sure.'

'And your friends?'

'I think that'll be good for everyone.'

'I'll go and get it,' she said. 'Make yourself comfortable.'

I walked around the big living room, which was dominated by a baby grand piano that was covered with framed photos. I walked over to take a look. Most of them seemed to be of a man I assumed was Chris Arnold, standing surrounded by horses. I didn't see any photos of Adrienne until I got to the fireplace mantle.

'Oh no,' she said, as she came in carrying a tray, 'not the family photos.'

'Do you play the piano?' I asked.

'I'm afraid not,' she said. 'This is actually my brother Chris's house. That is, it was. We haven't read his will yet, so I don't know what will happen to it.'

'What do you think will happen to it?' I asked.

'Well,' she said, setting the tray down on the coffee table, 'I know my brother Philip wants the place. But I think he's going to be disappointed.'

'You think Chris left it to you?'

'Either that, or equal parts to the four of us, but I don't think he'd want to do that to the rest of. Make us partners with Philip, I mean.'

'Philip seemed to think he had an interest in the horse,' I said. 'What's the horse's name, by the way. Bing didn't mention it.'

'My brother didn't usually name the horses,' she said. 'He left that to the people who bought them.'

'He didn't race horses himself?'

'No,' she said, 'he likes – liked – to breed them, but he didn't have the actual racing gene in him.'

'Is that why Philip would want to keep the horse?' I asked. 'To race him?'

'I really think the reason Philip doesn't want the horse sold is that I do.'

'So, it's like that?'

'Oh, yes,' she said. 'Do you have any brothers or sisters?'

'One of each,' I said. 'We don't speak much.'

'It must be easier that way.'

'It is.'

'And your parents?'

'My mother died recently,' I said. 'My father and I don't talk. My family still lives in Brooklyn.'

'Brooklyn,' she said. 'That's it. I've been trying to pinpoint your accent.'

'Is it bad?' I put my hand over my mouth, as if she had told me I had bad breath.

'No, it's hardly noticeable, except sometimes you drop your 'g's', and pronounce a word or two in an . . . odd way.'

'Where are you from?'

'Here,' she said. 'Nevada. My parents are dead. Have been for a long time. I actually raised my younger brother and sister. I'm glad my parents didn't live to see what an ass Philip has become.'

At that point Bing and Jerry came walking in.

'There's a bathroom right through there, if you want to wash up,' she said, pointing.

'Thank you,' Bing said. He and Jerry went through. Adrienne poured two lemonades and handed me one, then poured two more and left them on the tray for Jerry and Bing.

'So,' she said, 'you work in a Vegas casino. Must be a lot of women in your life.'

THIRTY-TWO

'There are a lot of women in Vegas,' I said, 'but no one special, right now. You?'

'Unattached, at the moment,' she said. 'Keeping my brothers from killing each other is a full-time job.' Then she put her hand over her mouth as she realized what she'd said.

'Oh God,' she said. 'I didn't mean—'

'It's OK,' I said.

Bing came walking into the room at that moment, then stopped short, as if he thought he was interrupting something.

'Come on in, Bing,' I said. 'The lemonade is very refreshing.' I pointed to the two glasses sweating on the tray.

'Jerry'll be along in a minute,' he said, snatching up one of the glasses.

'Mr Crosby,' she asked, 'what did you think of the horse?'

'Please,' he said, 'call me Bing. Jerry thinks the horse is very sound, and well formed.'

'Well then, could we go to the study and talk . . . money? Or do you want your . . . trainer involved in that part?'

'No,' he said, 'I can handle that myself. Gents?'

'Go ahead,' I said to Bing. 'If it's all right with the lady we'll wait here.'

'Of course,' she said. 'Make yourselves comfortable. If you want something stronger than lemonade there's a bar against that wall.'

'Thank you,' I said.

'Bing?'

They each carried a glass of lemonade out of the room with them.

'You want a drink?' I asked Jerry.

'No thanks, Mr G.'

I decided to stick with lemonade.

'What do you really think of the horse?' I asked.

'Well, he's a half to Crazy Kid—'

'A half?'

'Half brother,' he said. 'And he's put together well. I think it's a good buy.'

'For two hundred thousand?'

Jerry hesitated before he answered, then said, 'That depends.'

'On what?'

'First, does she have the right to sell it, or will he have to deal with that brother,' Jerry said, 'and second, the paperwork has to work out.'

'You mean, is he really a half to Crazy Kid?'

'Right.'

'Won't Bing need you for that?'

'I know a good horse when I see one, Mr G.,' Jerry said, 'but I don't know squat about papers. Mr C. is on his own there.'

'Well,' I said, 'it's his money, and he's bought horses before. And he has other trainers, right?'

'I suppose so,' Jerry said.

'Well, it didn't seem like he knew this one very well.'

'I think the trainer came to him with this deal,' Jerry said. 'Maybe they never had a horse together before.'

'You could be right.'

Surprisingly, Bing and Adrienne came back into the room. Seems they didn't need all that much time to hash out a price.

'I'll give you a call, Adrienne, probably in a day or two.'

'I'll be waiting to hear,' she said. They shook hands.

'I'm curious about something, Adrienne, if I may?' I said.

'By all means.'

'Are there any other buyers interested in this horse?'

'Not at the moment,' she said. 'If Mr Crosby doesn't buy it, though, I'm sure there will be.'

I nodded.

'Anything else?' she asked.

'Nope,' I said. 'I'm done.'

'I'll be in touch, Adrienne,' Bing said.

She walked us out to our car and stood there watching as we drove off, with her hands on her hips.

'What do you think?' I asked Bing.

'I'm worried about the brother,' he said. 'She says he has no claim on the horse.'

'I think he's probably a sore loser,' I said.

'He's a muscle-head,' Jerry said. 'Don't worry about him.'

'I wouldn't,' Bing said, 'as long as you're around, Jerry.'

THIRTY-THREE

When we got back to the Sands we all needed to clean up. I got one of the valets to take the car to get washed. Bing and Jerry went to their suites for showers, while I had mine in the locker room.

I'd taken most of my changes of clothes out of my locker lately without replacing them. All I had left were jeans and a t-shirt. I was going to have to go and pick up my laundry.

I called up to Jerry's suite to let him know what I was going to do.

'Comin' back later, Mr G?'

'Oh yeah,' I said. 'I've got no life outside of this place. I'll be back.'

'You oughtta get yerself a life, Mr G.,' he said. 'Maybe a steady girl.'

'A steady girl in Vegas, Jerry? With all these waitresses and showgirls around? No thanks.'

I told him I'd see him later and hung up.

My Caddy was in its parking spot, clean as a whistle, inside and out. I found the valet and tipped him extra, then drove home, stopping first to get the laundry.

When I got home I put my laundry away, setting aside a few things to take back to the casino. Then I had a cold beer and wondered if I should go back to my pit when I got back to the casino. After all, what more was there for me to do? I'd been so busy with Bing that I hadn't been able to fulfill my obligation to play host to Frank Junior.

On the other hand, Kathryn had specifically asked me to watch out for her husband. To that end I figured I should remain available to him until he decided to leave town.

But what about Jerry? He'd done what Bing had asked him to do, take a look at the horse. If we sent him home would the police end up looking for him and having him brought back? Were we even going to hear from the Sheriff's detectives again?

The fact that Hargrove had chosen to involve himself in matters made me nervous. Also, his laid-back attitude when he'd spoken to us at breakfast bothered me. What was that about? I couldn't see Hargrove, at this late date in his career, exchanging his bully boy tactics for a gentler hand.

I thought about having another beer but decided to skip it. I could have something when I got back to the Sands.

I left the house and started walking to my car, which was in my driveway, when I heard a voice.

'Hey! Hold it!'

I turned, saw three burly men walking across my lawn at me. The one in the front, calling out to me, looked familiar. When he got closer I could see his red face and recognized him as Adrienne Arnold's muscle-head brother, Philip. He looked mad, and so did the two muscle-bound idiots with him.

I know my limitations, and that day they were even more obvious. These three guys would undoubtedly bust me up if I let them get their hands on me.

I sprinted to my Caddy, leaped over the door into the seat and got it started. They all got their hands on the car as I backed out, yelling something, but I popped it in drive and took off, hopefully leaving them behind.

THIRTY-FOUR

I t wasn't that easy.

The three of them managed to get back to their car, a green sedan that apparently had something under the hood. They got behind me, but rather than chasing me, they seemed to be following. It looked like they were going to try to tail me to wherever I was going and brace me again there.

I had other ideas.

My neighborhood was full of small residential streets that you couldn't very well speed through, but since I knew where they were I was able to get into them quicker. Each time I took a turn on one of those streets, I got a little more room between us.

I finally made my way to Industrial Drive, a large multi-lane street that pretty much ran parallel to Las Vegas Blvd, referred to by some as 'The Strip.' Once I got on that multi-lane road I put my foot down. My plan was to come at the Sands from the back, hopefully losing my tail along the way.

*   *   *

I entered the hotel from the rear, made my way down a hall to the front lobby. I went to the door and looked out, trying to see if there was a green sedan being parked.

I moved back through the lobby to the casino, where I felt safe. But now what would I do about going home? And what did Philip Arnold have against me, anyway? It was Bing who was buying the horse, and Jerry who had embarrassed him. All I'd done was get knocked on my ass by the muscle-head. Why was he coming after me?

I briefly went by my pit to see how my replacement was doing, and saw that I wasn't being missed there.

I went into the bar for a beer and got the bartender to bring me a house phone.

'What are you doin'?' I asked Jerry when he answered.

'Watchin' TV.'

'You order room service?'

'I was thinkin'. Why, are you back?'

'Yeah, I'm in the bar.'

'You wanna go someplace to eat?'

'Yeah,' I said. 'Come on down. I'll take you for a good burger.'

'And fries?'

'And fries.'

'I'll be down in a few minutes.'

'I'll be in the Silver Queen bar.'

I hung up, picked up my beer and saw my worst nightmare come through the door: Philip Arnold and his muscle boys.

I had no place to go, so I sat tight as they approached. At least there were a few people in the lounge at that time of the day, and the bartender.

'Thought you got away from me, didn't you?' Philip Arnold said, accusingly.

'I hoped.'

'You must think I'm stupid,' Arnold said. 'Think I don't know where you work?'

'Mr Arnold,' I said, 'I have no idea how smart or dumb you really are. All I can say is, maybe you aren't as dumb as I thought.'

'Watch your mouth,' Arnold said. 'You don't have your big friend here with you, this time.'

No, I thought, but if I could stall long enough . . .

'What do you want, Mr Arnold?' I asked. 'What's so important you had to come to my home, and my place of business?'

'Maybe I just wanted to finish what we started.'

'What did we start?' I asked. 'You knocked me on my ass. That didn't satisfy you?'

'You tried to get in my way,' Arnold said. 'If you know what's good for you, you'll convince your Hollywood friend, Bing Crosby, to back off.'

'Why should he?'

'That horse is not for sale.'

'That's not what your sister says.'

'Look,' Arnold said, 'I ain't gonna tell you again.'

'You gonna beat me up in front of all these people?' I asked.

'We'll do that,' one of his friends said, 'and wreck this place at the same time.'

The three of them stared at me with the same vacant eyes. I had the feeling that inside all their heads they were dismembering me.

'Is there a problem here?'

The three men parted so they could see who was speaking behind them. Standing there were Dean Martin and Mack Grey. Dino had an easy going look on his face, while Mack was frowning. Both of them were ex-boxers, and Mack was almost as big as Jerry. Suddenly, my odds had more than evened up.

Arnold and his boys were trying to figure the odds when Jerry walked in and that was it, the odds swung firmly to my side.

'Hey, Mr G.,' Jerry said. 'This a party?'

'You were saying?' I said to Philip Arnold.

All he had left were the same words he'd used out in the Red Rock Canyon.

'This ain't over.'

As he turned to leave Jerry got right in front of him, chest bumped him.

'It better be over,' he said to Arnold, ''cause I don't care how many muscle-heads you got with you next time. I'll take you apart.'

Arnold tried to brazen it out and hold Jerry's look, but in the end he averted his eyes, moved around Jerry and skulked off to follow his friends who had gotten out of there quick.

'What did we just walk into, Eddie?' Dino asked.

'You guys just saved somebody from a beatin',' I said, 'and I think it was me.'

'No chance, Mr G.,' Jerry said. 'You woulda held your own til I got here.'

'Come on, guys,' Dean said, 'what's goin' on?'

'Mr G.'s takin' me for the best burger in town,' Jerry said to Dino and Mack. 'You guys wanna come along?'

'I could use a big burger,' Mack said to Dean.

'Sure, why not?' Dean said. 'I got a limo. Let's do it.'

THIRTY-FIVE

M y favorite burger place was way the hell out at a far end of Industrial Drive. I'd been there a lot, and taken many friends and girls there, but this was the first time I ever drove up in a limo with a Hollywood and Vegas legend.

The place was a little clapboard shack – the Burger Shack – that looked like it would blow away in a stiff wind. Getting out of the limo, though, the smell of meat and onions made my mouth water.

'Man, that smells good,' Jerry said.

There were picnic tables set up outside, and one was open. There was a line at the window, so I suggested Dean and Mack grab the table, and Jerry and I would grab the food. I also thought that Dean Martin standing in the line might attract attention. Maybe sitting at the table he'd be able to keep a low profile.

Jerry and I got on the back of the line. Our plan was to carry as many burgers and fries back to the table as we could.

When we got to the window and Jerry saw that they also had hot dogs he got himself two burgers and two hot dogs. And an order of fries. I got one burger and an order of fries for each of the rest of us, and piled some condiments on the tray. We managed to carry it all back to the table, and then Jerry went back for four beers.

'Thanks, pally,' Dean said, accepting a beer from Jerry.

Mack nodded as he took his, his mouth already full of fries.

We dressed our burgers and bit into them. They were so juicy that grease rolled down our hands.

'Wow,' Jerry said, 'this is a good burger.'

'I'll say,' Mack agreed.

'So tell me, Eddie,' Dino said. 'What was goin' on in the bar?'

'That guy is related to the dead man who was gonna sell Bing the horse,' I said. 'And there's a sister. She's taken over the sale, but this brother doesn't want it to go through.'

'Why was he gonna take it out on you?' Dean asked. 'And why'd he bring help?'

I told him what had happened out at the ranch.

'Well,' Dean said, 'they're lucky they backed off. The four of us would've cleaned the place up with 'em.'

'You got that right,' Mack said around a mouthful of burger.

While we were talking, Jerry finished both hotdogs and one of his burgers.

'How were the hot dogs?' Mack asked.

'OK, but not as good as Nathan's in Brooklyn.'

'You know, I spent a lotta time in Chicago,' Mack said, 'and those Chicago hot dogs are pretty good. I can't see how them skinny Nathan's dogs can be better.'

'Are you crazy?' Jerry asked. 'There ain't nothin' better than a Nathan's hot dog. Hell, even those dogs at Nedicks in the city are better than Chicago. I mean, you gotta put all that extra stuff on them to make them taste better, right?'

'All that stuff joins with the hot dog,' Mack explained, 'which is nice and plump.'

Jerry and Mack went off then, each extolling the virtues of Chicago and Brooklyn hot dogs. I thought I should probably stop them before they moved on to a pizza argument.

'When does Frank get to town?' I asked.

Both Jerry and Mack stopped and looked at me.

'Tomorrow,' Dean said.

'And that's Frankie's last night at the Flamingo?'

'Yep.'

I counted in my head.

'That makes five nights. The Flamingo booked a new singer for five nights?'

Dean stared at me.

'Never mind,' I said. 'That was silly.' A new singer named Sinatra, I told myself.

'Hey,' Dean said, 'I'm gonna go and get a burger for the driver. I forgot all about him.'

'I'll get it, boss,' Mack said. 'Somebody might spot you in line and cause a fuss.'

As Mack walked towards the shack, Dean called out, 'Bring him a beer, too.'

After we all finished our burgers – including the driver – we piled into the limo and headed back to the Sands. The inside of the car smelled like meat and onions. Not so bad. Jerry and Mack continued their hot dog debate, and then *did* move on to pizza.

THIRTY-SIX

The next morning the hotel was gearing up because Frank Sinatra was coming in. The steam room in the basement had to be ready. It pretty much belonged to Frank, and while any of the group – Dean, Sammy, Peter or Joey – was free to use it, nobody ever did unless Frank was there.

When I drove in from home I could see the hustle and bustle Frank's imminent arrival always caused.

I had gone home the night before, despite the fact Philip Arnold could have shown up with his two boyfriends at any time. Jerry offered to go home with me and sleep on the couch – 'like the old days' – but I refused.

'I don't think he's that dangerous,' I said.

'Well, if he does bother you,' Jerry said, 'remember, don't fight fair.'

I didn't have to worry about fighting fair or foul, since he never showed up.

As I crossed the lobby somebody called my name from the front desk. I headed over there. It was Charlie Slater, one of the concierges.

'Glad I spotted you,' he said. 'Somebody came in lookin' for ya this morning.'

'Who?'

'Cops.'

'Where are they now?'

'Mr Entratter's office. He told me to watch out for you.'

'To tell me to go up and see him, or to warn me off?' I asked. Charlie shrugged.

'You know who they were?'

'A couple of detectives,' Charlie said. 'I got no names, though.'

'Were they lookin' for anybody else?'

'Mr Entratter said they wanted to talk to Jerry, and to Mr Crosby.'

'And are either one of them up there?'

'I think Mr Crosby.'

'Have you seen Jerry?'

'He's that big guy that's friends with you, right?' Charlie asked.

'That's right.'

'I ain't seen him this mornin'.'

'OK, Charlie, thanks.'

I went to the house phone and dialed Jerry's suite. No answer. Next I dialed Jack's number. He answered.

'Are we in trouble?'

'No,' Entratter said, 'I said I didn't want to be disturbed. I've got Bing Crosby with me.'

'I get it,' I said. 'Is one of the detectives in your office; Hargrove?'

'That's right.'

'What the hell does he want? We haven't done anything.'

'I don't have all the answers.'

'All right, Jack,' I said, 'I might as well just come up.'

'And your friend?'

'I don't know where Jerry is,' I said. 'So for now, I'll come up alone.'

'OK, you do that.'

We hung up. I walked to the elevator and took one up to the second floor. Jack's girl just waved me in without saying a word.

THIRTY-SEVEN

'Well, look who's here,' Hargrove said. He was seated so he could see the door as I entered.

'Hello, Detective,' I said.

Bing Crosby turned in his chair and said, 'Good morning, Eddie.'

'Bing.' I looked at Jack. 'Is this why you were lookin' for me, Jack?'

'Come on in, Eddie,' Jack said. 'The detectives have some questions.'

I looked at the other detective in the room, and was surprised. I expected one of the other Las Vegas dicks, but instead it was one of the Sheriff's Department men. I didn't recall his name.

'You remember Detective Lewis, don't you, Eddie?' Hargrove asked. 'From the Sheriff's Department?'

'Sure,' I said. 'Nice to see you, Detective. Or is it?'

'I don't know, sir,' Lewis said. 'I guess we'll have to wait and see.'

'Sit down, Eddie,' Hargrove said. 'We were just asking Mr Crosby some questions about the other day in Red Rock Canyon.'

'What more do you think he knows?' I asked, while I remained standing.

'Well, that's why we ask questions,' Hargrove said.

'Well, maybe I can help clear up whatever's bothering you fellas,' I said.

'Oh, don't worry, Eddie,' Hargrove said. 'You'll get your turn.'

'Mr Crosby?' Detective Lewis said. 'You mind answerin' my last question?'

'And what was that question, Detective?' Bing asked.

'How long were you and Mr Epstein apart before he came back and told you he had found the victim?'

'Hold on,' I said. 'This is about Jerry?' I looked at Hargrove. 'You're tryin' to pin this on Jerry?'

'We didn't know about Mr Epstein's record when we spoke to you at the scene the other day,' Lewis said. 'Detective Hargrove was kind enough to fill us in on both of you.'

'So why aren't you trying to pin it on me, then?' I asked.

'You and Mr Crosby were together,' Lewis said. 'Or you say you were. That puts Epstein alone with the victim.'

'Yeah, the dead victim.'

'So he says,' Hargrove said. 'And we all know Jerry the Torpedo never lies.'

'Whatever you think of him, he's not lying now,' I said.

'That's what you say,' Hargrove said. 'I think Mr Crosby should answer the question.'

'It was only a few minutes,' Bing said. 'Hardly enough time to beat a man to death.'

'That's not for you to decide, Mr Crosby,' Lewis said. 'I've seen Epstein. He's certainly big enough to beat a man to death, especially if he's using a weapon.'

'What weapon?' I asked.

'We haven't determined that, yet.'

'Jerry couldn't have beaten that man to death and avoided being splattered with blood.' I looked at Lewis. 'Did you see any blood on him?'

Lewis looked over at Hargrove.

'We still need to talk to Epstein,' Hargrove said.

'I don't know where he is.'

'Not likely,' Hargrove said. 'You always know where he is. When he's in town you two are joined at the hip.'

'Sorry,' I said. 'Can't help you. I called his suite and he wasn't there.'

'His suite, huh?' Hargrove shook his head. 'How does a Brooklyn torpedo rate a suite?'

'I'm paying for it,' Bing said. 'He's my guest here.'

'That figures.'

'Gents,' Entratter said, 'I think we've all cooperated with you as much as we can, right now.'

'You think so?' Hargrove asked. He looked at me. 'Where's your buddy, Bardini?'

'How am I supposed to know?' I asked. 'You think these two check in with me with their every move?'

'We're lookin' for him,' Hargrove said, standing up. 'You let him know that . . . if you see him.'

'I'll pass that message along.'

'Mr Crosby,' Hargrove said, 'don't leave town.'

'Why not?' Bing asked.

'We might have more questions.'

'I think you might have to talk to my lawyer, in the future,' Bing said. 'I was nice enough to come down here to be questioned—'

'Just don't leave,' Hargrove said, cutting him off.

Hargrove looked at Lewis, who stood up and followed the Las Vegas dick out the door.

'They're gonna try to pin the Red Rock murder on Jerry,' I said.

'And sounds like they want Bardini for the Vegas killing,' Entratter said.

'Jesus,' I said, sitting down next to Bing. 'Jack, this time we're in the clear on both cases.'

'Then maybe you've got nothin' to worry about, Eddie,' he said.

'Somehow,' I said, 'I can't bring myself to look at it that way.'

THIRTY-EIGHT

I went back down to the casino floor while Bing stayed to talk with Entratter. I think they were going to try to get their lawyers together.

I needed to find Jerry and tell him what was going on, and then we needed to track down Danny and warn him. As long as the cops were looking at Jerry for the Red Rock murder, and at Danny for the Fred Stanley murder, they weren't going to be looking for the real killers.

While I was looking for Jerry in the casino I started to wonder, if both murders involved horsemen, maybe they were connected. And they both also involved Bing Crosby. I didn't know if the murders could have been done by the same person, but it was no stretch to think they were somehow connected.

I didn't find Jerry in the casino, the lounge or the coffee shop. I checked the race book, but he wasn't there either. I didn't know where else to look. If he left the casino where would he go? And how? The only time he ever left the Sands was when he drove my Caddy.

I went through the hotel lobby and out the front door, checked with the valets if they had seen Jerry get into a car, either a cab or a limo. There had been no sign of him.

Inside I went to a house phone, tried his suite again. No answer. Then I realized I needed tickets for Frank Junior's closing night. I didn't want to ignore Frank by not showing up for his kid's last performance. I called my contact at the Flamingo to make sure he held out four tickets for me. I was thinking me and Jerry, and then maybe Danny and Penny.

With that done I wondered if I should go ahead and leave the hotel and look for Danny. I started away from the house phones and stopped when I saw somebody in the lobby. She was just standing there, looking around, as if she didn't quite know what direction to go in. She was similarly dressed to the last time I'd seen her, but the shirt was a little dressier, and the jeans were very clean. The heels of her boots unnecessarily added to her height. The biggest difference was her hair, which was cascading down over her shoulders, shimmering as if she had just washed it.

I walked over, reached her as her head was turned and said, 'Miss Arnold?'

Adrienne Arnold turned her head to me quickly, her eyes wide, her mouth slightly open. The men in the hotel lobby were all looking at her.

'Oh! Mr Gianelli,' she said. 'You startled me.'

'What are you doing here?' I asked. 'Looking for Bing Crosby?'

'Um, no,' she said, 'actually, I came here looking for you. Is there someplace we can talk?'

'Complete privacy?' I asked. 'Or just someplace to sit?'

'Just somewhere to sit.'

'Sure,' I said. 'Come with me.'

I took her to the Garden Room, where we both ordered coffee.

'What brings you to Las Vegas, Miss Arnold?' I asked.

'First, I wish you would call me Adrienne,' she said. 'Second, I know I look like a country girl, but I do come to town quite often for various reasons.'

'I'm sorry, Adrienne,' I said, 'I wasn't judging you. At least, not harshly.'

'I should apologize,' she said. 'If I don't want to be judged I guess I should dress a bit differently when I come to town.'

'I don't see anything wrong with the way you're dressed.'

'Well . . . thank you.' She didn't blush, but she came close. I thought she was more of a country girl than she wanted to admit.

'That's very nice of you to say, considering where you live and work.'

'Now who's judging?' I asked.

'I only meant, you work with such beautiful women; showgirls, even the waitresses, they're all so . . . glamorous.'

'I think if you asked a bunch of these waitresses if they thought their jobs were glamorous you'd be surprised at the answers you'd get.'

'Perhaps, but the showgirls, surely . . .'

'Mostly they complain that their feet hurt,' I said. 'In fact, that's the same complaints you hear from the waitresses.'

'It's a problem I share with them, then,' she said.

'Maybe that's because of the boots.'

'Actually, it's when I try to wear regular shoes,' she said. 'My feet feel great when I wear boots.'

'I've been wondering about something,' I said.

'What's that?'

I leaned forward, which caused her to do the same.

'How tall are you when you're wearing boots?'

She smiled and said, 'Six one.'

I sat back, a little breathless. The waitress came with our coffee. We stared at each other while she was setting it down. In the past few years the women I had spent time with had either been waitresses, showgirls, or the occasional movie star.

This lady was a change of pace for me, and I still didn't really know what she did.

THIRTY-NINE

'I wanted to warn you,' she said.

'About your brother?' I asked. 'He's already been here, with a couple of his friends.'

'What happened?'

'I had a few of my friends with me, too.'

'Mr Crosby's trainer?'

'Jerry,' I said, 'and Dean Martin.'

'Dean Martin,' she said. 'That's an impressive friend to have.'

'And he used to be a boxer,' I said. 'Your brother backed down.'

'Yes, but don't depend on him staying that way,' she warned. 'Philip is mean.'

'Will he be mean just to me,' I asked, 'or to you, too?'

'Oh, he'll be mean to anyone who gets in his way,' she said. 'Or sometimes, just for fun. When we were kids, living on a farm, he'd torture animals to death.'

'Sounds like a great brother.'

'No, Christopher was the great brother.'

'Were horses his business?' I asked.

'Not always, but they were now. He started breeding them a few years ago, but was still working his regular job.'

'Which was what?'

'Investments.'

'And what's your business?'

'Antiques.'

'And Philip's business?'

'That's a little . . . hazy,' she admitted. 'We've always wondered what he's into, and why he's always broke.'

'So that's why he doesn't want the horse sold?' I asked.

'Not until he can figure out a way to get his hands on the money,' she said. 'Christopher wanted to keep him away from the profits of the horse sale.'

'Adrienne,' I said, 'would Philip have killed Christopher to keep him from selling the horse?'

She looked stunned.

'You haven't considered that?'

'No,' she said, 'not til now.'

'Christopher was beaten to death,' I said. 'Philip is quick with his hands. It seems to be the way he solves his problems.'

She hesitated, then said, 'Oh my God.'

She needed something stronger to drink so we went to the lounge. Didi was there and seated us, giving me a hard look as she did. I ordered two martinis.

'Cute,' she said. 'Is she going to poison my drink?'

'I doubt it.'

She rubbed her face, a masculine gesture I was surprised to see from her.

'If she did maybe I'd just drink it,' she said. 'How could one of my brothers kill the other?'

'We don't know that he did,' I said, 'but instead of looking at your brother the cops are tryin' to pin the murder on Jerry.'

'But why? He didn't even know my brother?'

'It's a long story,' I said. 'Jerry has a . . . checkered past.'

'One that has nothing to do with horses?'

'Exactly.'

'And your past?'

'Checkered, but for a different reason.'

Didi brought the drinks, set them down carefully, then stared at me, holding the tray down in front of her.

'Anything else, sir?' she asked politely.

'Not right now, thanks, Didi.'

She nodded and walked away.

Adrienne picked up the martini and sipped it gratefully.

'Have the police been in touch with you?' I asked.

'No, and I've wondered about that.'

'With their sights set on Jerry, there's no reason to bother you.'

'That doesn't sound like a very good way to run an investigation.'

'I agree. Do you know of anyone else who might have wanted to kill Christopher?'

'No,' she said. 'If it had been Philip who was killed, I may have been able to give you some names. He has a lot of people mad at him.'

I thought about that for a moment.

'Let's assume for a moment,' I said, 'that Philip didn't kill his own brother.'

'All right,' she said. 'That would make me feel . . . a little better.'

'OK,' I said. 'Which of the people who are mad at Philip would have killed Christopher to make a point?'

FORTY

'**M**y younger brother is the family accountant,' she said. 'I'll ask him.'

'He did Philip's books?'

She hesitated, then said, 'Not officially.'

'OK, I don't need to know the family details,' I said. 'But I would like some names that we can check out.'

'We?' she asked. 'Are you a detective, too, Eddie?'

'No, but I know one. A good one. If I give him enough information, he should be able to get to the bottom of things.'

'Do you need a client?' she asked. 'If he needs to be paid—'

'Don't worry about it,' I said. 'Bing Crosby's footin' the bill—'

'Not for my family, he isn't,' she said. 'If your detective is going to find out who killed my brother, I'm going to pay him.'

'I don't think Danny would object to bein' paid by a beautiful woman,' I said. 'In fact, I know he wouldn't.'

'I'd like to meet him.'

'I don't know if that's such a good idea.'

'Why? Is he one of those detectives with a flat nose and scars on his face? A big cigar in his mouth?'

'Actually,' I said, 'Danny's too handsome for his own good. I try never to introduce him to women I'm interested in.'

'Am I on that list, now?' she asked. 'Women you are interested in?'

'Let's say I find you interesting,' I said.

She smiled.

'You're very good at tap dancing with words, aren't you?'

'I have to be,' I said. 'I can't dance a lick with my feet.'

*   *   *

When we left the Garden Room I walked her to the front door of the hotel and had the valet bring her car around.

'I was serious about wanting to meet your detective,' she said.

'I'll make it happen,' I said. 'Where do you live?'

'I'll be staying out in Red Rock at my brother's place until I settle his estate.'

'Is there much of an estate to settle?'

'The house, some money, insurance, that sort of thing.'

'Anybody gonna get rich?'

'Not that much money, or insurance,' she said.

'And then there's the horse,' I said. 'Is it accounted for in the will?'

'We're reading the will tomorrow,' she said. 'I'll let you know.'

'You can call me here.'

'No home phone?'

The Valet drove her car up at that moment, blue '62 Pontiac Grand Prix. A nice car, but nothing flashy.

'I'll instruct them to give it to you if you call when I'm not here.'

I walked her around, opened her door and closed it after her, then leaned on it.

'Remember,' I said, 'the more information I have, the more I can get done.'

'I'll call you,' she said. 'Meantime, watch out for Philip.'

'I will.'

She put her hand over mine, then started the car and drove off.

The Valet, Tim Daly, came over to me and said, 'Nice lookin' piece, Eddie. New?'

'Very.'

'Well, toss her my way when you're done.'

I looked at him and said, 'I might keep this one around for a while, Tim.'

'Yeah,' Daly said, 'right. Tell me another one.'

He ran off to park a car.

I turned to go back inside when I saw Jerry walking towards me, in between cars.

'Where the hell have you been?' I asked.

'Went to the Horseshoe for breakfast,' he said. 'I didn't know I was under house arrest.'

'No, no, nothin' like that,' I said. 'I was worried.'

'About me? Aw, Mr G.'

'Well, we've got two dead bodies, and Philip Arnold walkin' around with his muscle-bound buddies.'

'I can handle them.'

'Just the same,' I said, 'I think you and me better stay together from here on out.'

'You gonna look out for me, Mr G?' he asked.

'We're gonna look out for each other, Jerry,' I said, 'like always.'

FORTY-ONE

We got in my Caddy and drove back down to Fremont Street, from which Jerry had just returned. He'd woken up that morning with a taste for the pancakes at the Horseshoe's coffee shop, and took a cab over there and back.

He didn't mind going back down there, though.

'I know why everybody likes the strip,' he explained, 'and I especially like the way Fremont Street feels.'

We managed to find a parking spot in front of the Apache Hotel, just down from the Horseshoe's corner entrance. We didn't go to the Horseshoe, but to Danny Bardini's office, first grabbing coffees for us and Danny, and hot tea for Penny.

As we entered carrying coffee and tea containers she smiled and said, 'Hi, Jerry.'

'I got you some tea,' he said, wanting her to know that he was the one who remembered.

'You're very sweet to remember,' she said, and he just about blushed.

'Boss in?' I asked.

'At his desk,' she said. 'Paying bills, so he's not going to be happy.'

'Well, I think I can keep him that way,' I said. Jerry and I went in.

'There's the big guy,' Danny said, accepting his coffee from me. He stood up and shook hands with Jerry warmly. They had started out with a slight mistrust of each other, and ended up liking each other, although neither would admit it.

'Still findin' bodies, huh, Shamus?' Jerry asked.

'You should talk, Gunsel,' Danny said. 'At least mine wasn't pummeled much.'

'Yeah, I like a clean kill better, myself,' Jerry said.

'Can we not discuss the state of dead bodies?' I asked. 'We've got more important things to do.'

'Like what?' Danny asked.

'We gotta solve these murders,' Jerry said.

'Why?' Danny frowned. 'I thought we were leavin' that to the cops?'

'That was the plan,' I said, 'but the Sheriff's dicks are lookin' at Jerry for Chris Arnold's murder.'

'Why?'

'Because they talked to Hargrove.'

'And I suppose they're lookin' at you for the trainer killing?' Danny asked.

'No,' I said, 'you.'

He frowned again, but said, 'Well, that makes more sense than you.'

'And they told Bing Crosby not to leave town.'

'Why? He didn't even find the body.'

'Might have something to do with the fact that he's still tryin' to buy the horse.'

Danny sat back in his chair.

'I can work the killing of the trainer,' he said. 'This is my turf. I don't know anything about Red Rock Canyon.'

'I talked with the sister today,' I said. 'She's gonna get me some names, people her brother Philip is in business with.'

'I thought the dead brother was Christopher?' Danny asked.

'He is, but from talking to Adrienne I think Christopher might have been killed as a warning to Philip.'

'Is he shady?'

'She said nobody was sure what his business was.'

Danny nodded and said, 'Shady. She can't think of anybody who would have wanted to kill Christopher?'

'No.'

'Could be she just sees him that way.'

'I thought of that.'

'What's her business?'

'Antiques.'

'And Christopher's business?'

'Investments, but he was getting out of that and into horses.'

'Racin' them?'

'Breeding them. Her younger brother is an accountant. She's gonna see what he knows about their brothers.'

'So I'll work the trainer killing and you and Jerry will work the Red Rock?'

'I suppose,' I said. 'You're the detective.'

'I'll supervise,' he said. 'You'll pretty much have to wait and see what kind of information she gets to you. So unless you wanna go back out there and prowl around the house . . .' He shrugged.

'Mr G. might wanna do that,' Jerry said.

'Oh? Why?'

'You ain't seen the sister,' Jerry said.

'Nice?'

'A looker,' Jerry said. 'Tall, stacked—'

'Yeah, OK,' I said, 'she's good lookin'. By the way, she wants to meet you.'

'Me? Why?' Danny asked.

'She wants to pay the freight on this investigation. I told her how good you are.'

'But you're the one lookin' at her brother's murder, not me.'

'You're supervising,' I reminded him.

'Right. Well, then, if I was you I'd drive back out there. Give the house a good once over, see what you find.'

'What are we lookin' for?' Jerry asked.

'Anything,' Danny said. 'Any of his records, letters, calendars; whatever you can find.'

'I should've arranged it when I saw Adrienne this morning,' I said. 'I'll have to call her.'

'Will she be there?' Danny asked.

'She told me she'll be staying there until they get the estate settled.'

'And the horse will be part of the estate,' Danny said.

'Probably.'

'Well,' he said, 'I guess I better head back over to the hotel where I found the trainer. Maybe somebody there saw something.'

'Can I use this phone to call her?' I asked.

'You got her number on you?'

I nodded. 'From when Bing first gave it to me.'

'OK. I'll see you guys when we have something to exchange.'

He walked out. I fished the number out of my wallet and picked up his phone.

'Jerry, can you still hear my Brooklyn?' I asked, before dialing.

'Not much, Mr G.'

'Do I, uh, drop my 'g's' when I talk?'

'Oh, yeah,' he said. 'That you do . . . especially when you been around me for a while.'

I shook my head and dialed the number.

FORTY-TWO

We drove out to Red Rock Canyon. Adrienne and I agreed on the phone that she'd leave the key for us. I think we both knew she'd be a distraction to me.

'Third time here,' Jerry said, as he cut the engine in front of the house.

We looked around outside first, and in the barn.

'Where's the horse?' Jerry said.

'They must have moved it someplace they could take care of it.'

'She didn't tell you that?'

'No.' We both wondered why.

There was still yellow police tape in the barn, but none on the house. I took the key from the rock she'd hidden it under and unlocked the front door.

Inside we split up. I took the office, going through the papers in the desk and the file cabinets. Jerry took the rest of the house.

I was sitting at the desk, leafing through things, when he came in carrying cans of Piels.

'Beer?' he asked. 'It's goin' to waste in the frig.'

I nodded. He handed me the beer and sat down across from me. I sat back.

'Find anything?' I asked.

'Some money stuffed into a coffee can in the kitchen. About five grand.'

'Emergency fund.'

'Nothing in the bedroom or the bathroom. There's another bedroom, must be for guests. There's nothin' personal in there.'

I sipped my beer.

'Anythin' in here?' he asked.

'A lot,' I said. 'A lot of paperwork. There may be something in here but I'm not seein' it.'

'Maybe we should take it all with us,' he suggested. 'You know somebody who could make sense of it?'

'No,' I said, 'well, maybe Adrienne does.'

'The sister?'

'Yeah, she says her younger brother's an accountant.'

'Did he work for the family?'

'I don't know.'

'We let him in here he may hide somethin',' Jerry said. 'You know, to protect his family.'

'Maybe,' I said. 'You may be right. We need somebody on the outside.'

'The Sands has gotta have some accountants,' he said.

'Yup.'

We stayed and drank our beer for a while. When my can was empty I put it aside and started going through papers again.

'Got an idea?'

'I'm just lookin' for papers that have something to do with the horse.'

'Want another beer?' Jerry asked. 'Frig is full.'

'No, thanks.'

He grabbed my empty from the desk and carried it with his back into the kitchen. I heard him pop another one, and then I heard the shot.

'Jerry!'

The sound of breaking glass reached me just a second after the shot. Or maybe it was the other way around. I don't know. Thinking back it could have been either way.

I got out from behind the desk and ran to the kitchen, calling his name again.

'Get down!' he shouted as I entered. I dropped to the floor immediately, skidded on the tiles and cut my knees on broken glass.

'Ow! Are you hit?' I asked.

'No,' he said. 'One shot, though, and a close one. Either he's a good shot and he missed on purpose, or I got lucky.'

We were both crouched down by the kitchen counter, which also had shards of glass on it.

'You got your gun?' I asked.

'Yeah. I thought it made sense to carry it, what with bodies droppin' all around us.'

'You know where the shot came from?'

'No, but the barn figures.'

'But if the shooter's in the barn why didn't he shoot us when we were there?'

'Maybe he wasn't in position yet.'

'Think he's waiting for us to poke our heads up?' I asked.

'Maybe.'

'You wanna go out the back?' I asked. 'I'll give him somethin' to shoot at.'

'You sure, Mr G?'

'Should we do it the other way around?'

'No,' he said, 'that wouldn't work.'

'Then you go.'

'If he's still out there, I'll get 'im, Mr G.,' Jerry assured me.

'Go!'

He scuttled across the floor and out of the kitchen. There was a door right there, but it wouldn't have been smart to use it. And he couldn't go out the front door. I knew if there wasn't another door, Jerry would make one for himself.

FORTY-THREE

I took a deep breath and then stuck my head up quickly. There was another shot, some more breaking glass that showered down on me. I hit the floor again, cut my hand, this time.

Get him, Jerry, I thought.

I wondered if I should pop up one more time, but thought that might be pushing it. Instead I found a yellow dish towel, and a broom in a corner. I hung the towel on the end of the broom and lifted it up. The shooter was either gone, or too smart to be fooled. I dropped the towel and broom, scuttled over to the door that led to the dining room, and got myself out of the kitchen.

Both the kitchen window and the front door were visible from the hayloft of the barn. I went to a front window and risked a peck outside. I didn't see Jerry, or anyone else. Hopefully the big guy was going around behind the barn.

I went to one of the back bedrooms, found an open window that Jerry must have used to get out, and went out the same way.

I worked my way around to the back of the barn, hoping I was retracing Jerry's steps.

I got around the back, flattened myself against the wall, and waited, listening intently. After a few minutes I heard Jerry's voice.

'Mr G!'

It sounded like he was out front. Was he OK? Or being forced at gunpoint to call me?

'Jerry?'

'Out front, Mr G.,' Jerry called. 'It's all clear.'

I walked around the barn and joined him out front.

'How can it be all clear?' I asked, my shoulders hunched, waiting for a bullet. 'He was just here.'

'Well, he's gone now,' Jerry said.

'Was he up there? In the loft?'

'Yeah,' Jerry said. 'He was using a bale of hay to steady his rifle.'

'So after he took the second shot at me, he left.'

'Looks like.'

'I don't get it, Jerry,' I said. 'Neither victim was shot. Why use a gun now?'

'I don't know, Mr G.,' he said. 'Maybe he's for hire. It seems to me he was a pro.'

'But he missed.'

'Pros miss, Mr G.,' he said. 'Sometimes.'

'Well,' I said, 'lucky for us.'

'Should we get out of here?'

'Yeah. No, wait.'

'For what?'

'There's one road in here and one road out, Jerry,' I reminded him.

'Right,' he said. 'We could catch him.'

'You go get the car.'

'What are you gonna do?'

'Go up in the hay loft and see if I can spot his dust.'

'OK. I'll pull the car over there.'

I ran into the barn and up the ladder to the loft. When I looked out I spotted a cloud of dust in the distance. Jerry pulled the Caddy up right in front.

'Anything?' he shouted.

'I'm comin' down.'

I considered jumping down into the seat from the loft, like in the movies, but in the end I chickened out. I hurried down from the loft by the ladder and got in the car.

'Go!' I said. 'Maybe we can catch up to him.'

He turned the Caddy in our own cloud of dust and took off down the road.

FORTY-FOUR

Jerry had the pedal to the metal and, from the look on his face, he was loving it.

We were kicking up so much of our own dust it was hard to see any clouds ahead of us, even though we were leaving most of ours behind.

'I think we're gainin' on him!' Jerry shouted.

He took his .45 out and put it in his lap.

'We get close to him you might have to take the wheel, Mr G.'

'If we kill him,' I said, 'we won't be able to ask who sent him.'

'So we'll try not to kill 'im.'

I stared ahead through the windshield, trying to see if we were catching up to him or not. Jerry had to run the windshield wipers from time to time to get the dirt off but it only seemed to be making it worse. I tried leaning my head out so I could look around the windshield, but I only ended up with sand in my eyes.

'Jerry.'

'What?'

'I don't think we're gaining.'

'We'll be at the highway soon,' he said. 'Let's see what happens then.'

What happened when we got to Highway 159 was that we didn't know which way he had gone. Jerry came to a stop and we looked both ways.

'Pick one,' he said. 'Where do they each go?'

'Either direction,' I said, 'takes you back to Vegas, eventually.'

'OK,' he said, 'then pick one.'

'That way,' I said, pointing to the direction we had come from town.

He turned right and stepped on the gas.

'Take it easy,' I said. 'We've got Highway patrol along here. The last thing we need is to get picked up by the cops.'

'Yeah, OK.'

By the time we came within sight of the city we had both long since given up the ghost.

'Tell me why somebody would try to kill you,' I said to Jerry.

'Me? Why do you think they were tryin' to kill me?'

'He shot at you, right?'

'Well . . . yeah, but maybe he thought I was you.'

'Excuse me, Jerry, but you and me, we don't look alike.'

'Maybe through a kitchen window, we do.'

'Yeah, maybe,' I said. 'OK, so why would anyone want to kill either of us?'

He shrugged. 'I dunno.'

'The only reason we'd be out there is if we were looking into Chris's death,' I said.

'The shooter would hafta know we were comin', Mr G.,' he said. 'He'd hafta be waitin' there for us.'

'OK,' I said. 'So who knew we were goin' out there?'

'Well, the Vegas Dick and his girl.'

'Danny and Penny, yeah,' I said.

'And who else?' he asked.

'Adrienne,' I said. 'She left us the key.'

'So she set us up?' Jerry asked.

'That's hard to believe,' I said, 'but what else can I believe?'

'Maybe,' he said, 'she told somebody.'

I looked at him.

'Like her brother?'

'Maybe.'

'Well,' I said, 'there's only one way to find out.'

'Yeah,' he said, 'ask her.'

'Right,' I said. 'Ask her.'

FORTY-FIVE

B ack at the Sands I called Adrienne's number from Jerry's suite, but got no answer.

'I'll try her again, later,' I said.

'Do we know where she lives?'

'No,' I said. 'She only told me she'd be staying at that house.'

'So maybe she ain't gone back, yet, and found the mess.'

'She might think we're dead.'

'She ain't gonna see no blood.'

'Maybe,' I said, 'whether she set us up or not, she'll call when she gets back. Maybe to see if we're dead, or to see if we're all right.'

I called the front desk, and told them where I was, told them to put through any calls for me to Jerry's suite.

'I gotta take a shower, Mr G.,' Jerry said, when I hung up. 'I got sand in the crack of my ass.'

'Yeah, me too.'

'You can take a shower after me,' he said.

I started to say I'd go downstairs and do that, and change, but remembered that I hadn't replaced the clothes in my locker.

'Yeah, OK.'

'Sorry I ain't got anything that would fit you, Mr G.'

'That's OK. I'll just . . . shake the sand out of my clothes.'

'I'll be quick,' he said, and went down the hall. The next moment I heard the shower.

I went to the bar and poured myself a small bourbon. I was sipping it when the phone rang.

'Yeah, hello?'

'Mr Gianelli? Eddie?'

'Oh, hello, Adrienne.'

'What the hell happened out here?' she asked. 'There's broken glass all over the kitchen, and what I think are . . . bullet holes? In the wall?'

'That's right,' I said. 'Jerry and I drove out, used your key to get in, and somebody took some shots at us.'

'Oh my God!' she said. 'Are you all right?'

'Yes, we're fine.'

'Did you . . . do you know who . . . why would anyone shoot at you?' she stammered.

'I don't know, Adrienne,' I said. 'Jerry and I were talking about that on the way back. Only a few people knew we were gonna be out there.'

'Including me, right?'

'Adrienne,' I said, 'did you try to have me killed today?'

'I did not,' she said.

'Did you tell anyone I'd be out there?'

'You said you told somebody.'

'I told my private detective friend,' I said. 'I don't think he'd try to have me killed.'

'What about his girl?'

'She wouldn't, either.'

'Who else did you tell?'

'Nobody,' I said. 'Who did you tell, Adrienne?'

She hesitated then said, 'I talked to my brother, Eric.'

'Is he the accountant?'

'Yes.'

'Where?'

'In Las Vegas.'

'His office is here in Vegas?'

'That's right.'

'Where does he live?'

'Henderson.'

'Where do you live, Adrienne?'

'Henderson.'

'Is that where you are now?'

'Yes.'

'I want to talk to Eric.'

'I can arrange that.'

'Today.'

'All right.'

'I want you to be there.'

'Why?'

'If somebody tries to shoot me again I want to be able to hide behind you.'

'Why would anyone—'

'Let's not go there again,' I said, as Jerry came walking in, dressed in clean clothes. He made a sign to me that I took to mean 'Is that her?' and I nodded.

'OK.'

'Give me your brother's address.'

'If we go there in the next three hours he'll be in his office.'

'That's where I'd like to talk to him.'

'All right. One hour?'

'Where is it?'

She gave me the address.

'Make it an hour and a half,' I said. 'I need to shower and change after driving out to Red Rock to get shot at.'

'Eddie, I'm so sorry . . .'

'If you didn't shoot at us,' I said, 'or hire it done, you don't need to be sorry.'

'Nevertheless . . .'

'Is there a place to have coffee near your brother's office?'

'Yes, right downstairs.'

'Let's meet there first,' I said. 'I want to talk to you before we go up.'

'All right.'

'I'll see you soon, Adrienne.'

'See you, Eddie.'

I hung up.

'If we get set up again we'll know it's her.'

'I'm gonna take a quick shower,' I said, 'and then we're gonna drive over there early.'

FORTY-SIX

Eric Arnold's office building was on 7th Street and Bridger, a few blocks from the El Cortez Casino. I wondered if he was a gambler.

I was sitting in the coffee shop downstairs when Adrienne came walking in.

'What'll you have?' I asked.

'Coffee and a Danish,' she said, leaning over to put her purse on the floor by her feet.

I waved the waitress over and ordered what she wanted, and asked for a warm up on mine.

'Where's your friend?' she asked. 'Jerry?'

'He's making sure nobody shoots at me.'

'Eddie,' she said, 'I didn't have anything to do with that.'

I stared at her for a few moments, then said, 'I believe you. Can you say for sure that Eric didn't?'

'I . . . want to say no.'

'But you can't.'

'Not for sure, no,' she said. 'I mean . . . there's always a possibility, I guess.'

'Your sister didn't know anything about this, did she?'

'About you going out to Red Rock? Why would I tell her?'

'I don't know. Why would you tell Eric?'

'I was talking to him about Christopher, and about Philip,' she said, with a shrug. 'I guess I just told him that you were going out there.'

'If Eric had a reason to send someone to shoot me,' I said, 'he'd have a reason not to want Chris's killer caught.'

'I don't know what that reason would be.'

'How do Philip and Eric get along?'

'Like brothers. They loved each other, they fought.'

'Does Philip bully Eric?'

'He did, when we were kids,' she said. 'Not so much as adults
. . . I guess.'

Her breakfast and my warm up came. I looked out the window.
Jerry actually was somewhere out there, making sure I didn't get
shot. Also checking to see if Adrienne had brought anyone with
her.

She ate her pastry like a man, no delicate little bites, no breaking
off little pieces. She made it look good.

We finished our coffee.

'I'm gonna go up and see Eric now.'

'OK,' she said, reaching down for her purse, 'let's go.'

'No,' I said, 'you don't have to come.'

'You said—'

'I changed my mind,' I said. 'Jerry's gonna come up with me.'
We went outside.

'You sure you don't want me to come up with you?' she asked.

'No, that's OK.'

'Is Jerry going to . . . knock him around?' she asked.

'What makes you think Jerry knocks people around?'

She shrugged.

'He's big,' she said, 'and he handled my brother Philip rather
easily.'

'Adrienne,' I said, 'before you go, give me your home address
and phone. I want to be able to reach you.'

'Oh, of course.' She fished around in her purse and handed me
a business card.

'This building is pretty close to Fremont Street and all the
casinos,' I said. 'Is Eric a gambler?'

'Yes, he is. Blackjack, mostly.'

'What about Chris and Philip?'

'Chris, no, Philip, yes.'

'OK,' I said. 'I'll call you.'

'Um, Eddie? Don't hurt Eric . . . any more than you have to?'

'I'm hopin' not to have to hurt him at all.'

She nodded, then walked to her car, which was several store-
fronts away. I watched her get in and drive away. When I looked
around Jerry was crossing the street towards me.

'She came alone,' he said, joining me on the sidewalk. 'Guess
you let her go because you believed her?'

'That's right.'

'You thinkin' with your dick, Mr G?'

'Jerry, the one thing I know about my dick,' I said, 'is that it never thinks.'

'Yeah,' he said. 'I getcha. Mine, neither. We goin' up?'

I nodded.

'We're goin' up.'

FORTY-SEVEN

According to the building directory, Eric Arnold, certified public accountant, had offices on the 7th floor. Also on his floor were two bail-bondsmen, an importer/exporter, and a private detective agency called All Night Eyes.

'High class,' Jerry said.

When we entered his office, a pretty secretary or receptionist looked up at us. I'd forgotten to ask Adrienne if her brother had partners, or employees. Damn. Now this girl was going to be able to identify us.

'Can I help you gentlemen?' She had a high-pitched voice that was kind of cute.

'Yes,' I said, 'we have an appointment with Mr Arnold.'

'Who shall I say is here?'

'Mr Gianelli and Mr Epstein.' I didn't have a choice. 'The appointment was arranged by his sister, Adrienne.'

'I'll tell him.'

She stood up, walked to one of two doors behind her, knocked and entered.

'Why didn't she use her intercom thing?' Jerry wondered.

'Maybe it's not workin',' I said.

The door opened again and she reappeared. She leaned against the open door with her hands behind her back. The position made her pert breasts even perter. And she knew it.

'You can go in,' she said, looking Jerry up and down. 'You're big,' she said, as we passed her.

'Yeah,' he said, ducking his head, as if that would make him smaller.

She closed the door behind us.

Eric Arnold stood up from behind his desk. He was tall, like his sister, but slender, a little younger. Bore no resemblance to the hulking Philip. He was wearing a blue suit, white shirt, blue-and-red tie.

'Mr Gianelli?' he asked.

'That's right.'

'Adrienne said you'd be by,' he said, putting out his hand. 'And this is your friend?'

'Jerry Epstein,' I said, shaking the accountant's hand.

He didn't shake Jerry's hand.

'You're the guy who found my brother,' Eric said.

'Yes,' Jerry said. 'Sorry.'

'Hey, I'm glad you found him,' Eric said. 'Have a seat. Tell me what I can do for you. Adrienne didn't say. Do you need legal advice?'

'No, Mr Arnold,' I said, 'that's not what we're here for.'

Eric spread his arms expansively and asked, 'Well, what then?'

'Adrienne said you might be able to tell us something about your brother Philip.'

'My brother Philip?' he said. 'What could I tell you . . .'

'Something about his business practices.'

He frowned.

'I don't understand,' he said, looking back and forth at us. 'Why would I tell the two of you anything about my brother?'

'Let me put this another way, Mr Arnold,' I said. 'We drove out to Red Rock earlier today to have a look around, see if we could find out anything about your brother Chris's death. While we were there somebody took some shots at us.'

'You're not the police,' he said. 'Why would you be looking into my brother's death? I really don't have to talk to you.'

'Yeah, you do,' Jerry said.

'Oh? Why's that?' Eric asked, looking at Jerry.

'*Because* we're not the cops.'

Eric Arnold looked at me, a helpless expression on his face.

'What is he talking about?'

'I think he means since we're not the cops we can do what we want,' I said. 'We don't have any bosses to answer to.'

The accountant swallowed and asked, 'Whataya mean, you can do anything?'

'I think Jerry's referring to the fact that he could break one of your arms or legs if you don't talk to us,' I said, 'and beat you to death with it, and nobody could stop him.'

'What?' Arnold asked, shrinking back in his chair. 'What?'

'Adrienne told you we were going out to Red Rock,' I said. 'I don't think she sent somebody out there to shoot us. That leaves you, and maybe anybody that you told.' I leaned forward in my chair. Jerry was sitting relaxed in his, one leg crossed over the other knee. 'Who did you tell, Eric?'

'I didn't tell anybody!'

'Then *you* sent the shooter out there to try to kill us.'

'What? No!'

'Well,' I said, 'it's one or the other.'

Jerry put his leg down and leaned forward.

'Wait, wait—' Eric said.

'I'm thinking Adrienne asked you for help with Philip, who's trying to queer the deal with Bing Crosby to buy your dead brother's horse,' I said. 'Only I don't think she knows that you and Philip are workin' together. Am I close?'

'Philip's my brother,' Eric said. 'Sometimes I help him with . . . with his books . . .'

'And what else?' I asked.

'Look . . . wait . . .' Eric stammered. 'I've gotta think.'

'We need less thinkin',' Jerry said, 'and more talkin'.'

Eric had a heavy oak desk, and Jerry wanted to make an impression on him. He put his right hand on the edge of the desk and, in one motion, shoved the heavy piece of furniture across the room, like it weighed nothing. That left space between Eric and us. The move even impressed *me*.

'Jesus!' Eric said, his eyes wide as the only buffer between him and Jerry disappeared.

'Start talkin',' Jerry said.

FORTY-EIGHT

'All I know,' Eric said, 'is that my brother Philip didn't want Chris to sell that horse.'

'Why not?'

'Philip saw ways of making a lot of money with it.'

'And Chris didn't?'

'Chris thought small,' Eric said, 'Philip thinks big.'

'And how do you think, Eric?' I asked.

'What?'

'Do you think big or small?'

Eric spread his arms.

'Look where I am. What do you think?'

'I think you're a blackjack player who keeps himself close to the action.'

'So I'm a gambler,' Eric said. 'Sue me.'

I studied him for a few seconds, then asked, 'Your brother Philip promised to cut you in, didn't he?'

'Cut me in on what?'

'On whatever he was plannin',' I answered. 'He wanted you to side with him against Chris and Adrienne.'

He didn't answer, but the look on his face said it all.

'Did you know he was gonna have your brother Chris killed?' Jerry asked.

'Hey, hey,' Eric said, waving his hands, 'Phil wouldn't do that.'

'Oh yeah,' I said, 'a brother wouldn't kill a brother? Not over a lot of money?'

'Philip has money,' Eric said. 'He wouldn't need to kill Chris for more.'

'Then maybe it was you,' I said.

'Me . . . what?'

'Maybe it was you who killed your brother for money,' I said. 'I'll bet you need it. I mean, after all –' I spread my hands, '– look where you are.'

'I never . . . I wouldn't . . .' He stopped short when Jerry put his big hand on his chest, pressed him back into the chair.

'When Adrienne told you Jerry and I were goin' out there, you called your brother Phil, right?'

'R-right.'

'And he sent someone out there to kill us, so we wouldn't find out he killed Chris. Or had him killed.'

'No,' he said, 'I don't know . . . if he sent somebody to shoot at you, but . . . but I can't believe he killed our brother. I won't believe that of Phil.'

'Why not?' I asked. 'Is he offering you that much money?'

'I'm . . . I'm . . . I do need a lot of money,' he said. 'You'd find that out if you tried. I'm not denying that. And Philip is going to help me. B-but he didn't kill Chris. He didn't!'

I reached out and touched Jerry's tree trunk of an arm. He removed his hand from Eric's chest.

'I believe you.'

He relaxed his shoulders a bit.

'I believe that you don't think Philip killed Chris,' I said.

'You . . . you think he did?'

'I can't think of anybody else with a motive,' I said, 'can you?'

'Well . . .'

'Come on, Eric,' I said. 'Don't clam up now.'

Jerry showed Eric Arnold his big hand, fingers splayed.

'Yeah, all right,' he said, quickly, 'Philip is in business with . . . some people.'

'Some people?' I asked. 'What people, Eric?'

'Um, the mob,' Eric said. 'Phil's in business with the mob.'

I looked at Jerry.

'Why doesn't it surprise me that we're gonna end up dealin' with the mob?'

FORTY-NINE

'**H**is name's Vincent DeStefano,' Eric said.

'What does he do?' I asked.

'I-I don't know.'

'You do your brother's books, right?' I asked. 'You must know something.'

'Well, yeah, but—'

'They're phony books, right?'

'R-right,' he admitted, reluctantly. He looked pained, but somehow relieved at having said it.

'So where are his real books?'

'I-I don't know.'

'He doesn't trust you, his own brother, with his real book?' I asked.

'N-No, it's not that . . . exactly . . . it's just that . . .'

'Yeah, it is,' Jerry said. He looked at me, but pointed at Eric. 'This guy's a boob, and his brother knows it.'

'Yeah,' I said, 'I think you're right.'

'Hey . . .' Eric said.

'So where do we find Mr Vincent DeStefano, Eric?' I asked.

'I-I don't know . . .'

'You must have an address for him?' I reasoned. 'In your brother's papers?'

'Yeah, but the papers are phony.'

'I'm bettin' the numbers are phony, but the addresses are real.'

He shrugged and said, 'OK. I-I'll get it.'

He got up and went to a file cabinet, took peeks over his shoulder a few times to see if we were watching him. We were.

'You come out of there with anything but paperwork and I'll make you eat it,' Jerry said, but with an easy-going smile on his face. Somehow, the smile made the threat even more menacing.

'I don't have anything . . .'

'Just get the info,' Jerry said.

Eric finally fumbled a file out of the drawer and brought it back to where we were sitting.

'Give that to me and something to write on,' I told him.

'And siddown,' Jerry said.

Eric sat, gave me the file and gave a pad and pen over to me. I found an address for DeStefano in Las Vegas. I also took down the phone number. I trusted myself more than him to write it down correctly.

'Here,' I said, and tossed the file back into Eric's lap, along with the pad. 'Now write down your brother's address and phone number.'

He hesitated.

'Do it, asshole!' Jerry snapped.

Eric wrote quickly, gave me back the pad. I stood up, looked at Jerry.

'He's gonna call his brother the minute we leave,' I said. 'Or DeStefano.'

Jerry looked at Eric.

'You gonna do that, you little puke?'

'N-no,' Eric said, blinking rapidly. 'I-I don't even know Mr DeStefano.'

Jerry felt he needed to reinforce the fear a little more so he produced his .45. Eric's blinking increased.

'If I hear you called your brother,' Jerry said, pressing his gun to Eric's forehead, 'or DeStefano, I'll come right back here and pull this trigger.' He pressed the gun harder against Eric's forehead. 'You got that, Mr Accountant?'

'Yeah, yeah, I got it,' Eric said, 'I got it.'

'I'm serious, asshole,' Jerry said. 'I don't care how scared you are of your big bad brother, or of Vincent DeStefano. I'll come back here and blow your brains all over the wall.'

Eric nodded jerkily.

'Tell me you believe me!'

'I believe you! I believe you!'

'Good man.'

Jerry removed his gun. The barrel left a round indentation on Eric's forehead. I wondered how long it would last as a reminder?

We went back out into the reception area. The cute little receptionist was still there. She looked Jerry up and down again. She apparently liked big men.

'Here,' she said, holding out a slip of paper to him.

'What's this?' he asked.

'My number,' she said, 'in case you wanna ask *me* any questions.'

'Uh . . .'

'He says thanks,' I said, grabbing the slip.

'I like a big man of few words,' she said.

Out in the hall I said, 'Here ya go,' and gave him the slip.

'What am I supposed ta do with this, Mr G?'

'Come on, Jerry,' I said. 'Don't tell me a girl never gave you her number before.'

'No,' he said, 'I don't get that kinda thing. You and Danny maybe, but not me.'

'Well . . . this is Vegas,' I said. 'Anything's possible.'

'So what do I do with it?'

'Put it in your pocket, just in case you end up with some free time.'

'You know,' he said, as we exited the building, 'with real girls, not whores, ya gotta talk to 'em. I ain't good at that.'

'Don't worry,' I said. 'I doubt that would be a problem with this girl.'

FIFTY

'Are we gonna go and see Philip now?' Jerry asked.

'Sure, why not?' I asked. 'There's no point in waiting, is there? Especially since he still might call ahead.'

'Maybe,' Jerry said, 'we should go and see DeStefano first?'

'Do you recognize the name?'

'No.'

'I think maybe we should find out just how connected DeStefano is before we go and see him,' I suggested. 'So let's see big brother first.'

He started the car and said, 'I gotta warn ya, Mr G. I'm gonna wanna smash his face in as soon as he opens his mouth.'

'I gotta warn you, Jerry,' I said. 'I'll probably let you.'

*   *   *

Philip Arnold had offices in a more businesslike section of town. His building was surrounded by other office buildings.

On the lobby directory he was listed as *Philip Arnold Consultants*. Adrienne had said his business was investments.

We waited for the elevator, stepped aside when it arrived to allow three men in suits to exit. They didn't look like accountants or lawyers. I had a feeling that while the building might be in a better neighborhood than Eric Arnold's was, the clientele was not much better. We got in and rode to the 3rd floor.

'This is a good floor,' Jerry said.

'Why's that?'

'If I have to hang him from the window by the ankles it's high enough to scare him, but low enough that he might survive if I accidentally drop him.'

We found his door and entered. He had a reception area, but there was no receptionist. That was probably good, because if she had been there she might have been underneath the overturned desk.

'I had a bad feelin' when those guys left the elevator,' Jerry said.

I nodded. We approached the closed door of Arnold's office, wondering if we were going to find another dead member of the family.

As we entered, we saw that he wasn't dead, but he was definitely the worse for wear.

'Whatayou want?' he demanded from behind his desk. He was holding a washcloth to his bruised and battered face.

'I think we ran into your friends in the lobby,' I said. 'Three guys with bad-fitting suits?'

He probed his mouth and said around his big hand, 'I think they loosened some teeth.'

'Why didn't you show them your muscles?' Jerry asked.

'Or sic your muscle buddies on them?'

'What the hell do you guys want?' he demanded. He opened a drawer and took out a bottle of scotch and a glass.

'No, thanks,' I said.

He ignored me, poured himself a drink, sipped it and then hissed as the liquor hit his sore lips and gums.

'We just came from seeing Eric,' I said.

'Oh yeah? What'd that pussy tell you?'

'He was very talkative,' I said. 'But I hope your friends didn't get all that you have to give already. Jerry would be really upset if you had nothing left for us.'

'Adrienne send you?' he asked, giving Jerry a wary look.

'We're working on her behalf,' I said.

'You guys ain't cops, and you ain't private detectives. Whataya want?'

'We'd like to know who killed your brother Chris,' I said, 'and who took some shots at us today out in Red Rock.'

'Well, for the first question, I don't know,' he said, 'and for the second, probably somebody who don't like you.'

'And that would be . . . you?' I asked.

Phil Arnold laughed, then hissed.

'Don't make me laugh,' he said. 'It hurts. You guys think I sent a shooter after you? I ain't got that kind of juice.'

'Balls,' Jerry said.

'What?'

'You ain't got that kinda balls.'

'So yeah,' Arnold said, with a shrug, 'maybe I ain't.' He poured himself some more scotch, sipped it carefully. His suit was disheveled, and there was blood on his white collar. 'But I also wouldn't have any reason to.'

There were two overturned chairs on the floor. We righted them and sat down.

'So who were the guys who roughed you up, Phil?' I asked. 'Collectin' on a bad debt, or do they work for Vinnie DeStefano?'

He was in the act of lifting the glass to his mouth, and stopped short to give me a sharp look.

'Where'd you hear that name?'

'We heard you're in business with him,' I said. 'We also heard that your brother keeps your phony books. But you don't trust him enough to let him keep the real ones.'

'I don't trust him to know enough to stay out of the rain. The fact that you bozos are here tells me I'm right. He can't keep his damn mouth shut.'

'Well, don't blame him too much,' I said. 'It was kinda hard for him to keep quiet with Jerry standin' on his chest.'

'You wanna see?' Jerry asked, with a smile.

'Hey, fellas,' he said, 'I been worked over enough for one day, don't you think?'

'Not by me,' Jerry said.

'Look,' he said, 'why don't we have a drink and talk about it, huh?'

'Sure, Phil,' I said, 'let's have a drink.'

'I got some glasses in the john,' he said. 'And I need to wash my face.' He pointed to the bathroom door.

'Go ahead.'

He got up, opened the door and went in. We heard the water turn on, and run . . . and run . . . and run . . .

'Crap!' I said, springing out of my chair.

It was a bathroom, all right, with another door that led to a back hallway. I ran out, looked both ways, listened for his footsteps, but he was gone.

FIFTY-ONE

'I wonder why he didn't do that with the other three?' Jerry asked.

'Maybe they were too smart to let him go to the john,' I said, glumly.

'Well,' Jerry said, 'we might as well go through this place.'

'Yeah, why not?'

As we tossed the place, not bothering to be neat because it was already in a shambles, Jerry said, 'Look on the bright side, Mr G.'

'Where's that, Jerry?'

'It's pretty clear he ain't got the balls to be behind his brother's murder.'

'That's clear to you?'

'Well, clear to me that he didn't do it,' he said. 'And clear that he don't have the juice to order it but sure didn't do nothin' to stop it, I bet.'

I went through the file cabinet while Jerry went through the desk, but I stopped, frustrated.

'I'll bet all this stuff is fake, to match his fake books,' I said.

'So what do you wanna do?'

I couldn't believe I was saying it, and not Jerry.

'I wanna get somethin' to eat.'

'No argument from me.'

I gave Jerry directions to a nearby diner that always reminded me of the Greek diners of my youth in Brooklyn. I figured he'd like it. I ordered a pizza burger platter and he ordered meat loaf with lots of brown gravy on the meat and fries. 'Wet fries' we called them when I lived in Brooklyn.

'Are we gonna go lookin' for him again, Mr G?' Jerry asked.

'Nope,' I said.

'Why not?'

'Seems to me he's on the verge of becomin' the next victim,' I said.

'Tell you the truth, Mr G., I don't think that would break me up none.'

'No, me neither, I guess.'

He popped a handful of dripping wet fries into his mouth.

'So DeStefano is our next move,' I said. 'We've got to find out who he is, what he's got to do with the Arnold family, or this horse.'

'You want me to make some calls?' he asked.

'Yeah,' I said, 'and I'll talk to Jack Entratter, see what he knows.'

'Maybe you should ask his girl, too.'

'Yeah, maybe I should.'

'I wonder how the dick did today?' he said.

'I don't know,' I said. 'Better than us, I hope.'

'Aw, Mr G., we didn't do so bad. We figured out these two brothers are limp dicks who couldn't swat a fly. But maybe somebody they got involved with killed their brother.'

I stared at him.

'One of these days,' I said, 'you're gonna let somebody see how smart you really are . . . I just hope it's me.'

He flashed a grin at me, brown gravy at the corners of it.

FIFTY-TWO

We went back to the Sands. Jerry went to his room to make some calls. I went to Jack Entratter's office. He wasn't there.

'He's on the casino floor,' his girl said. 'Somebody was cheating.'

'Where?' I hoped it wasn't any of my tables. If I'd been in the pit I would have noticed it.

'I'm not sure, Mr Gianelli.'

I searched my memory. That was probably the only time she'd ever called me by name. It was progress. I didn't want to push it.

'OK, thanks.'

I took the elevator back down, crossed the hotel lobby and entered the casino, looking for Jack.

I found him, but not near the tables, where I thought I would.

'Jack,' I said, 'what are you doin'?'

'Hear that?'

I listened. One of the slot machines was paying off, nickels pinging off the metal tray.

'That's the fifth jackpot today,' he said. 'Same machine. I'm tryin' to figure out how she's doin' it.'

The 'she' was a seventy-year-old, gray-haired grandmother who was happily scooping the nickels out of the tray and dumping them in her purse, which was almost as big as a suitcase.

'Five jackpots?' I asked.

He nodded.

'She's gonna need help carrying them out.'

'I'll help her,' he growled.

'What are you gonna do, kneecap her?'

He gave me a dirty look.

'What are you doin' here? Are you in trouble?'

'No,' I said, 'but I'm still workin' on Bing's problem.'

'Frank came in today,' he said. 'You got your tickets for tonight?'

'Yeah, I got 'em.'

'Good, 'cause I don't wanna disappoint him.'

'You goin'?'

'You know I don't go to shows in other places.'

'Yeah, but you're goin' to this one, right?'

He frowned, like he was in pain, and said, 'Yeah.'

'OK, look,' I said, 'forget about grandma for a minute. I got a question.'

'Go ahead, ask.' He folded his arms and kept his eyes on the old lady, but he was listening.

'You ever heard of a guy named Vincent DeStefano?'

He forgot about the grandma and looked at me.

'Where did you hear that name?'

'Came across it today.'

'In relation to what?'

'The murder of the horse guy out in Red Rock Canyon. Why, you know 'im?'

'I need a drink,' he said. 'Come on.'

He gave the slot machine lady one last look, then turned to head for the lounge. At that moment she hit again and he hunched his shoulders as the nickels started pouring out.

We got seated at a table in the lounge. It was late afternoon and starting to get busy. Didi dispensed with the dirty looks because I was with Jack. We both ordered bourbon.

'OK,' he said, 'listen up. You gotta stay away from Vince DeStefano.'

'Why?'

'Well, I'd tell you because I said so, but I don't think that would do it . . . would it?' He gave me a hopeful look.

'No.'

'I didn't think so.'

Didi came with our drinks. We leaned back and let her put them on the table.

'Thanks, doll,' Jack said.

'Sure, Mr Entratter.'

'She's cute,' he said, watching her walk away. 'You should try tappin' that.'

I stared at him.

'You already did,' he said. 'Why do I even talk?'

'DeStefano, Jack,' I said, sipping my drink.

'Damn it, Eddie, how do you get yourself into these situations?'

'Excuse me, Jack,' I said, 'but most of the time I'm mindin' my own business in my pit and *you* get me involved in these situations.'

'Yeah, yeah,' he said, rubbing his face with his left hand and picking up his drink with his right. 'OK, tell me how you got on to DeStefano . . .'

FIFTY-THREE

H e listened, working slowly on his drink as I told him what Jerry and I had done that day.

'But he didn't hang anybody from a window, or kill anybody?'

'No, Jack,' I said, 'but I think you missed the point of my little tale. Somebody tried to kill *us*. And I think it's connected to Vince DeStefano.'

'Look,' he said, 'I appreciate your dilemma, I do. But you gotta stay away from DeStefano.'

'You still haven't told me why.'

'Because he'll kill you, that's why. Just as soon as look at you, he'll kill you. And Jerry. And Bardini, if you get him involved. And his girl, what's her name?'

'Penny.'

'Yeah, Penny, her too.'

I finished my drink and put the glass down hard.

'Jack, you can't expect to drop a bomb like that on me and then just stop.'

'Kid,' he said, 'you been up against it a few times in the past few years, and I'll give it to you, you come out the other end. But this guy . . . even Mo Mo don't wanna mess with him.'

Jesus, I thought to myself.

'Jack, why don't I know this guy's name? How long's he been in Vegas?'

'Just a year or two.'

'How'd he get in here so quiet?'

'Mo Mo sent him in here, set 'im up on the quiet.'

'But if Mo Mo's afraid of him—'

'Jesus, kid, I didn't say that!' he told me, sharply. 'I never said that. All I said was that Mo Mo didn't wanna mess with him. And he don't. So he sent him here before he had to kill him.'

'Or before he killed Mo Mo, right?'

'Let's just say before he could try.'

'What's a connected guy like DeStefano doin' messin' with these morons?'

'I don't know,' he said. 'And I don't wanna ask him.'

'Well,' I said, 'I do.'

'Eddie—'

'Jack, damn it,' I complained, 'you're tying my hands.'

'That's better than having cement tied to your ankles at the bottom of Lake Mead.'

'That ain't gonna happen.'

'Why not?'

'Because Mo Mo's not gonna let it.'

'Mo Mo's not gonna get involved in this, Eddie.'

'Yeah, he is, Jack.'

'Oh yeah? Why?'

'Because Frank's gonna ask him to.'

Frank agreed to meet me and Jack in Jack's office. Entratter sent his girl home early.

'I think I'm starting to grow on her,' I said. 'She actually said my name today.'

'Forget it,' he said. 'She hates you.'

'Why?'

'You'll have to ask her.'

'I'm really not that interested in the answer,' I said.

When Frank arrived we all shook hands, and Jack poured us all a drink. Then we sat down and got to business.

'I need a big favor, Frank,' I said.

'No problem,' he said. 'Not after everything you've done for us. Whataya need, sport?'

'I need you to call Mo Mo and ask him for a favor.'

'What kind of favor?'

'There's a made guy in town,' Jack said, 'that Eddie needs to talk to. He wants . . . he'd like Mo Mo to arrange it for him.'

Frank looked at me. He was sitting comfortably in the chair, wearing gray slacks and an open collar polo shirt.

'What's this made guy's name?' Frank asked. 'Do I know 'im?'

'Vincent DeStefano,' I said.

Frank pursed his lips for a minute, then said, 'Never heard of the bum. What's he done?'

'I don't know that he's done anythin',' I said, 'but I wanna ask him. We got two murders on our hands that have something to do with Bing Crosby wantin' to buy a horse.'

'Hey, I heard about that from Bing,' Frank said. 'Not the murders, just that he was here to buy a horse. Tell me about the murders.'

So I did. I filled him in on everything Bing, Jerry and I had gone through over the past few days.

'So because you and Jerry were shot at you think DeStefano ordered the hit?'

'I think both Philip and Eric Arnold are too soft to have done it,' I said. 'DeStefano fits, but I need to talk to him, and look at him while I do it.'

'Jerry gonna go with you to see him?'

'Yes.'

'OK,' Frank said. 'I wanna come, too.'

'Hey, Frank—' Jack started.

'Naw, naw,' he said to Jack, holding one hand out, 'this sounds like too much fun to miss.' He looked at me. 'I'll set it up through Mo Mo, Eddie, but I gotta go along, or it's no deal.'

I knew Frank loved anything that had to do with made guys. And they also seemed to love being around him. They had a mutual admiration society going.

'OK, Frank,' I said. 'If you set it, you can come.'

'When do you wanna do it?'

'Tomorrow mornin' would be good.'

'Not in the mornin',' he said. 'We're all going to Frankie's show tonight, and then we're goin' out. Late night all around. How about the afternoon?'

'Sure, Frank,' I said. 'Make it in the afternoon.'

He practically leaped out of his chair.

'I'll go back to my room and make the call now,' he said. He started for the door, but turned and pointed at us. 'See you both at the Flamingo tonight, right?'

'Wouldn't miss it, Frank,' Jack told him. 'Either of us.'

Frank waved and left the room.

'If you let anythin' happen to him tomorrow . . .' Jack warned me.

'Hey, it's not my idea for him to come along.'

'It was your idea to ask him for the favor,' he rightfully pointed out, 'and now he's gonna be on the firing line.'

'He *loves* the firing line!'

'I'm just tellin' you,' Jack said. 'You and that big galoot of yours better be on your toes tomorrow.'

'Jerry's always on his toes.'

'Especially tomorrow,' Jack said. 'Now go. I'll see you tonight.'

I got up and left the office. I had to drive home and get dressed for the Flamingo. I'd bring back a few changes of clothes for my locker. If it was going to be a late night, like Frank said, I'd have to stay over.

I wondered as I went down in the elevator if Mo Mo would go along with this? Had he ever said no to Frank Sinatra?

FIFTY-FOUR

I woke the next morning with a raging headache and something strange in my mouth. When I reached in there to see what it was, it turned out to be my tongue.

Just as Frank had predicted, it had been a late night. Frankie had done his show, and then Frank went up and did a number, *then* invited Dino up for one. The Flamingo ended up hosting an impromptu meeting of the Summit, which didn't make Jack very happy.

Entratter begged off the carousing after the show, so both Franks, Dino, Jerry and I piled into a limo and did the town. Somewhere along the way, we picked up three showgirls. They fawned all over Frank and Dean until Frank practically ordered them to make a fuss over Frank Junior. In the end Junior ended up with one girl, and Frank with two. Dean managed to give his to Frank. None of the girls had the slightest interest in me, although one of them seemed to find Jerry's size interesting.

The phone rang and I grabbed my head with one hand, and the receiver with the other.

'Stop it,' I said. 'No more ringing.'

'Hey, Mr G.,' Jerry said. 'Look around your room will ya. And see if the top of my head is there.'

'It might be under the bed, but I'm afraid if I lean over to look, the top of *my* head will fall off.'

'What a night, huh?'

'You said it.'

'Ya wanna get some food?'

Shockingly, I did. Now that he mentioned it, I was starving.

'Sure, but I need a shower. Gimme half an hour.'

'When are we supposed to meet Mr S?' he asked.

I frowned.

'I don't remember. Did we set a time?'

'I think we did,' he said. 'I think when he took those two babes to his room he said, "See ya . . . sometime." I can't remember when or where.'

'Crap,' I said. 'OK, we'll have to eat in the building. Maybe it'll come to one of us.'

'Yeah, OK,' he said. 'Meet you in the Garden Room in thirty minutes.'

'I'll be the guy with the dark circles under my eyes,' I said, and hung up.

Surprisingly, I beat Jerry down to the restaurant. I had a pot of coffee and some cups on the table when he arrived. We were looking at the menu, getting ready to order, when Frank walked in.

'Hey,' he said, 'I didn't think you guys would remember we said we'd meet here. Scooch over, big guy.'

He slid into the booth next to Jerry and grabbed a menu.

'Coffee?' I asked, since we had extra cups on the table.

'Hell, yeah,' he said. 'How's the Spanish omelet here?'

'Really good,' Jerry said. 'I had one.'

'Think I'll have steak and eggs.' He put the menu down and looked at me. 'You look like you slept under a highway.'

'I don't know how you do it,' I said. 'The late night, the girls, the drinkin' . . .'

'Keeps me young,' he said.

The waitress came over to take our order. Her eyes widened when she saw Frank.

'Hey, sweetie. How about some steak and eggs?'

'Certainly, Mr Sinatra.'

I asked for the same. I wasn't sure she'd remember if I ordered something different than Frank. Jerry just ordered a couple of stacks of pancakes.

'OK,' Frank said, 'so I talked with Mo Mo last night.'

We hadn't discussed it at the Flamingo, or after the show. Frank had only been interested in Frankie's performance and showing the kid a good time after. He was as proud as a Papa could be.

'What did Mo Mo say?' I asked.

'Well, he wanted to know what the story was, so I told him everything you told me. He was really interested, especially when he heard Bing was involved.'

'And?'

'He went for it,' Frank said. 'DeStefano will be waitin' for us.'

'That's what I'm afraid of,' I said.

'No, it'll just be a meet and greet,' Frank said. 'Mo Mo's gonna ask DeStefano to do it as a favor to him.'

'That's great, Frank. Did he, uh, tell you anything about the guy?'

'He said to be careful, but he didn't fill me in.'

I looked at Jerry.

'We didn't have a chance to talk yesterday,' I said. 'You made some calls?'

'I heard the guy's a hard ass,' he said. 'Everybody I talked to said so, and one guy says he's crazy.'

'Entratter said even Mo Mo doesn't want to mess with him,' I told them.

'I got that impression,' Frank said, 'but I think it's because Mo Mo doesn't wanna have to kill him.'

The waitress came with breakfast, fawned all over Frank as she set his plate in front of him. His steak looked bigger than mine, and perfectly cooked.

'Thanks, babe,' he said to her, which sent her away tittering.

'Jerry,' Frank said, looking at his plate and not at the big guy, 'Mo Mo suggested you stay behind, at the hotel.'

'What?' Jerry looked away from his pancakes. That meant he was really upset. 'Why?'

'He thinks taking you along might . . . cause something to happen.'

'I can't let you and Mr G. walk in there without me, Mr S.,' he said. 'This guy DeStefano's gonna have some of his guys there.'

'I know that, Jerry,' Frank said. 'I'm only passin' along Mo Mo's suggestion.'

Jerry looked at me. We knew what Mo Mo's 'suggestion' meant.

'Jerry,' I said, 'how about you come along, but wait outside the building?'

'So I can come rushin' in when I hear the shots?' he asked. 'And you're already dead?'

'He's got a point, Frank,' I said. 'Two men have already been killed, and we've been shot at. But if you wanna go in without Jerry as backup—'

'Hey,' Frank said, 'fuck Mo Mo. If he thinks we're gonna walk into DeStefano's world unarmed and unprotected, he can go fuck himself. And if DeStefano doesn't like it, fuck him, too. How's that?'

'Suits me, Mr S.,' Jerry said, happily.

'That suggestion gets my vote,' I said.

'Just one thing,' Frank said.

'What's that?' I asked.

'One of *you* two is gonna tell Mo Mo we didn't take his suggestion,' Frank said, 'without tellin' him that I said he should go fuck himself.'

FIFTY-FIVE

Vincent DeStefano lived in Overton, Nevada, near Lake Mead. The sprawling house was new, had been built among the equally sprawling mesas and foothills.

Jerry drove the Caddy with me in the front, and Frank in the back. The other thing Frank had supplied were the directions on how to get there.

There were no front gates, so we drove up a winding driveway to the house. As we got out I spotted two men, on either side of the drive, wearing suits with guns underneath them. I didn't see them, I just knew they were there.

Jerry confirmed my suspicion.

'Heeled,' he said, 'under their arms.'

'They're not the only ones,' Frank said, with great satisfaction.

I turned and looked at Frank.

'You brought a gun?'

'Jerry brought a gun.'

'They'll expect Jerry to be armed,' I said. 'They'll frisk him and take it.'

'Maybe they won't frisk me,' Frank said.

'Yeah, they will,' Jerry said.

'Better let me have it, Frank,' I said. 'I'll put it in the glove compartment.'

I extended my hand back. He stared at it for a few seconds, then reluctantly took the gun from his jacket pocket and put it in my hand. It was a .38, with a short barrel.

I opened the glove compartment, stuck it in and slammed it. Briefly, I considered taking Jerry's .45 and putting it in with the .38, then decided against it. Let them find it when they frisked him.

'OK,' I said, 'time to go in.'

As if on cue, the front door of the house opened. A man came out and met us halfway up the concrete steps.

'Mr DeStefano is waiting for you,' he said. 'This way.'

We followed him up and into the house, then through the house and out the back. From there we saw an incredible view of the foothills. And I was pretty sure I could smell Lake Mead.

There was a round table with some chairs around it. It looked like patio furniture for a much less grand property than this. The person who had purchased it did not have the taste to match the house.

There was a man seated at the table, with two other men standing near him. They wore suits, and were undoubtedly armed. The seated man's lack of taste was clear in the white shoes, blue pants and mustard-brown t-shirt he was wearing. Especially the black socks.

My heart started to race.

'Frisk him,' DeStefano said, pointing at Jerry.

Jerry raised his hands. They patted us down and took Jerry's .45.

'The movie star, too.'

'Movie star?' Frank said, raising his arms.

'Singer, whatever,' DeStefano said.

'He's clean,' one of the bodyguards said. 'What about him?' jerking his thumb at me.

'Mr Gianelli doesn't carry, but pat him down.'

The guy did, in a half-assed manner, which I found sort of

insulting. I think I actually could have carried a gun in there and gotten away with it.

The man who had led us through the house was standing off to one side, hands folded in front of him.

'Are you Vincent DeStefano?' I asked.

'That's right,' he said. He looked like what a bulldog would look like if it were human. Hunched, rounded shoulders, big jaw, thick chest, but short, bandy legs. 'You're Gianelli?'

'That's right.'

'You're here because Mr Giancana asked me to give you ten minutes of my time.'

'Ten minutes?'

'And it's worth ten minutes of my time not to rub Mo Mo the wrong way.'

'Then we better get started,' I said.

'I know you?' DeStefano asked Jerry.

He shrugged.

'What's your name?'

'Jerry Epstein.'

'A Jew,' DeStefano said. 'From where?'

'Brooklyn.'

'I heard about a big Jew from Brooklyn,' DeStefano said.

'Good things?'

'Bad things.'

'Good,' Jerry said.

'Mr Sinatra,' DeStefano said, 'it's a pleasure to have you in my house. I have quite a few of your records.'

'Thanks,' Frank said. He looked a bit off balance. I think he'd intended on showing this mob guy why he and Mo Mo were friends, and the guy's compliment threw him.

'You know a family named Arnold?' I asked DeStefano.

He took his eyes from Jerry and looked at me.

'Arnold,' he said. 'I know some brothers.'

'Chris, Phil and Eric.'

'I know Phil and Eric,' he said. 'Never met Chris.'

'Did you have Chris killed?'

'I said I never met Chris.'

'I know that,' I said. 'That wasn't my question.'

'Why would I have some guy I don't even know whacked?' he asked.

'You're in business with Phil Arnold, right?'

'We have had some dealings, yeah.'

'And Eric?'

'He's his brother's accountant.'

'That's it?'

'That's it.'

'Does Phil owe you money?'

DeStefano sat back. 'Lots of people owe me money.'

'Is Phil Arnold one of them?' I asked.

He didn't answer.

'Is it a lot of money?'

He looked at his watch.

'See, somebody killed Chris Arnold,' I said. 'Beat him to death. I think it has something to do with Phil's business dealings, which you just admitted you're involved in.'

'Doin' business with the guy don't mean I killed his brother.'

'It don't mean you didn't, either,' Frank said, wanting to be part of the conversation.

'You're right,' I said. 'It doesn't *necessarily* mean you killed his brother.'

DeStefano looked at his watch.

'You got a few minutes left.'

I wasted a few seconds of that time studying him.

'He called you, didn't he?'

'Who?'

'Philip,' I said. 'He called you yesterday after we left the office. He told you we'd be coming to see you.'

'What makes you say that?' DeStefano asked.

'I don't think you would've agreed to see us otherwise.'

'I told you why I agreed.'

'Yeah, Giancana,' I said. 'But, you see, I think you would've tossed us out of here already if that was the case. You and Phil are partners, aren't you?'

'I said we had some dealings.'

'And that's all you're willin' to admit to?'

'Time's up, Gianelli,' he said, looking at his watch again, 'and now I am gonna have you tossed out.'

His two bodyguards started for us.

'Don't try it,' Jerry said.

'Back off, pally!' Frank chimed in. He put his hands up.

They stopped. Apparently they'd heard about the big Jew from Brooklyn, as well. I don't think the skinny guy from Jersey backed them off, any.

'Boss,' said the man who had shown us the way.

'It's OK, Sid,' DeStefano said. 'Just show our guests out.' He looked at me, then at Frank. 'You'll tell Mo Mo I gave you the ten minutes I promised, right?'

'I'll tell 'im,' Frank said.

'Good.' Then he looked at Jerry. 'You ever think about leavin' Brooklyn lemme know.'

Jerry didn't answer. We followed Sid out.

As we approached the Caddy Frank said, 'Well, what did that accomplish?'

'Mr G?' Jerry said.

'DeStefano and Phil Arnold are partners,' I said.

'So you're sayin' he didn't have Arnold beat up?'

'No,' I said. 'If he had, Philip wouldn't have warned him about us. In fact, I don't think DeStefano had anythin' to do with killin' Chris.'

'Why not?'

'He was way too calm about seein' us, and about the questions I was askin'.'

'Then who did have Philip Arnold beaten up?' Frank asked. 'And his brother killed?'

'I don't know,' I said, as we piled into the car under the watchful eyes of Sid – who handed Jerry back his gun – and the two outside bodyguards. 'I think we may be back to square one.'

FIFTY-SIX

We drove back to the Sands, but didn't get out of the car right away. It was as good a place as any to talk.

'Did the two of you notice something back at DeStefano's?' I asked.

'Like what?' Frank asked.

'Like while we were talkin' to him neither one of us mentioned that there was an Arnold sister; let alone two,' I said.

'Adrienne,' Jerry said.

'There's an Adrienne Arnold?' Frank asked.

'Yeah,' I said. 'She took over the negotiation with Bing about the horse.'

'And DeStefano said he knew the Arnold brothers,' Frank said.

'Phil and Eric,' I added. 'But not Chris.'

'But he knows *about* Chris,' Jerry said.

'If he knows the Arnold boys – about all the Arnold boys – wouldn't he know about her?' I asked.

'And there's another?' Frank asked.

'Yeah, but she lives in Europe, so she's out of the picture. But Adrienne lives here . . . he'd know about her.'

'Maybe,' Jerry said.

'Not necessarily,' Frank said.

I looked at Frank.

'Well,' he said, 'you know Adrienne Arnold and you didn't mention her.'

We sat in silence for a few moments, Frank drumming out a rhythm on the back of my seat.

'I guess,' I said, after a few moments, 'that was a question I should have asked him.'

'Well,' Jerry said, 'you did only have ten minutes.'

'Ten minutes?' I repeated, looking at Frank. 'That was all you could get me?'

'I didn't know about that part. Sorry.'

'Yeah, well . . . that's OK.'

'Those guys at the house,' Jerry said.

'What about them?' I asked.

'None of them came out of the elevator at Philip Arnold's building.'

'You're right.'

'DeStefano could have used local muscle,' Frank said. 'Couldn't he?'

'I doubt it,' Jerry said. 'He didn't look like he needed any extra help.'

'And any of those guys looked capable of knocking Phil Arnold around.'

'So what's next for you guys?' Frank asked.

'What's next for you?' I asked.

'I got a show to do tonight. Frankie and me are leavin' tomorrow,' he said. 'Headin' home. You guys can come to the show if you have time, but I'll understand if you can't make it.'

'Well then,' I said, 'Jerry and me will have to try and find Phil Arnold again. Only he can tell us who knocked him around.'

'Or,' Jerry said, 'we could talk to Adrienne again.'

'And what?' I asked.

'We could ask her the question you didn't ask DeStefano. If she knows him.'

'Good point.'

We all popped our doors and got out of the Caddy.

'Thanks for your help, Frank.'

'Guess I didn't help all that much,' he said.

'Yeah, you did,' I said. 'The ten minutes was enough to tell us DeStefano didn't rough up Phil or kill Fred Stanley.'

'That's not definite,' Frank said. 'Is it?'

'No,' I said. 'It's just what I believe. I'll have to run it by Danny.'

'Good idea,' Jerry said. 'After all, he's the dick.'

'Yeah, he is,' I said. We went inside the Sands.

'I should tell Jack what happened,' I said, as we entered the hotel.

'I can do that,' Frank said. 'I want to see him one more time before I leave, anyway.'

'OK,' I said. 'Thanks. He won't get mad at me if he sees you're OK.'

'Aw, was he worried?'

'Yeah,' I said, 'he thought I'd get you . . . damaged.'

'I'll make sure he knows I'm undamaged.'

'I'm glad you didn't try to act like a gangster when we were there,' I said.

'I'm not an idiot, Eddie,' Frank said. 'Catch you later, pally. See ya, Jerry.'

'Later, Mr S.'

Frank headed for the elevator.

'Where to boss?' Jerry asked.

Good question.

FIFTY-SEVEN

We needed to find Phil Arnold again. Where to look? Where did he live?

'You were right,' I said to Jerry.

'I was? About what?'

'We need to talk to Adrienne again.'

'You wanna do that with me,' Jerry asked, 'or without me?'

'Let's do it together,' I said.

'You sure?'

'Yeah.'

'Where?'

'She gave me her number, and her address.'

'You wanna call her?'

'No,' I said. 'I think we should just . . . drop in on her.'

'Now?'

'Right now.'

He grinned.

'Back to the Caddy!'

I was surprised to find that Adrienne Arnold lived in a brand new building, walking distance from the strip. From her door to the Dunes was about a ten minute walk.

'We goin' up?' Jerry asked, as we stood in front of the building.

'Huh? Oh, yeah. I was just finding it odd that the Arnold who lives closest to a casino is Adrienne, when the two brothers are supposed to be gamblers.'

'You think she's a gambler?'

'That would explain why she still wants to sell the horse even though her brother Chris was murdered.'

'Maybe the whole family gambles.'

'That's what I'm startin' to think.'

We went inside, found a young, uniformed doorman standing behind a desk.

'Help ya?' he asked.

'We're lookin' for Adrienne Arnold.'

'Who ain't?' he asked, with a silly grin. 'She's hot.'

'Yeah, she is. Is she also in?' I asked.

'Nah, went out early. Ain't come back, yet. Believe me, I been watchin' for her.'

'Any idea where she went?'

'Sure,' he said, 'if she ain't home, she's at the Dunes, hittin' the blackjack tables. If she's not there, just keep tryin' casinos.'

'The lady is a gambler?' I asked.

'You kiddin'?' he asked. 'She's jonesin'.'

'Does she play all day?'

'Oh, yeah,' the man said. 'She can be gone for hours.'

'OK,' I said. 'Thanks.'

We went back outside, stood in front.

'Want me to wait here while you go lookin' fer her?' Jerry asked.

'Naw,' I said, 'we can both go lookin' for her.'

We walked down the block and got into the Caddy.

*   *   *

The Dunes was located at the southernmost tip of the Strip. Along with the Sands and the Desert Inn it was known as one of the Kings of the Strip.

It didn't have the success the other two had, though. Not right away. Not even booking Frank into their showroom could help. However, when they started their first topless review, that put them on the map. From that day on they were a huge success.

I knew they were planning to spend some money on a huge neon sign the following year, '64. It would be one hundred and eighty feet high and shoot 'electric lava' into the sky every minute. It would lead the way toward lighting the Strip.

Inside the Dunes we split up.

'If you find her, then find me,' I said. 'Unless you wanna question her.'

'I'm the muscles, Mr G.,' he said. 'You're the brain. I'll find you.'

The Dunes ran a lot of blackjack tables. Jerry took one end of the room and I took the other. I got lucky and hit the jackpot. I found her seated at one of the high stakes tables. I watched her play for a while. She was in my world now. There was nowhere to hide.

She was occupying the middle spot. She played with her body leaning forward, watching every move the dealer made, oblivious to the fact that the eyes of all the males at the table were on her. She played with intensity, shaking her leg, biting her lip, tensing her shoulders. She'd go from elation to despair from hand to hand. The doorman was so right. She was jonesing for it. Blackjack was her drug of choice.

I spotted Jerry across the room and waved to him. He started over.

I moved up behind her, but before I could say a word the pit boss spotted me. We weren't friends, but we were usually cordial to each other. He had been watching the dealer. Maybe he was suspected of cheating, or maybe he was new.

Charlie was about my age, but that was all we had in common. Mostly because he was a prick.

'Hey, Eddie,' Charlie said. 'Whataya doin', checkin' out my dealers?'

'Hi, Charlie,' I said. 'No, just spotted a friend. Hey, Adrienne.'

She turned and froze when she saw it was me.

'Hello, Eddie.'

'Wanna take a walk?' I asked.

'No, I can't,' she said, 'I'm uh, on a—'

'Don't even try to tell me you're on a roll,' I said. 'You just ate a twenty when the dealer made twenty-one. You need to take a break, get some air. Believe me, I know.'

Before I knew it Charlie had come around from behind the tables. He was a big guy and he got in my face.

'Hey, Eddie, it ain't like you to try and steal a mark.'

'I'm not stealing anybody, Charlie. I just wanna talk to her. She'll be back.'

'She better be,' he said, jabbing his forefinger into my chest. He was about to do it again when Jerry grabbed the finger.

'Want me to snap it off, Mr G?' he asked.

'Hey, Eddie . . .' Charlie said, to me, looking worried.

I looked at him.

'You know, Charlie, part of your problem is you look at people as marks. They're people. Sometimes they need to take a break. She's takin' a break.' I looked at Jerry. 'Let him go.'

Jerry released Charlie's finger.

I took Adrienne by the elbow.

'Let's take a walk.'

'I'll lose my seat,' she said, 'my chips . . .'

'They'll all be here when you get back, right, Charlie?'

'Yeah, yeah,' Charlie said, 'right, go ahead. Get some air.'

'See?' I said to Adrienne. 'Come on.'

FIFTY-EIGHT

Jerry and I walked Adrienne out on to the street, in front.

'You told me your brother Eric was a gambler,' I said. 'I found out Philip is, too. But you didn't tell me that you were, also.'

'You didn't ask me.' She was rubbing her upper arms, although it wasn't cold. She was feeling the urgency of having to get back inside.

'You told me you lived in Henderson. So you lied about that.'

'I didn't lie,' she said. 'I have a house in Henderson.'

'We talked with Eric and Philip, Adrienne,' I said. 'That led us to Vincent DeStefano. You know him, don't you?'

'Um, yes, I know Mr DeStefano.'

'Funny,' I said, 'when we talked to Vince he didn't mention knowin' you. How well are the two of you acquainted?'

She averted her eyes and said, 'Pretty well.'

I was afraid I knew what 'pretty well' meant.

He was partners with Philip, Eric was their accountant, and Adrienne was his . . . girl? DeStefano was definitely involved with the entire family.

'What's Vince's connection with the horse, Adrienne?'

'The horse?'

'Chris's horse?'

'Vince? Nothing.'

'He's partners with Phil, right? And Phil thinks he's got a piece of the horse?'

'Phil thinks he's got a piece of everything, Eddie,' she said. 'He's all talk.'

'And Eric?'

'Like I told you, Eric does Philip's books.'

'Yeah, the real set and the queer set.'

'I don't know anything about that,' she said. 'Look, I'm just trying to sell the horse.'

'Because you need the money?' She didn't answer. 'You owe money, Adrienne?'

'Doesn't everybody?'

'No,' I said, 'you owe big money, don't you? And the sale of the horse was gonna bail you out? Was Christopher gonna help you when he sold the horse?'

'O-of course,' she said. 'He was my brother.'

'So are Phil and Eric. Were they gonna help you?'

'They can't even help themselves.'

'What about Vince? Was he gonna help you?'

'Vince would help me . . . if I asked.'

'But you haven't?'

'No.'

'Why not?'

'Because I don't want anything to do with him anymore.'

'And Phil?'

'Him, either.'

'What about Eric?'

'Eric's confused. He lets Phil use him.'

'Do you try to help Eric?'

'Sometimes.'

'And you all gamble,' I said. 'You all play blackjack, right?'

'So?' she said. 'It's Vegas, right? Look, I have to go back in. I don't have much more time. I have to . . .'

'Ya have to what?' Jerry asked her.

'She has to move,' I said. 'To another casino. She has to play here for a certain amount of time, and then move, right, Adrienne?'

She looked at her watch. This woman was so different from the other one I'd met, the first Adrienne.

'Can I go?' she asked.

'Sure, Adrienne,' I said. 'Sure. Just tell us one thing. Where do we find Phil? We went to his office yesterday, but he ran away from us.'

'That's no surprise.'

'What's his home address?'

'I told you yesterday.'

'You told us his work address, but we never got around to his home address.'

'OK,' she said. 'When I give it to you can I go back in?'

'Sure,' I said. 'Sure, Adrienne, you can go back in.'

'What was that all about?' Jerry asked in the car. 'That stuff about movin' from casino to casino.'

'She's chasing the hot table,' I said. 'Tryin' to find her luck. Some people will sit at one table for days, trying to beat it. Others go from table to table, waitin' for their luck to change. Adrienne is one of those.'

'That's sick, ain't it?'

'Maybe it is. I'm not a psychiatrist, so I don't know for sure. Some gamblers are just superstitious. Don't you have any superstitions in your life? Like when you play the horses?'

'No.'

'That's because you're too well adjusted, Jerry.'

A well-adjusted leg breaker for the Mafia. Who knew?

FIFTY-NINE

Philip Arnold had a house on Palomino Lane, near Ranchero Drive. It had to be a house, an estate really, that he couldn't afford, unless the whole Arnold family had more money than I knew about. And hadn't mentioned it.

No, it seemed to me all the trouble was stemming from the fact that they needed money. All of them. On the other hand, it looked like Vince DeStefano had all the money he needed. But that was the problem with money. The more you had the more you wanted, the more you wanted the more you needed. I learned that from dealing with gamblers for so many years.

We stopped at the front gate.

'He's gonna hafta buzz us in,' Jerry said. 'Since he ran from us yesterday, I don't think he's gonna do that. Especially if he's holed up here.'

'Let's park away from the gate and look for a way in.'

He backed the Caddy up. We parked under a tree a few hundred feet along the road. Then we got out and began to walk the wall, looking for a likely place to climb over.

'Wait,' Jerry said after we'd walked a while. 'I can boost you up here, and then climb.'

'How?'

'The wall's crumbling here,' he said, pointing. 'I can get a foot-hold.'

'OK, let's try it.'

He not only boosted me up, but when I put my foot in his cupped hands he almost tossed me over.

I laid flat on top of the wall and extended my hand.

'I'll pull you down,' he said. 'I got it, Mr G. Go ahead.'

The wall was seven or eight feet high, but by hanging from my hands first I only had to drop a foot or two. I waited and soon Jerry appeared at the top. When he lowered himself he only had to drop inches.

'Any dogs?' he asked.

'I haven't heard any.'

'I hate dogs.'

'How can you hate dogs?'

'When you been chased and got by as many junkyard dogs as I have, it's real easy.'

'Well, like I said, I don't hear any. Come on. Let's get to the house.'

As we trotted to the house he asked, 'Think you can get the truth out of him this time?'

'No,' I said, 'I think you can.'

When we got to the house it was huge, lots of stucco and stone with many windows and stairways.

'This guy's got more money than we thought,' Jerry said.

'Or not as much as he wants people to think,' I said. 'Front door?'

'No,' Jerry said. 'Something with lots of glass.'

'French doors.'

'I guess.'

'This way.'

We went up one of the stone stairways, which led to a path. We followed that around until we found a large swimming pool. That's where we found a pair of French doors.

'There you go,' I said. 'You gonna pick the lock?'

'Yeah,' he said, and put his elbow through the glass. 'There ya go.' He reached in, unlocked the door and we walked in.

'Arnold!' I shouted. 'Philip, it's Eddie Gianelli.' I looked at Jerry. 'Find the front door and stay there so he can't run out.'

'OK.' He took out his .45. 'Here.'

'No, you take it,' I said. 'I'll be fine.'

'Be careful.'

I nodded, and we split up.

When we had gotten to Philip's office I had half expected to find him dead. Even I was getting paranoid about me and Jerry finding bodies together.

But this time I was expecting to find him worked over. I actually would have preferred that.

I checked several rooms before I found an office, and that's where he was. He was seated behind a huge cherry wood desk. His head was cocked to one side and there was a blood trail from the left corner of his mouth. I checked for a pulse and didn't find any. In fact, his skin felt cold. Jerry would know better than me, but I thought he'd been dead since yesterday. Maybe when he ran from us at his office he'd come straight back here and battened down the hatches.

Only not hard enough.

SIXTY

I found Jerry by the front door and led him back to the office. He studied the body for a moment, touched the skin, felt for a pulse, then straightened.

'He's been dead since yesterday,' he said. 'Maybe last night.'

'What killed him?'

Jerry looked again.

'I don't wanna move him or touch him,' he said. 'I see a little blood on his chest. Can't tell if he was stabbed or shot.'

'A shot might've been heard.'

'Depends on what caliber,' Jerry said. 'Depends on what time of day, who was home, what kind of neighbors he has—'

'I get it,' I said. 'OK, now we gotta figure out what to do. Too many people know we were lookin' for him. Eric, Adrienne, DeStefano. If we don't call the cops one of them will.'

'Not DeStefano.'

'No, maybe even him, if he's tryin' to play the straight citizen here in Vegas. If we don't call the cops – and I mean Hargrove – he'll come lookn' for us.'

'If we do call him he'll grill us, anyway.'

'But at least we'll have the fact that we called him on our side.'

'You could leave and I could call him,' Jerry suggested.

'No, that would only work the other way around,' I said. 'Remember, me brains, you brawn. You leave and I'll call them.'

He walked away from the desk and came to stand next to me.

'We might as well stick together, Mr G.,' he said. 'Whichever one of us stays, they'll come lookin' for the other one, anyway.'

'We got another problem, though.'

'What's that?'

'We broke in,' I said. 'I don't think Hargrove will let that go. It'll give him somethin' to throw us in a cell for.'

'I didn't think of that.'

'OK, so a bunch of people knew we were looking for Philip, but we could always say we got here, the gate was locked, and we couldn't get in.'

'So we leave him for somebody else to find?' Jerry asked. 'Or do we make an anonymous call?'

'I vote for the anonymous call,' I said, 'but after we take a look around.'

'Make sure you don't leave no prints, Mr G.,' he reminded me.

'What can we do about the wall?'

'They ain't gonna fingerprint the whole wall,' he said. 'We just gotta worry about the French doors and anything we touch from now on.'

'Gotcha,' I said. 'I'll look around here, you take the upstairs.'

'I'll find the master bedroom,' he said. 'Probably won't be anything else important up there.'

'Let's be as quick as we can, before somebody sees the car and makes a call.'

'Right.'

He left the office and I got started.

* * *

It was hard to search the desk with a dead body seated at it. It was also difficult to rifle through drawers when you're holding a handkerchief in your hand.

I did the best I could, then moved on to the file cabinets. I kept thinking that if I had phony records and real records then I would keep the real ones at home. That was probably why I wasn't a crook. I found a bank statement in a drawer that indicated Philip Arnold had a safety deposit box at a Las Vegas branch of City National Bank.

I didn't find anything interesting in the file cabinet. I figured anything that would help us was probably in that safety deposit box.

I left the office after a few minutes and ran into Jerry coming back down.

'Nothin',' he said.

'Let's get out of here.'

We retraced our steps and wiped prints off the French doors. Let the cops think that whoever killed him broke the window to get in.

We climbed the wall again to get to the car. I half expected to find police waiting for us when we dropped down off the wall.

We scrambled into the car and got away from there.

Along the way I told Jerry about finding the bank statement.

'I'll bet there's somethin' in that box that him and his brother've been killed over.'

'Yeah, so how do we get to it?'

'We don't,' Jerry said. 'I ain't never broke into a bank, Mr G. You know anybody?'

I shook my head.

'No bank robbers in my phone book,' I said. 'But his brother or sister can probably get in there after he dies.'

'Yeah,' Jerry said, 'if they ain't killed before that.'

SIXTY-ONE

Everything started and ended at the Sands.

It was late afternoon when we got back there. We'd started out very early going to see Vince DeStefano, even though it felt like days ago to me.

We had stopped along the way at a pay phone. I had disguised my voice and called in a disturbance report at Philip Arnold's address. Even said I thought I'd heard breaking glass.

We sat parked in the lot for a few minutes.

'I hate finding bodies.' I looked at my shaking hands.

'I know how you feel, Mr G.,' Jerry said. 'Ain't my favorite thing, neither.'

We sat quietly for a few moments.

'What do we do now?'

'I'd still like to talk to Adrienne some more,' I said, 'but think we need to spend some time around people.'

'Alibis?'

I nodded.

'We'll need an alibi for last night—'

'We got alibis for last night, Mr G. We wuz at the Flamingo for Frank Junior's Show, and then we went out with Mr S.'

'That's right,' I said. 'Jesus, that seems like days ago to me. OK, but we still need 'em for the rest of the afternoon. We don't know when the cops will find him, or when Hargrove will get called in, but when he does he'll come after us. That much I'm sure of; and he'll try to place us here today.'

'We can't alibi each other,' Jerry said. 'Believe me, I know that never works.'

'We've got some people we can ask,' I said. 'Let me work out the details. You go to the horse book and make sure you're seen.'

'Have you seen me, Mr G?' he asked, spreading his hands.

'Yeah, you're right. Mount Rushmore would have more trouble bein' seen.'

We got out of the car and started toward the casino, but I put my hand on his arm.

'Not the front door,' I said. 'We don't want some valet or bell boy tellin' the cops when we came walkin' in.'

'Good thinkin'.'

We went behind the casino and entered that way. In fact, Jerry was able to veer off and go right to the horse book with a 'See ya later.'

'Stay there until I come for you,' I said. 'We don't wanna talk to anybody until we have alibis for today.'

He nodded and I went into the casino.

I had a few choices for alibis. I could ask Bing, Frank, Dean or Jack Entratter. However, first I had to find out who was still around.

Even if Frank had left, it would take the cops a while to check with him, because he'd be in Palm Springs.

When I got to Jack's office, like the day before, he wasn't there. The girl looked at me.

'Still trying to catch that slot granny at it,' she said, with a shrug.

'Got it,' I said. 'Thanks.'

Probably the most civil exchange of words we'd ever had. We were practically dating.

Jack saw me coming, but then frowned at the old lady.

'Back today?' I asked.

'She's been at it for days,' he said. 'I know it's only nickels, but it's the principal of the thing. I *know* she's cheatin'.'

'Well, I need to talk to you. It's important.'

'Where?' he asked.

'Someplace where it's just the two of us.'

'There's no game in the VIP room,' he said. 'Let's go there.'

The Sands had a room in the back that was reserved for big money private games. This was where Jack Entratter treated his 'whales' to whatever kind of game they wanted.

The silence in the room fell over us like a blanket. That was good. I had the feeling if he could hear the nickels striking the tray I'd lose him.

I told him about finding Philip Arnold's body. Told him how, when, where, and what we did. I'll give him credit. He could have blown his top, but he listened intently.

'So where's Jerry?'

'In the horse book.'

'You both need alibis for today.'

'Right.'

'You didn't do nothin',' he said, 'but you need alibis. Well, you did break into the man's house. That broken glass is gonna be blamed on the killer.'

'Hopefully. We wiped away any fingerprints.'

'All right,' he said, scratching his head. 'Who'd you have in mind? Me?'

'Well, I work for you. I was thinkin' maybe Frank or Dean.'

'Frank left with Junior today,' he said. 'Dean's leavin' tomorrow.'

'Bing?'

'He can't leave until the police tell him,' he said, thoughtfully. 'We need two people, one for you, one for Jerry.'

'I could ask Dean.'

'What about your P.I. buddy? That wouldn't surprise anybody.'

'I haven't talked to him since yesterday when we split up. He's been working the trainer's death, but we could work somethin' out, I guess.'

'You and Jerry can't alibi each other,' he said. 'Hargrove wouldn't go for that.'

'No, he wouldn't.'

'What about Mack Gray? You could talk to Dino about using Mack for Jerry.'

'That's good,' I said.

'No,' he said, 'they'd wanna know where they went, they'd expect people to remember two guys like them.'

'They can say they stayed in and watched some movies, had some beers.'

'Movies?'

'Jerry likes them, and Mack's been in some.'

He thought a moment, then said, 'OK. That'd take care of Jerry for last night. What about today?'

'Horse book,' I said. 'Casino. He and I were in the Dunes earlier.'

'OK, that's good. Somebody there will remember seein' him. Now how about you?'

'I'll use Dino or Danny, whoever it works better with.'

'You need a girlfriend, Eddie,' Jack said.

'Yeah, Hargrove would buy that in a minute.'

'Well,' Jack said, 'get busy tonight, maybe even work your pit. It'd be good if you were working when the cops came to talk to you.'

'Yeah, OK,' I said. 'I've been gettin' itchy to work, anyway.'

'Or maybe you can help me catch this slot granny at her game,' he said.

'I'll give it a try.'

SIXTY-TWO

I couldn't see it.

It looked to me like granny was just lucky. It was odd but she just kept hitting jackpots. I recommended we take her in the back and sweat it out of her.

'That's what we'd do to somebody we thought was cheatin' at one of my tables, right?' I asked him.

'We can't do that to an old lady, Eddie,' Jack said. 'Believe me,
I thought about it already.'

'Well, I don't know what she's doin',' I said. 'I've gotta go.'

'Where are you off to?'

'I'm gonna drop in on Adrienne again and see if I can squeeze
the truth out of her,' I explained. 'I've got more of a handle on her
now that I know she's a blackjack player.'

'You takin' Jerry with you?'

'Not this time.'

'OK, I'll put him and Mack Gray together. Let them work out
their song and dance.'

As I starred from the room he said, 'Work out your alibi first;
and let me know!'

I called Dino's suite and Mack answered. I told him what we
needed and he said if it was OK with Dino it was OK with him.
He checked with his boss and got the OK. He said he'd be right
down.

I met him in the lobby and took him to the horse book. We
figured he and Jerry would stay there a few hours, play some horses,
have a few drinks. When the cops asked around in there, people
would say yeah, they saw the two big guys in there playing horses.
Maybe they'd be a little vague about the time.

I called Danny's office from a desk phone and Penny answered.

'He's been in and out since you left yesterday, Eddie,' she said.
'He's still working on the murder of that trainer.'

'Has he found anything yet?'

'He went back to the hotel. He's working the building and the
area. What do you need? Can I help?'

I told her what had happened because I trusted Penny. She listened
without comment, then said, 'So you want Danny to alibi you?'

'That's it.'

'Hargrove won't buy that,' she said. 'He'll just think your friend
is covering up for you.'

'My other choice is Dean Martin, but the cops'll think the same
thing.'

'You have another choice.'

'What's that?'

'Me.'

'Penny,' I said, 'Danny'll kill me . . .'

'I'll clear it with him,' she said. 'And I only come into play if
and when the cops ask.'

'Oh don't worry,' I said. 'They'll ask.'

'OK, then,' she said. 'Just tell me what we were doing all night and all day . . . as if I don't know . . .'

Alibi set up, I left the Sands and got to drive my own car, for a change. I drove to Adrienne's building first and talked to the same doorman.

'Hey, man,' he said. 'You find her?'

'I did, thanks,' I said. 'She told me to drop by later, though, so here I am.'

'You're in luck,' he said. 'She came in about an hour ago. I think she's gonna recharge her battery and then get back to it.'

'What apartment is she in?'

'She didn't tell you?'

'She did,' I said, 'but you know us gamblers.' I pointed to my head. 'Lots of numbers.'

'Tell me about it.'

'If you don't wanna tell me her apartment just call her and tell her I'm here.' I took out a ten, folded it up and held it out to him. 'But I really would like to surprise her.'

'I thought you said she told you to come by?'

'She did,' I said, 'but I didn't call ahead to say when.' I took out a second ten.

'OK sure, man,' he said, taking the money. 'Six F.'

'Thanks.'

In the elevator I started to worry. If there was a body waiting for me in her apartment, I had just hung myself out to dry. The doorman would definitely remember me and Jerry from earlier today, and remember me and my twenty dollars now.

I just had to hope she was alive.

I knocked on her door and held my breath. I released when she opened the door. She was wearing a robe, and her hair was wet, so she was fresh from a shower or bath.

'Come on in,' she said. She didn't seem surprised I was there. I wondered if she had already heard about Philip? If not I wondered if I should tell her and then question her, or question her and then tell her.

SIXTY-THREE

'Would you like a drink?' she asked.

The apartment was very large, but still could have fit into a Sands suite. She went into the kitchen and opened the freezer.

'Sure.'

'You like vodka?' she asked. 'I keep it really cold.'

'That's fine.'

She set the bottle on the counter, then opened the frig itself.

'I love fruit juice with it,' she said. 'Grapefruit, cranberry or orange?'

'Orange.'

She made me a screwdriver and then added cranberry juice to her glass. She came around the counter, out of the kitchen, and handed me my drink.

'Here's to truth,' she said. 'I assume that's what you're here for.'

'The whole truth and nothin' but,' I said, and we clinked glasses.

How we ended up in bed is still fuzzy to me.

Somehow, with the gambling addiction, Adrienne seemed a little more real to me. Before that she was different from the other girls in Vegas, something I hadn't seen before, outside of my world. Somehow, that had made her both desirable and unattainable. But when her feet of clay showed she came crashing back down to earth, where I lived.

And we ended up in bed, rolling around with our feet of clay tangled up . . .

She lit a cigarette and blew smoke at the ceiling.

'You want one?' she asked.

'No, thanks,' I said, lying on my back. 'I used to smoke when I was a kid, but I quit.'

'I'd like to quit, too.'

I turned my head and looked at her. She was sitting up with her back against the headboard. Her red hair was down, covering her shoulders and partially hiding her pale breasts. She had her left arm folded beneath her breasts, the other hand up, holding the cigarette.

Her lipstick had been rubbed off, and her eye make-up smudged. The room smelled like sex.

'Why would you quit?' I asked. 'On you it's sexy; dead sexy.'

'Sexy,' she said, 'yeah, right.' She picked a piece of tobacco off her tongue with the last two fingers of her right hand.

I sat up and looked around the expensively furnished bedroom. 'Adrienne,' I said, 'how did we end up here?'

She looked at me and said, 'I was wondering the same thing. You were telling me about Phil being dead, I started to cry, you held me . . . here we are.'

'I'm sorry . . .'

'For what?' she asked. 'I took advantage of you. What is it about death that makes you want to feel alive?'

'Adrienne—'

'Come on,' she said, getting to her feet, 'let's go back into the living room. We can't talk here. We'll end up fucking our brains out . . . again.'

Her bare buttocks twitched their way across the room where she grabbed her robe and put it back on.

'I'll have drinks waiting,' she said, and left the room.

SIXTY-FOUR

I got up, found my clothes on the floor, pulled some of them on, carried my jacket and shoes back out to the living room. She handed me a glass of vodka, no juice. It suited me.

'I need the truth, Adrienne,' I said. 'Your brothers, DeStefano, what kind of business were they in together?'

'Phil fancied himself a developer,' she said. 'That's Developer, with a capital 'D'. Only he was small time and didn't know it. The best he could do was a lower case 'd', until he met DeStefano. He had just come to town and was trying to get a foothold in different businesses. I guess you know what he really was.'

'I know.'

'Somehow, Phil convinced him he could help. Only it was Phil who needed help. He was broke.'

'What about the rest of the family?'

'We all had our own money for a while,' she said. 'Our parents died years ago, left us all a nice chunk of change. But we gambled it away – all but Chris. He put his to good use, even multiplied it. Then he decided to breed horses, and he came up with this one.

'Phil realized what Chris had, and he wanted Chris to race the horse, not sell it. Race it, and after it earned a million then breed it. Phil always had big time ideas and no money; Chris had money, but small ideas.

'They should have joined forces,' I said.

'They might have except they both wanted to be in charge.'

'So nobody was in charge.'

'Phil tried to get me and Eric on his side, and our sister Elizabeth.'

'Where is she in all this?'

'She's the smart one,' Adrienne said. 'Lives in Europe with her husband. Doesn't gamble. Doesn't even talk to the rest of us. Sends a postcard, sometimes.'

'But Phil tried to recruit her, too?'

She nodded, lit another cigarette, then pulled the belt on her robe tighter and picked up her drink. Her red hair was tousled and she brushed a lock from her eyes. A damned sexy gesture.

'He tried to recruit all of us, but Eric could only do the books. He had no influence with Chris.'

'But you did?'

'I had some,' she said. 'I'm not proud of it, but Christopher was going to help me out when he sold the horse. You see, I'm more like him than Phil. I'm kind of small time too in my thinking. Phil sees turning the horse into five million in a few years. Me, I wanted fifty thousand next week.'

'So you still say Phil wouldn't have killed Chris?' I asked.

'I told you,' she said, 'he's small time. Murder is big time.'

'So would he get DeStefano to do it for him?'

'No,' she said, 'I don't think so.'

'Well, could he have owed DeStefano enough money to get himself killed?'

'Phil owes money all over town,' she said. 'Any one of them might have killed him for it.'

'But not DeStefano.'

She hesitated, then said, 'Vince and I were . . . tight for a while. A short while. I wasn't above trying to use him to feed my habit. But Vince is not a gambler – not a casino gambler, anyway. And he didn't like that I was. So in the end he gave me ten grand, a pat on the butt and sent me on my way.'

She crushed her cigarette out in a glass ashtray on the kitchen counter.

'Chris was business minded, but he still wanted to make a profit next week, not in five years. He wanted to sell the horse, and reinvest in other horses. Let whoever bought the horse race it. See, if it flopped on the track then it would be worth nothing. Chris didn't have the gambling gene. He always went for the sure thing.'

'So sellin' the horse to Bing Crosby was a sure thing.'

'That was how it looked.'

'Adrienne.' I sat down and pulled on my shoes and socks. 'You've got two dead brothers now. And Bing Crosby has a dead trainer. Now the same person might not have killed them all, but I think the same man was behind them. You can't point me in any direction?'

'I told you,' she said. 'Phil owed money all over town. Maybe he mentioned the horses to one of his partners, and maybe they thought killing the trainer and Chris would get Phil the horse. I don't know.'

'Who would know? Eric?' I asked.

'I think the only person who knew all of Phil's business was Vince.'

'Do you think you could get me in to see Vince for more than ten minutes?' I asked. 'Maybe without all the bodyguards?'

'Without them?'

'I don't want to get to him,' I said, 'but without them around there might not be so much posturing, on his part.'

'I don't know,' she said. 'I could try.'

I put on my jacket. Her scent was all over me. I wished I could stay so we could drink and fuck all night and forget about everything else. I thought she might have felt the same way.

'I have to go,' I said. 'Will you try with Vince?'

'I'll give him a call,' she said. 'If he agrees I'll probably have to go with you.'

'I don't want to put you in danger.'

'Don't worry,' she said. 'Vince won't hurt me. I can't promise the same for you, though.'

'I'll take my chances.'

I headed for the door, then stopped and looked at her. A parting word? Kiss goodbye? It was awkward.

'Just go, Eddie,' she said. 'Do what you have to do. I'll call you.'

'OK,' I said. 'Uh, thanks.'

She was pouring herself another drink as I went out the door.

SIXTY-FIVE

I left her building and drove to my house instead of the Sands. It was late, but not late for Vegas. I figured I'd change for work, go in and spend some time in the pit. I wondered if the police had found Phil's body, and if Hargrove was hard at work yet? I knew his first move would be to look for me and Jerry.

It was getting dark when I pulled up in front of my house. As I entered I knew something was wrong. The place felt different. You know how when you live alone your home feels one way, and when something changes the way it feels you can tell? There had been some excitement in my living room on more than one occasion. I think there might have even still been a bullet in the wall, somewhere.

I looked around. Everything seemed to be in place, but I had the feeling someone had been there. It didn't feel like they were still there. I didn't feel the urgency to get out. I walked through the house carefully, finally determined that it was empty. I turned on the light in the kitchen and got myself a beer.

Somebody had been in my house. What for? I walked around with the beer in my hand. This time with the lights on. I saw a couple of signs in the bedroom that someone had searched. I have a thing about dresser drawers. They have to be closed tight. Two of mine were slightly ajar.

Also, when I looked in them, I could see that someone had rifled through my undies.

Whatever they were looking for had to be small enough to fit in a drawer?

I didn't have a good enough eye to narrow it down further than that, but I knew who did.

This time when I called Danny he was in his office. He got to my house in twenty minutes.

'What's missin'?' he asked.

'Nothin',' I said. 'All I know is they looked through my underwear.'

'Did you touch anything else?'

'The refrigerator. For a beer.'

'Got any more?'

'Help yourself.'

He grabbed a Piels from the frig and then we walked the house. It wasn't until we got back to the kitchen that he saw something.

'You close your cereal boxes after you use them, right?'

'Well yeah,' I said. 'Otherwise the cereal gets stale. Jerry made me start doing it.'

'Well, you've got an open box of cereal on top of your frig.'

'Anything else?'

He ran his hand over my kitchen counter, showed me the granules of sugar on his palm.

'They went through my sugar bowl?'

'Might even have dumped the whole thing on the counter to go through it,' he said, brushing his hands off in the sink. 'Better chance, though, they just stuck their fingers in and wiggled them around. Still got sugar on the counter.'

'So now we're smaller than a sugar bowl,' I said. 'Anything else?'

He looked around a bit more, then shook his head.

'Maybe if I spent another hour walkin' around, but—' I stopped him there, because something hit me.

'We don't need you to do that,' I said. 'Small enough to fit in a sugar bowl.'

'Diamonds?' he asked. 'Rubies?'

I shook my head and said, 'A key.'

SIXTY-SIX

'A key,' Danny said, 'to what?'

'A safety deposit box, I think.'

We'd gone down the block from me and around the corner to a bar I'd been in once or twice.

'Hey, Eddie, long time,' the bartender said.

OK, so more than once or twice.

'Two beers, Arnie.'

He set us up and we got back to the business at hand.

I told Danny about getting into Philip Arnold's house, finding him dead, and then discovering the bank statement mentioning the safety deposit box.

'Whoa, back up,' he said. 'Don't skip over the part about the dead guy. What did you and Jerry do when you found him?'

'We wiped the place down, got out of there, and called it in to the police anonymously.'

'You know, sooner or later, Hargrove's gonna get on to that.'

'Yeah, I know,' I said. 'Jerry figured he'd been dead since last night, but we set ourselves up with alibis for this afternoon, anyway.'

'What else did you do today?'

I started from the beginning, told him about DeStefano.

'Wait, wait, you took Frank Sinatra with you to see the mob guy?'

'Frank loves mob guys,' I said. 'Plus he got us the meet through Giancana.'

'OK,' he said, 'go ahead.'

I gave him the rest of the story, and then accounted for the remainder of the day.

'Sounds to me like the dead guy and DeStefano have got some bad enemies,' he said. 'Maybe DeStefano's next.'

'Well he's got guys around him all the time,' I said, 'although I *am* using Adrienne to try to set up a meeting without them.'

'You really think he's gonna go for that?'

'I don't know,' I said. 'It depends on just how tight he used to be with Adrienne.'

'Adrienne,' he said. 'She wanted to meet me, right?'

'Yeah,' I said, 'we'll work that out.'

'Well, when is she settin' up this meet?'

'Hopefully tomorrow.'

'Yeah, well, let's hope you can keep that meeting and you're not in jail.'

We finished our beer, ordered two more.

'OK, so tell me what you think is in the safe deposit box?'

'I don't know. Something worth killin' three people for.'

'I thought this was all about a horse.'

'So did I. But what if it's not?'

'Go on.'

'What if the whole horse thing is just a coincidence?' I asked.

'Or, better yet, a smokescreen.'

'To hide what's really goin' on.'

He looked at me. 'So what's really goin' on, Eddie?'

'I don't know,' I said. 'Maybe Vince knows. Maybe I'll get the chance to ask him. So, what've you been doin' since yesterday?' I asked.

'Lookin' for witnesses,' he said. 'First in the hotel itself, and then outside. I've been goin' door-to-door.'

'That sounds boring.'

'It's called legwork, my friend. It's what bein' a detective is all about.'

'OK, so what has your legwork gotten for you?' I asked.

'It's gotten me nobody who saw the trainer, Red Stanley, get to the hotel.'

'Not even a cab driver from the hotel?'

Danny spun around on his stool a couple of times, looking annoyed.

'There are two cab drivers I haven't been able to get to yet,' he said, finally. 'One's a family man, apparently, henpecked like hell. His wife got him to take a few days off, take her and the kids away. I'm waitin' for him to get back.'

'And where'd they go?' I asked. 'Can't you go to them?'

'Florida.'

'Who goes from Las Vegas to Florida for vacation?' I asked.

'You got me.'

'What about the other one?'

'Him,' Danny said, as if he hated the guy. 'He got fired. I'm still lookin' for him.'

'So you've pretty much been chasing two cabbies around for two days?'

He pointed his finger at me.

'This is the dirty part of the job, Eddie,' he said. 'Believe me, I've been in places that have never seen soap.'

'OK, OK,' I said, 'I'm just pokin' at ya. Findin' a body is no bed of roses either, you know.'

'Yeah, I know,' he said.

'Besides, don't we already have a cabbie who saw Stanley hustled into a dark car?'

'We do, but he didn't see any faces. I'm still lookin' for somebody who can describe these two jamokes. I'm hopin' that's one of these missin' cab drivers.'

'I hope you're right.'

'You're gonna have to deal with Hargrove sooner or later.'

'Hopefully I can give him a killer.'

'Before another body shows up.'

'I just hope if the fired cabby did see somethin', he's not in hidin'. That'd just make him that much more trouble to find. He probably found a hole and pulled it in behind him.'

'Yeah, but you're good at findin' holes, Danny,' I said. 'Nobody can hide from you in Las Vegas. Not for very long, anyway.'

We finished our drinks and I settled up with the bartender.

'You know,' I said, when we got outside, 'if the next victim is DeStefano it might get the cops off my back and lookin' at the mob.'

'So you just wanna hope he's next,' he asked, 'or set it up? Jerry can make the hit.'

'You know, Jerry likes you,' I said. 'He'd never make a remark like that about you.'

'Hey, I like the big buy, too. I was just kiddin'. I mean . . . you don't *wanna* kill DeStefano, do you?'

'Of course not.'

'OK.'

We started back to my house, where our cars were.

'I'm just sayin' if somebody did kill him, it would take some heat off us. That's all.'

He looked at me.

'I'm just sayin',' I said.

When we got back to the cars he asked me the question I didn't want him to ask.

'So what kind of alibis did you and Jerry set up? Do you need my help?'

I looked at him and smiled. 'Here's the part you're gonna find funny.'

SIXTY-SEVEN

I went back to the Sands and did a late shift in my pit. Jerry was nowhere in sight. Maybe he and Mack Grey had found something else to do, or maybe they really were in his room watching movies. Maybe they actually got along.

I kept my eyes peeled for Hargrove, or any other cop. When they didn't show up by three a.m. I started to wonder what was going on? Phil's body must have been found by now.

It was almost four a.m. when Jack Entratter appeared as I was getting ready to hand my pit off. He looked as if he had dressed quickly after somebody woke him up. His suit and white shirt were wrinkled, and he wasn't wearing a tie.

'Eddie,' he said, waving to me.

My replacement moved into the pit and I joined Jack on the casino floor.

'What's up, Jack?'

'I just got woke up by the cops,' he said. 'They were lookin' for you and Jerry.'

'Hargrove?'

'No,' he said. 'I don't think Hargrove would've called. He would've wanted to surprise you.'

'Are they comin' here?'

'Yeah,' he said. 'I called our lawyer, he's on his way, too. Can you think of any reason why you shouldn't be here when they get here?'

I scratched my cheek and said, 'It might not be so bad if it's not Hargrove. Maybe he's . . . off.'

'Yeah, maybe.'

'I'll get a hold of Jerry. He's probably in his suite.'

'I'm wonderin' Jack said, 'if we should bring Bing in on this?'

'Let's not wake him and Kathy up just yet,' I suggested. 'We can do that if the cops ask for them.'

'OK,' Jack said. 'I'm goin' to my office to take some bicarbonate before they get here. Although I doubt very much it'll help.'

'I'll come up after I talk to Jerry,' I said.

'Yeah, OK.'

He didn't ask me to come to his office and make the call. I was glad. Let him have his bicarbonate in peace.

I decided to go to Jerry's suite instead of calling. I only had to knock once and he answered.

'Hey, Mr G.'

'Guess I didn't wake you.'

'Naw, come on in.'

As I entered I noticed that the TV was on, and Mack Grey was asleep sitting up on the sofa.

'How long has he been asleep?'

'I think he nodded off halfway through *The Charge of The Light Brigade*.'

There was a room service tray with a metal pot of coffee and a few cups.

'Anything left in there?'

He nodded. 'Might even still be warm.'

I poured and sipped. Just warm enough not to be cold.

'What's up? Cops around?'

'That's what I came to see you about,' I said. 'They'll probably be here within the hour. Called Jack Entratter already.'

'Hargrove?'

'That's the odd part,' I said. 'It's not him. Not yet, anyway.'

I noticed we were both speaking in hushed tones so as not to wake Mack.

'So what do we do? Wait for them to come lookin'?' he asked.

'No, I told Entratter we'd come down to his office and wait.'

'That's real cooperative of us.'

'Yeah, it is.'

'You talk to the sister?'

'Adrienne,' I said. 'Yeah, we . . . talked. She's gonna try to come up with a name for us, somebody doin' business with her brother and DeStefano who might be targeting Vince next. She's also tryin' to get me a meeting with Vince.'

'She's bein' helpful, too.'

'Yeah,' I said. 'We're all bein' so damned cooperative.'

'What should we do with Mack?' he asked.

'Let's just let him sleep, for now.'

'OK,' Jerry said. 'I'll change.' He was wearing a t-shirt and trousers. I knew he'd want to change into a sports jacket, though. Even if he wasn't going to wear his gun beneath it – I hoped. Jerry was only casual when he was at home.

I finished my lukewarm coffee while waiting.

'I'm ready,' Jerry said, when he reappeared.

'Jerry . . .' I said, eyeing him.

He held his jacket open and said, 'No gun, Mr G.'

SIXTY-EIGHT

When we got to his office Jack was taking two aspirin. 'On top of the bicarb,' he said, putting down the glass of water. 'Does wonders.'

'I'll pass,' Jerry said.

'Me, too.'

We both sat.

'Well,' Jack said, 'this is a switch.'

'Whataya mean?' I asked.

'You guys really haven't done anythin' wrong, and you're still in trouble.'

Jerry held up a huge forefinger and said, 'We did break into the dead guy's house.'

'Well, compared to murder, that's not much of a charge,' Jack said.

At that point the phone rang. Jack picked it up, said, 'What?' listened, then said, 'Thanks,' and hung up. 'Two detectives are on the way up.'

'Do we know them?' I asked.

'We'll know when they walk in.'

We waited, heard the elevator, then the footsteps and some unintelligible words. Presently, two men wearing suits walked in, both looking like they'd been awake for many hours. Happily, neither of them were familiar to us. No Hargrove.

'Mr Entratter?' one of them said.

'That's right,' Jack replied, standing.

The detective shook Jack's hand, took a quick look at us.

'I'm Detective Maddox, this is my partner, Detective Lang. I'm the one who spoke to you on the phone. Sorry to have to wake you.'

'That's all right,' Jack said. 'Murder's a serious business.'

'Yes, it is,' Maddox said. 'I assume these are the two gents we talked about?'

'That's Eddie Gianelli, one of my pit bosses,' Jack said, 'and Jerry Epstein, a friend of his who is a guest with us right now.'

Jerry and I both stood up.

'Stay seated, guys,' Maddox said. 'We just have a few questions.'

We sat back down.

'You gents know a man named Philip Arnold?'

'We know him,' I said.

'How?'

'We were helping another of our guests, Bing Crosby, buy a horse from a man named Chris Arnold. As you probably know, he was killed a couple of days ago.'

'We do know,' Lang said. 'That's how we got on to you.'

'We got a flag that cases involving anyone in the Arnold family should be referred to Detective Hargrove,' Maddox said.

'We know Hargrove,' I said. 'Where is he?'

'He's off, today,' Maddox said, 'but when he gets in this morning he'll find a note on his desk.'

Great.

They asked us when we last saw Philip, what the circumstances were, and then what we had been doing last night. We told the truth, that we'd gone to the show at the Flamingo and then for a night out with Frank and company.

When they asked what we'd done during the day Jerry gave them Mack Grey's name, and I reluctantly gave them Penny's name and contact info. Reluctantly, because when I told Danny that I'd be using Penny as my alibi – that she had *volunteered* – he hadn't been real happy about it. But there was nothing he could do about it, because he knew if he told Penny she couldn't do it, she'd just dig her heels in.

'But don't use her unless you absolutely have to,' he told me.

'I'll do my best,' I promised.

So much for my best.

The detectives finished their interview in about twenty minutes. They thanked Jack Entratter for his assistance in gathering us in one place, then thanked us for our time.

'I'm sure Detective Hargrove will be in touch when he gets to his desk in the morning and catches up,' Maddox said.

'I'm sure he will,' I said.

They said good-morning and left. We waited until we heard the elevator come and go.

'Wow,' Jerry said, 'good cop and quiet cop.'

'Well,' I said, 'I'm sure Hargrove will play the bad cop very well.'

'You fellas and your other buddy, Bardini,' Entratter said, 'better try to wrap this thing up today. The only way you might stay out of jail is to hand Hargrove the killer.'

I looked at my watch.

'Have you slept?' Entratter asked.

'No.'

'You?' he asked Jerry.

'No.'

'You both might as well catch four or five hours,' he said.

'Three would be more like it,' I said. 'In four or five hours Hargrove will be here lookin' for us.'

'OK,' Jack said, 'so three hours. Do it, and then go catch a killer.'

Jerry and I stood up and headed for the door.

'You'll have to get Mack off your sofa,' I said, as we walked to the elevator.

'Let him sleep,' Jerry said. 'He won't bother me. Are you gonna be in the hotel?'

'Yeah,' I said, 'I'll go down to the desk and get a room. I'll meet you at seven forty-five . . . but not in the lobby. We might accidentally run into Hargrove.'

'The café?'

'No,' I said. 'The parking lot, by the car. We'll get somethin' to eat and figure out our next move. I'm too tired to figure it out now.'

'Me, too,' Jerry said. 'I've seen enough TV to last me a long time.'

SIXTY-NINE

I got into bed at five a.m.

The phone rang at seven fifteen.

For a moment I debated about answering it. What if it was the cops? Hargrove? I answered it.

'I've been lookin' for you,' Danny said.

'At seven a.m.?'

'I haven't been to bed at all. Do you wanna know why?'

'Definitely.'

'I found the fired cab driver. He's our guy.'

'Did the cabbie see anybody's face?'

'He was in line behind the cab they pulled Stanley away from.'

'So he got a clear view of his face.'

'He did.'

'And is he able to describe it?'

'He is, and he did.'

'And?'

'He said he has a face like mashed potatoes,' Danny said. 'Like somebody who'd spent his life in the ring. And this cabbie should know. He used to fight middleweight.'

'Could he be more specific?'

'Six three or four, big mashed nose, square jaw, and startling blue eyes.'

'Startling?'

'Yeah, he said "startling".'

'Jesus, I haven't seen anybody like that this whole time.'

'Sorry,' Danny said. 'I was hopin' that would be helpful.'

'Look, Jerry and I are gonna be on the move today,' I told him, 'tryin' to avoid Hargrove. You wanna meet us for breakfast?'

'Gee, that's just what I need to start my day, watching that guy wade through stacks of pancakes. Of course I do.'

'OK, let's make it someplace Hargrove would not look for us.'

'OK, that means not anywhere near a casino,' Danny said.

'Yup.'

'I got just the place.'

* * *

Just as my favorite burger place was out of the way, so was Danny's favorite place for breakfast. Well, one of his favorite places. It was in one of those long, silver diner things, but it was more than a diner.

Jerry and I pulled up in front, found Danny standing outside, leaning against the front of his Chrysler. We had driven way out on Highway 159, even going past the turn-off that headed out to Red Rock Canyon.

As soon as we pulled up I could see Jerry's head go up, his nostrils flaring. He smelled the place before I did.

'Ham,' he said, as Danny walked over.

'You said it,' Danny said. 'Ham omelets. It's their specialty.'

'How's the pancakes?'

'Out of this world. Come in, I'm starving. Been workin' all night.'

We went inside and found a small, cramped empty space. A man came out of the back and he and Danny hugged like long-lost brothers.

'Ham omelets for me and my friends,' Danny said, 'and a couple of stacks of pancakes for the big guy.'

'Comin' up, Danny.'

The guy – about Danny's age, which was a few years older than me – came back out with coffee, got us all filled up and then went to cook.

'Wow,' I said. 'Good coffee.'

'Yeah,' Jerry said, nodding his approval.

'That's just the beginning,' Danny assured us.

Danny's friend came out with all three omelets and the pancakes at the same time, and managed to deliver it all hot. He followed immediately with perfect toast.

'Anythin' else, guys, just let me know.'

We started to eat, and Jerry and I both heartily approved.

'If the food's this good why is this place so empty?' I asked.

'Oh, Lenny can't have too many people knowin' about this place,' Danny said. 'He's wanted.'

'Wanted?' I said.

'In about half a dozen states.'

'For what?' Jerry wondered.

'We don't talk about that,' Danny said.

'OK,' I said, 'then talk about our problem. Tell Jerry what you told me.'

'You tell 'im,' Danny said. 'I'm eating.'

I gave Jerry the description Danny had gotten from the fired cab driver.

'By the way,' I asked Danny, 'why'd he get fired?'

'He loses too many fares.'

'Wait a minute,' Jerry said, chewing his pancakes.

'What?' I asked.

'That day out on the road, when that driver almost forced us off the road?'

'Yeah,' I said, 'the killer.'

'I started to tell you I thought I saw something . . .'

'What was it?'

'Here,' he said, waving his hand in front of his face. 'I thought I saw like . . . a big . . . nose . . .'

'Like a potato?' Danny asked.

'Yeah . . . I guess . . . I thought I was just . . . ya know, seein' things, what with all the dirt and dust . . . damn it. I shoulda said somethin'.'

'Why?' I asked. 'It's not like we've run into a guy with a nose like that. But at least now we know he's probably the Red Rock killer.'

'But we were thinkin' the Red Rock killer wasn't also the killer of the trainer.'

'He coulda been,' I said, 'if he killed the trainer the day before.'

'We don't know the time of death,' Danny said.

'No, but the police do. It could've been potato nose, or whoever his partner was when they picked up the trainer at the airport.'

'Were there two guys in the car out in Red Rock?' Danny asked.

I looked at Jerry and he shrugged.

'Some pair of detectives you guys make,' Danny said.

'He's the brains,' Jerry said, jabbing his fork toward me, 'I'm the muscle.'

'And you're the detective,' I said. 'So what do we do now?'

SEVENTY

We couldn't very well search Las Vegas for a guy with a nose like a potato. At least, that was what Danny said. 'We'll have to wait until he turns up.'

'That could take a long time.'

'Probably not,' Danny said. 'They're still lookin' for the key.'

'What key?' Jerry asked.

'Safe deposit box key,' I said. 'I forgot to tell you, somebody searched my house. They were lookin' for somethin' small enough to fit in a sugar bowl.'

'A key,' Jerry said, chewing. 'Makes sense.'

'You know,' Danny said, looking at Jerry, 'every time you come to town I gain weight. How come you don't?'

'I have a fast metabolism.'

Then Danny looked at me.

'You know sometimes I think you're right.'

'About what?'

'He is smarter than he looks.'

We lingered over coffee.

'You're gonna meet with Adrienne and see if she can get you another meeting with DeStefano, right?' Danny asked.

'Right.'

'Well, watch for the man with the potato nose,' he said. 'If he works for Vince, chances are Vince is behind the killings.'

'Tryin' to get a horse?' Jerry asked.

'Or the key,' Danny said.

'If he's got people lookin' for that key,' Jerry said, 'then who's got it?'

'It was Philip's,' I said. 'Who would he give it to for safe keeping?'

'Not Chris,' Danny said. 'They were at odds.'

'And he was at odds with Adrienne, so that leaves her out.'

'Eric?' I asked.

'From what you tell me, Phil didn't trust Eric with important stuff.'

'So if it ain't family,' Jerry said, 'who is it?'

The question hung in the air for a few moments, then Danny said, 'Unless Phil had a really close friend, it would have to be family.'

'Well . . .' I said.

'What?'

'There's still one family member,' I said.

'There is?' Danny asked.

I nodded. 'Another sister. Younger. Doesn't live in Vegas, doesn't gamble. Apparently, has a whole different life.'

'That makes sense,' Danny said.

'I don't get it,' Jerry said. 'If she's got a whole different life . . .'

'Phil might've mailed her the key,' I said.

'If he did,' Danny said, 'DeStefano might figure it out the way we did.'

'But then he'd have to find her,' I said.

'And who knows where she is?' Danny asked.

'Adrienne,' I said, 'and maybe Eric.'

'Well, you're already gonna talk to Adrienne,' Danny said. 'Why don't I talk to Eric?'

'You ain't workin' on the killin' of the trainer anymore?' Jerry asked.

'All three killings are connected,' Danny said. 'Red Rock, Vegas, it don't matter. If it doesn't have to do specifically with the horse, it has to do with the key.'

'I can see Chris and Phil bein' killed over the key,' I said. 'But why Fred Stanley? If he was just a trainer . . .'

'Didn't you say,' Danny said, 'that it was Stanley who took this horse idea to Bing Crosby?'

'Did I?' I asked. 'I guess that's what he said.'

'Then talk to Bing again,' Danny said. 'Find out if Fred Stanley had a connection to the Arnold family. And if not, how he came to hear about this horse.'

'OK,' I said, 'you talk to Eric, Jerry and I will go to Adrienne and Bing. But we all have to do this while avoiding Hargrove. If he puts us in a little room somebody can still get killed over this key.'

'If that happens while we're in custody,' Danny said, 'we'll be in the clear.'

'That's not the way I wanna get in the clear, Danny,' I said. 'I don't want Adrienne – or her innocent sister – to get killed.'

'OK,' Danny said. 'Let's move, then.'

'OK.'

Outside the diner Danny said, 'Do me a favor, guys.'

'What?' I asked.

'Next time we meet, no food, huh?'

I grinned, looked at Jerry, who stared at Danny and said, 'Now you're just talkin' crazy.'

SEVENTY-ONE

We split up.

Danny went his way, we went ours. We agreed to use Penny to pass messages, and if we were going to meet, it would be at her place.

I decided to see Adrienne before I saw Bing. She was the one whose life might be in danger because of a key.

'What if there ain't no key?' Jerry asked.

'What?'

He kept his eyes on the road.

'I said, what if there ain't no key? We're wrong, and they're lookin' for somethin' else.'

'Something else that would fit in a cookie jar?' I asked.

Jerry shrugged.

'A piece of jewelry?'

'All this for . . . what? A ring? A watch?'

Jerry shrugged again.

'I'm just sayin' what if?'

'You're right,' I said. 'It could be somethin' else. Let's see what Adrienne has to say about it.'

'Where we gonna find her? She's probably gonna be casino hoppin' again.'

'If she is we'll track her down,' I said, 'but let's start at her apartment.'

'OK, Mr G.'

The same doorman was on duty.

'Hey, you're back,' he said. 'She's in. She ain't gone to the casino today. What'd you do, cure her?'

'I don't think so,' I said. 'We're gonna go up.'

'Well, I—'

I gave him a ten and he waved us to the elevator.

When she answered her door she looked worried, and scared.

'I've been trying to find you,' she said.

'Why?'

'Somebody broke into my house.'

'This place?' I asked.

'No, my house,' she said. 'In Henderson. My cleaning lady called. The place is a mess. It's like they were . . .'

'Lookin' for something?' I asked.

'Yes,' she said, 'like the place was searched.'

'They searched my house, too. Nobody's been here?' I asked. 'Maybe while you were out?'

'It's not generally known that I own this place,' she said. 'I use it . . . I only use it . . .'

'I know,' I said. 'When you need to get to the casinos.'

'Yes.' She averted her eyes. Her gambling made her ashamed.

'Well then, that's good,' I said. 'Means the three of us are safe here.'

'Safe?' she asked. 'From who?'

'Let's sit down, and we'll explain . . .'

'So you think Phil has a safety deposit box at City National and some people are looking for the key?'

'That's what we think,' I confirmed. 'Unless you can think of something else that small, someone might be looking for.'

'Like what?'

'Well, Jerry suggested a piece of jewelry.'

'I don't know of a piece of jewelry worth killing for that I own, or Phil owned.'

'What about Eric?'

'Forget it. He's the worst gambler of all of us. He's got nothing.'

'There's one more person I can think of,' I said.

'Who?'

'Your sister Elizabeth.'

'What? Elizabeth? She's in her own little world, but—'

'Phil might've mailed the key to her, that's all I'm sayin',' I told her. She really couldn't accept the idea that her sister might be involved. 'She probably has no idea what's goin' on.'

'W-what do you want me to do?'

'Just call her and ask.'

'But what do I tell her?'

'Nothing,' I said. 'As little or as much as you want, Adrienne. Just ask her if Phil mailed her a key.'

'A-all right.'

'Did you ever tell her that Chris was dead?'

'Yes, I called and told her . . .'

She paused, her words catching in her throat.

'Jerry, get her somethin' to drink, will ya?'

'Sure, Mr G.'

I was surprised when, out of everything she had available, he chose to bring her a glass of brandy. We got her seated with the glass.

'What's happening to my family?' she asked. 'What did they get themselves into?'

'Whatever it is,' I said, 'I feel it has to involve Vince DeStefano.'

'Oh, God.' She put the glass down and buried her face in her hands. 'I did it,' she said, her voice muffled.

'What?'

She raised her tear-streaked face to us and said, 'I did it. I brought Vince into our lives.'

Up to that point I had been under the impression that Phil had brought Vince into their lives.

'I met him in a casino and started to . . . to see him. It was exciting at first, and I introduced him to Phil. By the time Vince and I were done with each other, he and Phil were . . . friends.'

'What about Eric?' I asked.

'Phil introduced them.'

'Well, if I was you, Adrienne, I'd call Eric and warn him to stay out of sight until this is all over. That is, if you know where he is.'

'A-all right,' she said. 'I'll call Elizabeth and Eric.'

'And Vince,' I added. 'We still wanna have that meeting.'

'OK. I'll do it in the bedroom, and then fix my face.'

'Fine,' I said. 'If your sister has the key have her send it to you as quickly as possible.'

'All right.'

She stood and took the glass of brandy with her, heading for her bedroom.

'Oh, and one other thing.'

She turned to look at me.

'You were gonna get me some other names of people Phil might've been in business with. Somebody else who might have had a reason to want him dead.'

'I know that Phil – and Eric, too – had borrowed money from a man named Lenny Markwell.'

'Markwell,' I said. 'OK. I'll look into that.'

We both kept our eyes on the doorway, even after she went through.

'Mr G. . . .' Jerry said.

'I know.'

'If I was Vince DeStefano, I wouldn't be done with somethin' like that for a long time.'

'Well, maybe she was done with him.'

'Still, I don't see him just lettin' her go.'

'I know what you mean.'

We looked at each other.

'You know that name she gave you? Markwell?'

'Yeah,' I said. 'He's a local loan shark.'

'Sharks break bones,' Jerry said, because he was an expert on the subject. 'They don't kill people who owe them money.'

'I know that,' I said.

'Well, what do we do now?' he asked. 'No matter how fast Elizabeth sends the key we ain't gonna have it for a couple of days.'

'Depending on where Elizabeth is.'

'We don't know?'

'She just said she's in Europe with her husband.'

'It'll be days before we see that key,' Jerry said, shaking his head. 'We just gonna wait?'

'No,' I said, 'we've got to do somethin'. We can't just wait for somebody else to die. We'll take our meeting with Vince.'

'We? You think he's gonna agree to see you alone. And let you bring me along?'

'How about we don't tell him?'

SEVENTY-TWO

We got a couple of drinks for ourselves while we waited. Seemed to me I'd been drinking a lot more lately. When I moved to Vegas years ago I was both a drinker and a smoker. I'd pretty much cut those two vices down to almost nothing. Over the past few years I'd gone back to drinking a bit – beer, and an occasional bourbon – but still stayed away from the cigarettes.

When she came back out almost fifty-five minutes later – Jerry had suggested at the half-hour mark we check to see if she had run out on us – her make-up was perfect and she had composed herself. Still, she poured herself another brandy and lit a cigarette. The way she inhaled the smoke and expelled it, you could see she was still churning inside.

'All right,' she said. 'Elizabeth said she got an envelope in the mail from Phil weeks ago.'

'The key?' I asked.

'She claims she never opened it. Now she says she doesn't want to. She agreed to send the whole thing on to me by international messenger. Still, it might take two days.'

'What about Eric?'

'I couldn't get him on the phone,' she said. 'Not at home, and not at work. He's either in a casino or he's—'

'In hidin',' Jerry said.

'I was going to say "dead",' she said, 'but I hope you're right, Jerry.'

'And what about Vince?'

'Vince agreed to meet with me.'

'You? Alone?'

'Yes.'

'Did you ask him about me?'

'I did. He said there was no reason to meet with you.'

'Why did you arrange to meet with him, then?' I asked.

She shrugged.

'I thought you'd come along, anyway.'

'I will,' I said.

'Mr G.—'

'I know, Jerry,' I said. 'He won't be alone.'

'You won't be, either.'

'Yeah, you'll be there,' I said, 'but we'll have to set it up so the advantage is ours.'

'How do we do that?' Jerry asked.

'By controlling the time and place.' I looked at Adrienne.

'I'm supposed to call him back and arrange that,' she said. 'He was in a hurry to get off the line. He said to call back in two hours.'

I looked at Jerry, who looked back at me. I found the silence on both our parts very loud.

'OK,' I said. 'We have some stuff to do. We'll pick out a place and be back in two hours.'

'Are you sure you can't . . . stay?' she asked.

This time I felt Jerry look at me, but I didn't return it.

'No, Adrienne,' I said, 'but we'll back before the two hours.'

'OK.'

'Keep tryin' Eric,' I suggested. 'He has to be warned.'

Jerry and I left. I knew we were thinking the same thing. If she hadn't been able to get Eric, and DeStefano hadn't been able to talk, why had she been in the bedroom on the phone for almost an hour?

We had two hours to figure out a place for the meeting, someplace where Jerry would have a good line of sight on us.

'And I need to be close,' Jerry said to me as we left Adrienne's building. 'If the shooter out at Red Rock was from DeStefano, he'll probably use him again. He won't have to be close. Me, with my forty-five, I'll have to be closer.'

I was starting to think I was a fool to have come away from the first meeting with Vince DeStefano believing that he was not involved. Unless somebody else came out of the woodwork, he was the likely suspect . . .

'Why'd she give us that loan shark's name?' Jerry asked.

'And why was she on the phone for almost an hour?' I asked.

'You think she's settin' us up?'

'I think the only person I'm ready to trust over the next few hours is you,' I said. 'So we're gonna have to watch our backs.'

'I got yours, Mr G.,' he said, 'and I know you got mine.'

I suddenly remembered something, and opened the glove compartment. There was Frank's .38.

'I definitely have got yours, Jerry.'

SEVENTY-THREE

We drove around. I didn't want to get a drink, and I didn't want something to eat. Neither did I want to sit and watch Jerry eat. So we compromised. I stopped where he could jump out and grab a hot dog.

Here,' he said, getting back in the car. He handed me a container of coffee.

'Thanks.'

'Where to?' he asked.

'Someplace where we can park so you can eat.'

'It's OK, Mr G., I can eat and drive.'

'I don't want you takin' out a bunch of tourists with my car,' I said. Then, on the spur of the moment, I said, 'Pull in here!'

'What's this?'

He pulled into the parking lot of a two story building that had just recently been completed, but wasn't open yet. We were at the northern end of the Strip, not exactly considered prime real estate.

'This is gonna be The Westward Ho Casino and Motel,' I said. 'They're gonna call it The Friendliest Casino in Las Vegas.'

'What's gonna make it so friendly?'

I took the top off my coffee and sipped it.

'It's gonna be the only casino *motel* on the Strip,' I said. 'Also, they're supposed to have some really cheap food specials.'

I knew the Westward Ho was owned by brother and sister, Dean and Murray Peterson, as well as Faye Johnson. They had hired Hans Dorweiller to manage it. I didn't know him, but I'd heard some good things. He would go on to manage the place for forty years.

Jerry ate his hot dog and studied the two-story motel building.

'Not gonna be very big, is it?' He looked around. 'Pretty deserted here. When's it supposed to open?'

'This year.'

We both sat and stared at the building.

'You thinkin' what I'm thinkin'?' I asked.

'Yeah,' Jerry said, 'but who says we get to pick the place? What if DeStefano tells Adrienne where he wants to meet her?'

'Well, she got him to agree to the meet,' I said. 'We'll have to hope she can get him to agree on the place.'

We drove back to Adrienne's with a half-hour to spare, decided to park down the block, across the street, and watch.

'She may have called somebody as soon as we left,' Jerry said.

'Maybe,' I said. 'Let's just sit here for about twenty minutes and see what happens.'

Nothing did.

'Let's go up,' I said. I opened the glove compartment, took out Frank's gun and stuck it in my belt. I knew Jerry had his .45 on him.

We entered the building and the doorman smiled at us.

'Hey, guys,' he said. 'You're gettin' to be regulars.'

I took a twenty out and held it out to him.

'Who do I have to kill?' he asked.

'The lady get any visitors while we were out?' I asked.

'Nope,' he said. 'She's all alone up there.'

'Is there another way up?' Jerry asked.

'Freight elevator, but I can tell from here that nobody used it while you were away. Nope, the lady is alone.'

Jerry took the twenty from me and stuffed it into the doorman's breast pocket forcefully, then kept his hand there.

'If she ain't,' he said, 'I'll be back.'

Adrienne opened the door and looked relieved.

'Oh my God, I didn't think you were going to make it. What do I do?'

'Call Vince,' I said, 'and here's what I want you to tell him.'

She was on the phone for fifteen minutes, then came back out from her bedroom.

'Well?' I said.

'He agreed,' she said. 'He'll meet us there tomorrow morning at nine a.m.'

'He wouldn't meet tonight?'

'No,' she replied. 'He said he didn't want to meet in the dark.'

'Well, OK,' I said. 'Daylight's good. At least we'll be able to see who he brings with him.'

'B-but . . . when will you be here? We're going together, right?' she asked.

'Yes,' I said. 'I'll be here at eight thirty.'

'And Jerry?'

'Don't worry about Jerry,' I said. 'He'll have his own job to do.'

Out in the hall, as we left, Jerry said, 'What's my job gonna be, Mr G?'

'What it always is, big man,' I said. 'To keep us alive.'

SEVENTY-FOUR

'You think it's a trap?' Jack Entratter asked. Jerry and I had gone back to the Sands, called Jack in his suite and asked him to meet us in his office so we could tell him what was going on.

'Think about it, Jack,' I said. 'Why would Vince DeStefano agree to meet me at a time and place of my choosing?'

'Well, the way you paint this broad he's doin' it for her.'

'I can see a man like DeStefano makin' a fool of himself for a woman like Adrienne Arnold,' I said. 'I can't see him puttin' himself at risk for her.'

'Maybe,' Jack said, 'he doesn't see you as much of a risk.'

'He knows Jerry's with me, and he knows who Jerry is,' I reasoned.

'All right,' Entratter said, 'if he's gonna set a trap for you, why bother to let you leave his house the other day?'

'He didn't wanna shit where he lives,' Jerry said.

'True,' I said, 'and there was also the fact that Frank was with us. Killing Frank Sinatra – aside from the publicity it would cause – would be like a smack in the face to Mo Mo.'

'So after you went to his house you said he was innocent,' Jack said. 'Now you're sayin' he's behind the killing?'

'I think he had them done, yeah,' I said. 'For himself and for the person he's workin' with.'

'And that would be . . . the woman?'

I shrugged.

'Why would she want her own brothers dead?'

I knew Jack loved his brother, who had been killed years earlier in the service of Legs Diamond.

'Why not?' I asked. 'It wouldn't take much to make me hire somebody to kill mine. But with her it's gotta be money. She and her brothers are all gamblers. I think she and Phil both wanted that horse, or at least a piece of it, and Chris wouldn't come across.'

'So she's lyin' about her and DeStefano bein' done,' Jack said, 'and he backed her up when you went to see her.'

'He didn't back her up, he acted like he didn't even know she existed. If he knew her brothers, he had to have met her, or seen her, at least once. And after once there's no way he could've ignored her.'

'So you think the woman is settin' you up.'

'That's what I think.'

'Then how do you wanna play this? You wanna send in the cops?'

'They won't get anything,' I said. 'We can't prove anything. No, I want to go in there and meet with him, and get him to admit he had Chris and Phil killed, and Fred Stanley too. And I want him to admit that he did it for her.'

'He's gonna have a rifle on you,' Jack said.

'It's Jerry's job to find him, and make sure he doesn't kill me.'

'You goin' in unarmed?'

'Frank left his gun in my car,' I said, patting my pocket.

'How many torpedoes you think DeStefano's gonna have with him?'

'Well,' I said, 'I know one I'm hopin' he'll have.'

'Potato nose,' Jerry said. 'He'll have the rifle. Then there was the three we saw at Phil's place, and the three we saw at Vince's place.'

'Seven? You and Jerry against Vince DeStefano and seven guns? That's crazy.'

I frowned. That was exactly what I had been thinking while Jerry counted them off.

'OK then,' I said, 'I've got another idea.'

SEVENTY-FIVE

At eight twenty-nine the next morning I knocked on Adrienne's door. Once again the doorman – the only one I'd ever seen on duty – said she was alone. I gave him another twenty.

She opened the door and gave me that phony look of relief, again. I realized she was probably sorry she'd ever laid eyes on me and Jerry the day we went out to Red Rock with Bing Crosby. She'd been forced to deal with us, so now she probably thought she was doing so for the last time.

'Where's Jerry?'

'I told you yesterday. He has his own job to do. Come on, let's go.'

On the way down in the elevator I asked, 'Have you heard from Vince today?'

'No, nothing.'

I didn't believe her; but then we were at the point in our 'relationship' where I didn't believe anything she said.

We left the building, got into my Caddy and drove to the northern end of the Strip, to the deserted site of the soon-to-be Westward Ho Motel and Casino.

We got out of the car and looked around.

'Why are we so early?' she asked. 'Vince won't be here till nine.'

'Don't kid yourself,' I said. 'He's here now.'

As if to make a liar out of me a black limo pulled into the parking lot from the other end. It stopped about fifty feet away. I looked around. The only place a man with a rifle could have been was on the roof of the Motel building, unless he was so confident that he was positioned across the street on a higher building. An expert shot could probably have taken my head off from somewhere in the Riviera or the Stardust.

The limo stopped. The driver's side door opened and a man got out. He walked to the back and opened the door. Two more men got out. They all had normal sized noses.

'So much for meeting us alone,' I said.

'What do you want to do?' she asked. 'Run?'

It was almost as if she was baiting me.

'No,' I said, 'we'll see it through.'

The last person out of the car was Vince DeStefano. He was

easily the shortest person in the parking lot. He and Adrienne together would have attracted a lot of curious eyes.

One of the men waved at us to walk over.

'Wow,' I said, 'he's really trying to call the shots after agreeing to meet when and where we said.'

'Should we walk?'

'Oh yeah, no point in playing hard to get now. But stay on my right.' That put the Westward Ho on my left.

'Why?'

'If there's a guy with a rifle, I'm thinking he's on the roof of the motel. I don't want you between him and me.'

'How gallant.'

First she tried to bait me, then a little hint of sarcasm, and all a little too soon, I thought. I still could have jumped in my Caddy and gotten out of there. Then Vince would've given her hell.

I was tempted, just to screw with her.

As we got close I could see the smile on Vince's face. A man only smiles like that at a woman.

'Adrienne,' he said.

'Hello, Vince.'

'Come stand beside me.'

She gave me a look then that was unmistakable. It said 'sucker' as she walked over to stand beside her man. He put his arm around her and kissed her cheek. She had to duck her head to make it easier for him.

'Wow, you two make an odd couple.'

DeStefano laughed.

'I know you had her, Eddie, but she's mine. Make no mistake about that.'

'Should we frisk him, boss?' one of the men asked. It was the same guy who had searched me at the house.

'Eddie doesn't carry, but go ahead.'

The guy gave me the same kind of careless frisk he'd given me at the house. Armpits, waist, legs and ankles. Jerry had been right. They missed Frank's gun, which I had tucked into my belt at the small of my back.

'OK, Eddie,' DeStefano said, 'where's Epstein?'

'He's around.'

'I've got four other men spread around this place,' he said. 'You'll never see him alive again.'

'We'll see.'

He looked at Adrienne.

'What about the key?'

'Eddie was right,' she said. 'Phil mailed it to Elizabeth. She's sending it back to me.'

'Good. Then we don't need Eddie anymore, do we?'

SEVENTY-SIX

I almost went for the gun in my belt, but it was too soon. He hadn't said anything incriminating, yet.

'So, it's been you and Adrienne all along, huh, Vince?' I asked. 'She needed her brother out of the way, so she came to you.'

He tightened his arm around her waist.

'You're a Vegas guy, ain't you, Eddie?' he asked.

'Depends on what you mean by that?'

'Women,' he said. 'You go through lots of women, don't ya? You ain't got just one.'

'No, I don't.'

'Well, I do,' he said, squeezing her again, possessively. 'And that means somethin' to me.'

Man, I thought, she really had him wrapped around her little finger.

'It means you kill when she wants you to?'

'It means,' he said, with feeling, 'you do whatever she wants you to do, no matter what.'

'Like killin' her brothers?'

'Eddie,' he said, 'I'd kill her mother if she wanted me to.'

'Aw, honey,' Adrienne said, 'my mother's dead, but thank you.'

Wow, I thought, he's henpecked and she's crazy.

'What about the trainer?' I asked. 'Why was he killed?'

'That was kind of an accident,' he said. 'My men were just supposed to hold him until after the deal for the horse was made with Crosby. We just didn't want him havin' an expert with him.'

'And then you and your goon showed up,' Adrienne said.

'So Chris and Red Stanley were killed because of the horse,' I said. 'Why'd you have Phil killed?'

'Like you said,' DeStefano said, 'my lady asked.'

'What about it, Adrienne?' I asked. 'Why Phil?'

'The key,' she said. 'The idiot wouldn't give it up.'

'And what's in the box?'

'That's none of your business,' she said, then leaned over and kissed DeStefano on the cheek. 'I'm bored, hon.'

'Eddie,' he said, 'all I have to do is raise my arm and you're dead.'

'The man with the big nose?' I asked.

'So you saw him that day,' he said. 'Yeah, he's pretty good with a rifle. You won't feel a thing. I promise.'

Grinning, he lifted his arm. Then he frowned.

'Bang,' I said, and pulled Frank's gun from behind my back.

It all happened so fast. The other three men went for their guns. In all the situations I'd found myself in with Jerry over the past three years, I hadn't shot anybody. In this instance, I had no time to think. I pulled the trigger.

One man went down. He had pulled his gun first, but when the bullet hit him it flung his hands over his head and his gun went flying. Before I could do anything there were shots and the other two men fell dead on the parking lot surface.

'Hold it, Vince!' someone shouted.

DeStefano had been going for his belt. He stopped short as uniformed cops suddenly appeared from nowhere, led by Detective Hargrove and his partner. I saw another man following them, carrying a shotgun microphone. Hopefully, they'd gotten every word.

'Gimme the gun, Eddie,' Hargrove said.

I handed it to him, wondering how mad Frank would be if I didn't get it back?

'You missed, Mr G.' Jerry told me later.

'What?'

We were at the Sands, taking the elevator to go up and see Bing and Kathryn Crosby, just hours after the business in the Westward Ho parking lot. I was trying to stop shaking. I'd never shot anyone before. This was the first time . . . or so I'd thought.

'I pulled the trigger,' I said. 'Point blank range.'

'You took out one of the limo's headlights.'

'Then how—'

'I got the first guy with the rifle I took off the shooter.'

Jerry had not only snuck up on the shooter, knocked him out and disarmed him, but he'd done the same to two other DeStefano men who were in hiding. Vince had lied when he said he had four more men. Now I was finding out that Jerry was also a dead shot with a rifle.

'Good thing you're an expert with a rifle,' I said.

'Actually, I'm not real good with rifles. Just handguns.'

'But—'

'He would've outdrew you,' Jerry said. 'I had to take the shot.'

'So, you were . . . lucky?'

'No,' he said, 'you were.'

The cops had taken out the other DeStefano men when they continued to go for their guns even after the cops had identified themselves. I didn't remember it that way, but there was yelling and shooting going on, so maybe I did get lucky.

When we knocked on Bing's door Kathryn opened it and invited us in with a smile.

'What ho, men?' Bing asked from behind the bar. 'News?' He was wearing one of his golf shirts. Kathryn was wearing a peach-colored silk blouse, white pants and heels. She had her hair up in a bun and smelled like she was right out of a bath.

'Good news,' I said. 'You can leave whenever you want.'

'You found the killer?' Kathryn asked.

'We got him this mornin', with the help of the police,' I said.

'I'll make drinks and you tell us the whole story.'

'OK, but make mine a club soda.'

The three of them had martinis while I explained what had happened, and why.

'So you solved it,' Kathryn said, 'and handed it to the police. They must have been very grateful.'

I thought about seeing Hargrove the night before and the hours it took us to explain everything and convince him we were right. He hated to pass up a chance to jail us, but it was worth it to him to nail Vince DeStefano.

'We want to show those Chicago gangsters they can't come to Vegas and run wild,' he'd said.

Not outside the casino business anyway, I thought.

'So what's in the deposit box?' Kathryn asked.

'We don't know,' I said. 'The cops are gonna find out, but there's no guarantee Hargrove will ever let us know.'

'What do you think?' Bing asked.

'Papers,' I said. 'Records of shady deals that will hurt DeStefano, or maybe prove real estate fraud. That was another business Philip Arnold was dabbling in.'

'And what happens to the horse?' Bing asked.

'I don't know,' I said. 'I guess along with all the other property the Arnolds own it'll be tied up in legalities for a while.'

'Too bad.'

'Maybe you could buy it later, from the estate,' I suggested.

'It would be too old by then to start it racing,' Bing said. 'I guess we have to write this trip off as a loss.'

'Well, you had some excitement,' Jerry said.

'Son, at my age that's the kind of excitement I can do without.'

We shook hands with Bing, and got kissed on the cheek by Kathryn, and said our goodbyes. They'd be leaving the next day.

On the way down in the elevator Jerry said, 'So we're never gonna know what the big deal about the key was? What's inside the box?'

'Probably not,' I said. 'Hargrove is not the sharing kind.'

Maybe, I thought, some day I'd get the answer from him . . .

EPILOGUE

Las Vegas, December 2004

b ut it never happened.
Hargrove stayed a bastard till the day he dropped dead
. . . of a heart attack at sixty. And I always had an open invitation to a cell. Luckily, that never happened either.

Danny and I watched a DVD, Frank smiling while he sang with
Mitzi Gaynor, then Frank, Dino and Crosby with Mitzi. Then he
said he had to get back to Penny before she sent out a search party.

I walked him to the door.

'Thanks, Danny,' I said. 'That sure brings back a lot of memories.'

'Like when Bing tried to buy that horse?'

'Yeah,' I said, 'still burns my ass that Hargrove never told us
what was in that box.'

'What?' He was looking at me funny.

'The safe deposit box,' I said. 'We never found out what was in it.'

'Jeez, Eddie,' he said. 'Hargrove told me that the next time I
saw him. I-I thought you knew.'

Now I looked at him funny.

'What the hell's wrong with you? I've only been bellyachin'
about that for years.'

Danny shrugged.

'I guess I just thought —'

'Well, what was it?' I asked. 'What was in it?'

'Papers,' he said, with a shrug. 'Deeds to prime real estate that
got turned into casinos later. They woulda made a killin' if they
hadn't gone to jail – or in Phil's case, died.'

'Jesus,' I said, disappointed. 'That's just about what I figured.'

'So what's the big deal, then?'

'I just thought . . . maybe it'd be somethin' . . . ya know, big.'

He punched me in the arm and said, 'I gotta go, Eddie. Merry
Christmas.'

'Merry Christmas. Give Penny my love.'

He nodded, and left. I walked back to the sofa, sat down and
picked up the remote. I was going to watch the DVD again when
the phone rang.

'Hello.'

'Hey, Boss,' Jerry said. 'Merry Christmas.'

'Well, well, another early Christmas visit from a friend. Happy Hanukkah, buddy.'

'Who beat me to it?'

'Danny was just here. Brought me a DVD of the Frank Sinatra Show for Christmas. He and Penny are gonna be out of town when the big day comes.'

'Yeah, well, I got my own appointment on Christmas, so I thought I'd call ya now. Your present's in the mail.'

'So is yours,' I said. 'Watching this DVD made me think back to that time when Bing Crosby tried to buy the horse.'

'That whole thing started out great, with you takin' me to Del Mar, and then it turned into a mess.'

'Yeah it did.'

'So how you been feelin', Mr G?'

'OK, Jerry,' I said. 'Diabetes is under control, so's the blood pressure. Say, when you gonna come out? It's been a few years.'

'Yeah, I know,' he said. 'I, uh, I got some stuff to take care of, but maybe, uh, next year . . .'

'What's goin' on, Jerry?'

'Whataya mean?'

'Come on, big guy. We've known each other a lot of years. I know when somethin's on your mind.'

'Well . . . I went to the doctor last week and they . . . found something.'

'What?'

'A lump . . . a mass, they called it.'

'Jerry—'

'Now don't worry, Mr G.,' he said. 'I'm goin' into the hospital to get it removed, and to get a . . . whatchamacallit . . .'

'A biopsy?'

'Right, a biopsy.'

'Do they think it's cancer?'

'Nah, they don't think it's nothin', but they wanna take it out, just in case. You know how doctors are . . .'

'Jeez, Jerry . . . I'm sorry . . .' I did some math. Jerry was in his mid seventies. He still had plenty of life ahead of him. I was glad they didn't think it was serious, but still . . . Jerry was alone . . .

'That's where I'm gonna be on Christmas Day,' he said. 'Might as well get it taken care of. I got no family to see around the holidays . . .'

'Well, you know,' I said, 'I don't have any family here, either. Why don't I figure on spending the holiday in Brooklyn? I could come a few days early. You could take me for some Nathans, and pizza . . .'

'. . . and bagels,' he said.

'Right.'

'Mr G.,' he said, and I could hear the relief in his voice, 'that would be really great.'

'Hey, Jerry,' I said, 'that's what old friends are for. To have each other's backs, right?'